Matches Made in Scandal

Disgraced...yet destined for passion!

The Procurer is the woman everyone in the *ton* is talking about. Reputed for her utmost discretion, she makes the impossible come true.

She excels at finding fresh starts for the women she chooses to help, but little does she know that her scandalous matchmaking has wildly sizzling results...until it's her turn!

Don't miss this scorching new quartet from Marguerite Kaye!

From Governess to Countess

Has Count Aleksei Derevenko hired herbalist Allison as a governess, mistress... or something more?

From Courtesan to Convenient Wife

Lady Sophia is the *ton*'s most notorious courtesan... until she accepts a new role as a duke's convenient bride!

His Rags-to-Riches Contessa

Luca del Pietro has hired Becky Wickes to help avenge his father's death...but will she be his downfall or his redemption?

All available now!

Author Note

When I told my fabulous editor, Flo Nicoll, that I wanted to set one of the Matches Made in Scandal quartet in Venice, she asked me to consider including the Carnival, as it would make a spectacular backdrop to the burgeoning romance. At that point, other than the iconic masks, I had no idea what Carnival was. Reading up on it, I became utterly fascinated, and as you'll see, without Carnival, there would be no story. So as always, I'm indebted to Flo.

If you follow me on social media, you'll know that I'm a big fan of musicals, thanks to my mum force-feeding me and my many siblings Doris Day films when we were kids. It is so obvious it hardly needs stating, but of course my heroine, Becky Wickes, is my tribute to Eliza Doolittle. However, much as I adore Audrey Hepburn's version of her in *My Fair Lady*, she's not nearly tough enough. So I added a pinch of Helena Bonham Carter's portrayal of Mrs. Lovett in *Sweeney Todd*.

My third big influence while writing this book was Nicolas Roeg's classic film *Don't Look Now*. Venice is portrayed as a city of deception, where nothing is as it seems, a city of beauty and decay, light and shade. I watched this poignantly tragic film many times. But I promise, without giving anything away, that Becky and Luca's book has a much, much happier ending. I hope you enjoy it—I certainly had enormous fun writing it.

MARGUERITE KAYE

His Rags-to-Riches Contessa

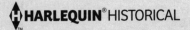

HARLEQUIN® HISTORICAL

Recycling programs
for this product may
not exist in your area.

ISBN-13: 978-1-335-52291-7

His Rags-to-Riches Contessa

Copyright © 2018 by Marguerite Kaye

Printed in U.S.A.

Marguerite Kaye writes hot historical romances from her home in cold and usually rainy Scotland, featuring Regency rakes, Highlanders and sheikhs. She has published over forty books and novellas. When she's not writing, she enjoys walking, cycling (but only on the level), gardening (but only what she can eat) and cooking. She also likes to knit and occasionally drink martinis (though not at the same time). Find out more on her website, margueritekaye.com.

Books by Marguerite Kaye

Harlequin Historical

Scandal at the Midsummer Ball
"The Officer's Temptation"
Scandal at the Christmas Ball
"A Governess for Christmas"

Matches Made in Scandal

From Governess to Countess
From Courtesan to Convenient Wife
His Rags-to-Riches Contessa

Hot Arabian Nights

The Widow and the Sheikh
Sheikh's Mail-Order Bride
The Harlot and the Sheikh
Claiming His Desert Princess

Comrades in Arms

The Soldier's Dark Secret
The Soldier's Rebel Lover

Visit the Author Profile page
at Harlequin.com for more titles.

For Wendy Loveridge, for being such a loyal and supportive reader, a wise and wonderful woman, and a wise and wonderful friend.

Prologue

London—Autumn 1818

The woman The Procurer had come in search of had once been a regular street performer in the piazza at Covent Garden. The Procurer had seen her in action several times, and had been impressed by her skills and ability to work the crowd, particularly admirable in one so young. Becky Wickes's looks, no less than her sleight-of-hand tricks, had always drawn a large audience, for she was dramatically beautiful, with huge violet eyes, sharp cheekbones, a sensual mouth and a lush figure. When she passed the hat round she garnered a healthy collection of coins, though about a year ago, by The Procurer's reckoning, she had abruptly disappeared from her usual pitch. It was clear now, from the very public scandal in which she was embroiled, and which the gutter press had naturally made the most of, what she had been doing in the interim.

The Procurer entered the infamous rookery of St Giles in the wake of her guide, a local urchin, son of one of her less salubrious contacts. Her target had not been at all easy to trace, but then people who so desperately needed to disappear rarely were. With very good reason in this case. Members of the royal family, even minor ones, had a long and powerful reach. It had been a very grave mistake on Miss Wickes's part to be caught in the act of fleecing one such.

The Procurer sidestepped the foul sewer which ran down the middle of the narrow alleyway, executing another sidestep in order to avoid landing on the rotting carcase of a small mammal she did not care to identify. A gaggle of rough-looking men were drinking from pewter tankards outside one of the rookery's many gin shops. She could feel their sharp, curious glances stabbing like knives in her back. Her black cloak was plain enough, but the quality of the wool would be sufficient to make her stand out. As would her looks. The Procurer was indifferent to her singular beauty, but she was not fool enough to deny its existence.

As her child guide led her ever deeper into the rookery, the alleyway narrowed. Hatches from the cellars had been flung open to allow the fetid air to escape the subterranean living areas. Even one woman rescued from this ocean of misery and deprivation was a victory, however small. As her guide pointed to the open door of a dark and gloomy close, The Procurer resisted the impulse to scatter her purse of loose change at the feet of the raggle-taggle band of followers her progress had attracted. When she was done here, and returned to safer streets, there would be ample time for dispensing such alms. To do so now might jeopardise not only her mission but her personal safety.

'Stay here and do not move,' she told the boy firmly. 'You remember what you are to do if I do not return within the hour?'

Waiting only on his nod of affirmation, she ascended the worn steps to the third-floor landing, rapping sharply on the first door to the right. There was no answer. Accustomed to encountering both suspicion and fear during this critical first meeting, The Procurer knocked again, listening intently. Yes, there was someone on the other side of the door, she could not so much hear as sense the tension emanating from them. 'Miss Wickes,' she said quietly, her tone conciliatory, 'I come alone, and as a friend.'

After a brief pause, the door opened a fraction. The woman who peered at her in the dim light bore little resemblance to the one The Procurer recalled from Covent Garden. Her formerly glossy mane of black hair was dull, piled in a tangled knot of curls on top of her head. Her violet eyes were darkly shadowed, the slant of her cheekbones so pronounced she looked almost gaunt. 'What do you want? Who are you?' Her panic was evident from the way her eyes darted over The Procurer's shoulder.

'I merely wish to speak to you, Miss Wickes.' The Procurer stuck her foot against the jamb just in time to prevent the door being slammed in her face. 'You need not be alarmed. I am not here to have you clapped in irons, but to put a proposition to you.' Taking the woman completely by surprise, she pushed her way in. 'Now, do you have the makings of a cup of tea? I would very much appreciate one.'

A startled peal of laughter greeted this remark. 'Would you indeed?' Hands on hips, Becky Wickes surveyed The Procurer through narrowed eyes. 'What in the devil's name is a woman like you doing in a place like this? Who are you?'

'They call me The Procurer. Perhaps you have heard of me?'

Becky felt her jaw drop. 'All of London has heard tell of you.' She studied the intruder in her expensive wool cloak more carefully. 'You aren't how I pictured you. I thought you'd be much older. I certainly didn't think you'd be a beauty.'

'Then both our expectations have been confounded, Miss Wickes. Despite your own very striking beauty, you bear little resemblance to the woman I used to admire, performing in the Covent Garden piazza.'

'That's because I ain't working the piazza no more,' Becky said, deliberately lapsing into the harsh accent of her cockney roots. 'What I'm wondering,' she continued in her more cultured voice, 'is what *my* appearance has to do with your appearance here?'

The Procurer, however, did not seem inclined to explain herself. Instead she nodded approvingly. 'I knew, from watching you perform, that you were an accomplished actress. It is reassuring to know that you have also an excellent ear.'

'You saw me on the stage? I've not trod the boards for nearly five years.'

'I was referring to your performances in Covent Garden piazza. I confess, your strong local accent was something which did concern me. I am vastly relieved to discover it is not a problem.'

'That is indeed a relief,' Becky responded in a

mocking and flawless imitation of The Procurer's own accent with its faint Scottish lilt.

'I do not intend any slight or offence,' The Procurer said. 'Firstly, for reasons which will become clear, it is important that your voice does not betray your humble origins. And secondly, I am relieved because your facility with language indicates that you will find a foreign tongue as easy to master as the accent of those who call themselves our betters here in London.'

Becky snorted. 'Judging from your own accent, madam, I'd say that you are in the other camp.'

'I would have thought that you would know better than to judge by appearances, Miss Wickes, for they can be very deceptive. The performer I observed executing those sleight-of-hand tricks was a very confident, almost arrogant individual. Very different from the female standing before me now. Your alter ego had a certain air about her, one may say.'

'One might.' Becky eyed her astonishing visitor with respect. Any doubts she'd had about the woman's claim to be the mysterious Procurer vanished. 'Most people only see what you want them to see.'

'That is my experience, certainly.'

'So there's another woman behind The Procurer, then? I wonder…'

'I suggest most strongly that you dampen your curiosity.' The frigid tone made Becky take an instinctive step back. 'The first of my terms,' The Procurer continued, 'is that you will neither speculate nor enquire about me. And before you answer, let me assure you, Miss Wickes, that I will know if you do.'

Formidable, that was what the woman was. Well, so too was Becky, but she also knew there was a time for facing up to people, and a time for backing down. If she wanted to hear what The Procurer had to offer, then she'd better comply with The Procurer's terms. 'Fine,' she said, throwing her hands in the air. 'No questions. You have my word. And it can be relied on, I promise.'

She was rewarded with an approving smile. 'I believe you. Now, to business. *Do* you have tea?'

'I do, though I reckon you'll think I'm serving you dishwater. If you will sit down I'll see to it.'

The Procurer took a seat at the table, pinching off her gloves and unfastening her cloak, making no effort to disguise her surveillance of Becky's spartan room. That clear, frankly intimidating gaze took in every detail: the rickety bed with its cast-iron headboard and thin cover wedged into the corner; the tin kettle on the hearth and the battered teapot beside it; the mismatched china cups and saucers which Becky set out on the scarred table with the wobbly leg. 'I had heard that until your major faux pas you were rather successful in your... Let's call them endeavours,' she said, as Becky sat down opposite her, 'but I see none of the trappings of that success here.'

'Major faux pas!' Becky repeated scornfully. 'That's one way of putting it, and a lot more generous than some.'

'I've seen the reports in the press. Written with a view to selling copy rather than telling the truth, of course. I prefer to rely on my own sources, Miss Wickes, and I believe I know enough of your circumstances to think that you have been, if you will forgive the pun, dealt a very poor hand.'

'But one I dealt myself,' Becky said bitterly.

'Really?' The Procurer raised one perfectly arched brow. 'I was informed that the plan was hatched by a certain Jack Fisher.'

Becky gave a scornful snort of laughter. 'Your sources, as you call them, are impressively well informed. It was his idea all right.' Her face fell, and her mouth thinned. 'But it was my decision to go along with it, all the same. Even though I knew—but there, it's done now, and at least I've had my eyes opened where Jack Fisher is concerned. I should never have trusted him.'

'Console yourself with the fact that it is a mistake countless women have made with other such charmers.'

Was that the voice of experience she was hearing? Becky opened her mouth to ask, remembering her promise not to do so just in time. 'Well, *I* won't be making that mistake again,' she said instead. 'Once bitten twice shy, as they say.'

'I prefer my own mantra. Onwards and upwards.' The Procurer took a dainty sip of her tea, her face registering mild distaste.

'I did warn you,' Becky said, surprised to discover that she could be embarrassed over a stupid thing like tea. 'Dishwater, like I said, not whatever exotic blend you're used to.'

She expected a polite denial. She was surprised when The Procurer smiled ruefully. 'My apologies. I am fortunate enough to have a friend in the tea trade who indulges my passion for the beverage.' She set the cup to one side. 'Tell me, have you always resided here in St Giles?'

Becky shrugged. 'Here and hereabouts. It's the safest

place to be, for those of us born and raised here, and the most dangerous for unwelcome visitors who were not. How did you find me? Was it Jack who tipped you off?'

'I have not had the misfortune to meet your paramour. In fact I'm reliably informed that he is en route to the New World.'

'I would rather you'd been reliably informed that he was on his way to the underworld,' Becky said sharply. Flushing, she covered her mouth. 'I don't really mean that.' The Procurer raised an enquiring brow. 'Don't get me wrong, he's a lying, cheating—' She broke off, digging her nails into her hands. 'I wish I'd never set eyes on him. I fell hook, line and sinker for his handsome face and his charming ways and his lies. He played me like a fish, and I was gullible enough to believe every sweet nothing he whispered in my ear.'

Becky forced herself to unfurl her fingers, acutely aware of the cool gaze of the woman sitting opposite her. 'I've learnt my lesson,' she said with a grim little smile. 'From now on, whatever happens in the future, it'll be down to me and me alone.'

She'd meant to sound confident. Defiant. But something in her voice or her expression betrayed her thoughts. The Procurer reached across the table, briefly touching her fingers with her own. 'It can be done, Becky. A fresh start. A new you.'

'You sound so certain. How can you be so sure?'

'Trust me, I speak from experience.' The hand was withdrawn. The Procurer was all business again. 'You can escape from here. The proposition I have for you will reward you sufficiently to set you up for life, whatever life you choose to lead, without having to rely on any man. Are you interested?'

'What do you think?'

The Procurer eyed her coolly. 'I think, Miss Wickes, that despite acting foolishly, you are very far from being a fool. A woman from your disadvantaged background, who has survived by her wits rather than succumbing to the many lucrative offers a beauty such as yourself must have been presented with is very much to be admired. I think that you deserve a second chance and I am in a position to offer you just that. As it so happens I am looking for someone with your unique combination of talents.'

A second chance! For two weeks Becky had been in hiding from the authorities, constantly dreading a knock on the door, left to take her chances by the man she had naively trusted, quite literally, with her life as it turned out. Hope flickered inside her. Becky tried to ignore it. 'I want no part of it, if it means using my skills at the gaming tables to line someone else's pockets.'

'Isn't that precisely what you did for Jack Fisher?'

'It is, though I never knew it. Until I met Jack, my only aim was to keep belly from backbone. It was his idea, to move from the piazza to the tables. It took him a year to persuade me, and I only ever did it because I believed the pack of lies he spun.'

'Had you been less principled, Miss Wickes, with a talent such as yours, you would not be living in a place like this. Pray accept my compliments, and my assurances that the assignment I have in mind for you does not require you to use your most considerable skills to enrich my client in any monetary sense.'

'Thank you. I appreciate that. I'd like to know what it is your client does require of me.'

'Some ground rules first, Miss Wickes. I must have your solemn promise that you will never disclose the details to anyone.'

'That I can easily promise. I told you, I've learnt my lesson. Trust no one. Rely on no one except myself.'

'A commendable maxim. You should also know that you have no obligation to disclose any details of your life or your history to my client unless you choose to do so.'

Becky's eyebrows shot up. 'He doesn't know who I am?'

'I have a reputation for making the impossible possible. My clients come to me with complex and unusual problems requiring unique solutions. Solutions they cannot, by implication, come up with themselves. He need know nothing more than you choose to tell him.'

Becky frowned. 'So he doesn't even know you're talking to me?'

'Nor will he, unless you accept the contract offered. The reward for which, as I mentioned, is considerable.'

She quoted a sum so large Becky thought she must have misheard, but when she asked to repeat it, the number was the same. Becky whistled under her breath. 'That's enough to set me up for life, and then some. I'd never have to work again.'

'A life-changing amount.'

'A life-saving amount! Enough to get me far from here before they find me and make an example of me by stretching my neck.' Becky finished her cold tea and fixed The Procurer with a defiant stare. 'Robbery and fraud, they'd hang me for, you know, and they'd have every right. I cheated. It doesn't matter that he could well afford to lose, I still cheated.'

'You did not act alone. Your partner in crime...'

'Is halfway across the Atlantic by now with his pockets full of gold,' Becky said impatiently. 'What a fool I was.'

'Love can make a fool of the best of women, sadly.'

'Love! It doesn't just make a fool of us, it makes us blithering idiots. I thought the earth, moon and stars revolved around Jack Fisher. All I ever wanted was to make him happy. Was that love? I was certainly in thrall to him.' To Becky's shame, tears smarted in her eyes. She brushed them away angrily. She'd cried enough tears to mend the most broken of hearts. 'Never again. I've learnt my lesson the hard way. As you have, I reckon,' she added pointedly.

For the first time, The Procurer failed to meet Becky's eyes. 'To continue with my rules of engagement,' she said brusquely, 'if you accept this assignment, my client will require your unswerving loyalty. He will also require you to complete the terms of your contract to the letter. The terms, as I mentioned, are generous. I should caution you, however, that you will be paid only upon successful completion of your assignment. Half measures will not be rewarded. If you leave before the task is completed, you will return to England without any remuneration.'

'Return to England?' Her anger and embarrassment forgotten, Becky leaned forward eagerly in her seat. 'Where am I to go? Is your client a foreigner? Is that why you mentioned my—what did you call it?—ear for language? I can't imagine—'

'No, I don't expect you can,' The Procurer interrupted, laughing softly. 'Let me enlighten you.'

Chapter One

Venice, Kingdom of Lombardy–Venetia—
November 1818

Drizzly rain was softly falling as Becky embarked on the final stage of her long journey from London, which consisted of the short sea crossing from the nearby mainland port of Mestre to the island of Venice itself. The black gondola which she had boarded with some trepidation a few hours ago made her think of a funeral barge, or some sort of huge menacing aquatic creature with a vicious golden beak. The crossing was choppy, and the *felze*, the poky little cabin which straddled the central seats, afforded her no view of her destination. Clutching gratefully at the gondolier's hand as she climbed the narrow flight of slippery stairs on the jetty, she felt completely disoriented.

The first thing she noticed was that the rain had stopped. The sky had turned from leaden grey to an eerie brackish pink, tinged with pewter. The waters of what she assumed must be the Grand Canal were no longer churning but calm, glinting green and brown and grey, echoing but not mirroring the sky. The air felt heavy, making everything sound muted and muffled. She felt as if she were in a shadowland, as if the gondola had transported her to some mystical place.

Casting around her, Becky began to distinguish the buildings which slowly emerged from the mist, as if voile curtains were being pulled back from a stage set. Somehow she hadn't imagined that the houses would look as if they were actually floating on the water. Their reflections shimmered, creating a replica underwater ghost city. There were palaces as far as the eye could see, jostling for position on the Grand Canal, encrusted with intricately worked stonework as fine as lace, adorned with columns, a veritable menagerie of stone creatures prowling and crouching, standing sentinel on the flat rooftops.

She shivered, entranced, overawed and struck by an acute attack of nerves. She had been travelling for weeks. The journey had been meticulously arranged, leaving her little to do but hand over her travelling papers to be validated, keep an eye on her luggage and get herself from carriage to boat to carriage to boat, the world changing so quickly and dramatically before her eyes that she could only marvel at the different vistas, listen to the changing notes and tones of the languages, all the while trying to appear the world-weary traveller lest anyone mistake her for a flat and try to rob her of her meagre funds.

But now she was in Venice, her final destination, about to meet the man on whom her carefree future depended. Conte Luca del Pietro lived right here, in the Palazzo Pietro, on whose steps she was now, presumably, standing. By the looks of it, it was one of the grandest palaces of all those which lined the Grand Canal. Craning her neck, Becky counted three storeys, which seemed to consist almost entirely of tall glass double doors, separated by columns. A balcony ran the length of the first floor. Lions stood guard all along the parapet of the roof. There was a coat of arms on a shield right above the huge arched double doors, which were being thrown open by two servants in green and gold livery. A third, imperious member of the household, clearly a butler or major-domo, made his stately way to her side. '*Signorina?* If you please, come this way.'

Stomach clenched with nerves, knees like jelly, Becky followed in his wake as the servant led her into the Palazzo Pietro, where she was relieved of her travelling cloak, hat and gloves. The hallway was patterned in a complicated mosaic of black and white tiles. The walls were hung with tapestries. The ceiling, soaring high above her, was elaborately corniced. There was a chandelier so enormous she couldn't imagine how it could be secured so as not to crash to the ground. She barely had time to register anything else as she was swept up a staircase with an intricately carved balustrade, three short flights set at right angles to each other, before they reached the first floor. The middle one of five sets of double doors was flung open.

'Signorina Wickes, Conte del Pietro,' the servant announced, nudging her forward.

The doors were closed behind her. The room in which she stood was staggering. The ceiling was painted with a host of angels and cherubs, peeping from behind fluffy white clouds, gambolling naked in the celestial blue sky, and haughtily strumming on harps and lyres. Another breathtakingly beautiful chandelier glittered and sparkled, reflecting the light which streamed in through the windows on to the highly polished floor. Shelves of decorative china and plates lined the walls. There were clusters of chaises longues, sofas and chairs, scatterings of tables bearing busts, ormolu clocks and garnitures. Outside, the canal had changed colour again, now buttery yellow and seaweed green.

Dazzled, Becky did not notice the man at first. He must have been sitting in one of the chairs facing out of the window. But as he got to his feet and began to make his way towards her, she forgot all about the opulence of her surroundings.

'Luca del Pietro,' he said, making a slight bow. 'I am delighted to make your acquaintance, Miss Wickes.'

Becky dropped into a curtsy, her knees all but giving way. Rising awkwardly, she followed him, taking the seat he indicated by the window, aware that she was staring, but unable to drag her eyes away from the man who was throwing himself carelessly into the chair opposite, one long boot-clad leg crossed over the other. A count, The Procurer had informed her, the product of an Italian father and English mother. Becky had imagined—blooming heck, it didn't matter what she had imagined, this man couldn't be more different.

His hair was raven black, silky soft and too long for current fashion, reaching the collar of his shirt. His brows were thick, fiercely arched, his eyes a warm chocolate brown. A strong nose, sharp cheekbones, a decided chin. A small, meticulously trimmed goatee beard of the style favoured by Walter Raleigh, appropriately enough, for this man looked more like a pirate than a count. Dangerous—yes, very. And wild—that too. Then he smiled at her, and Becky's stomach flipped. Dear heavens, but that smile would melt ice.

'I must tell you, Miss Wickes, that your appearance is not at all what I expected.'

He spoke English with a trace of an Italian accent. His lips were pale pink against the clean, precise line of his beard, sensual, almost feminine. Not that there was anything at all feminine about the Count. Quite the contrary. There was a litheness, a suppleness in the sleek lines of the body lounging with catlike languor in the chair that made her think of him pacing the decks of a ship with the same feline grace. Becky, who had been certain that experience had numbed her to all male charms, was alarmed to discover that she was wrong.

'Conte del Pietro,' she said, relieved to hear that her voice sounded surprisingly calm, 'how do you do?'

She was rewarded with another of those smiles. 'I do very well now that you are here, Miss Wickes. Will you take some refreshment? We have a great deal to discuss. Though perhaps you are tired from the journey. Would you like to see your room first?'

Becky shook her head decisively. She had regained her composure—or near enough so that this stranger wouldn't notice, she hoped. First impressions were more important than anything. This was no time for first-night nerves. The stage was set. Now she had to deliver the required performance. She smiled politely. 'I'm not one bit tired, thank you very much.

What I am is extremely curious to know exactly what it is you require of me. So if you don't mind, let's get down to business.'

Luca couldn't help it, he laughed. Despite all the tales he'd heard of the woman who called herself The Procurer, despite the personal recommendation he'd managed to extract from a very senior member of the British government, and despite the enormous advance he'd already paid, part of him had doubted that the woman would deliver anyone suitable, let alone this extraordinary female sitting opposite him. *To business*, Miss Wickes insisted, but Luca was in no mood to proceed just yet. 'I know from the time I've spent in England,' he said, getting to his feet to pull the bell rope at the mantelpiece, 'that you like to take tea before you do anything. Tell me, how was your journey?'

'Gruelling,' she replied in a tone that made it clear she was in no mood for small talk. 'But I'm here now, so if you don't mind…'

'All in good time,' Luca said as his major-domo arrived with the tea. He could sense her impatience watching the tea service being laid out with the slow, deliberate care with which Brunetti executed every action. When finally the doors closed behind the servant again, he was pretty sure he heard Miss Wickes exhale with relief. 'Would you like to pour?' he asked her, sitting back down.

To her credit, she did not demur. To her credit also, she did not falter in the ritual, spooning the tea from the lacquered caddy, pouring the boiling water into the silver pot, the milk into the china cups with the steadiest of hands. Evidence of her skills with the cards, or a genteel upbringing? Luca wondered. Her accent was not the cut-glass, clipped tone of the English aristocracy which he found so grating, but nor did it have the burr of a peasant woman—which was hardly surprising, and a great relief. Venice was no place for a rustic of any nation. 'You are from London?' he hazarded, since he knew that was where her journey had commenced.

Miss Wickes paused in the act of raising her teacup to consider this. 'Yes.'

'You have lived there always?'

'Yes.' Miss Wickes set down her cup. A lustrous jet-black curl fell forward over her forehead. She brushed it impatiently away, before treating him to a prim smile. 'Something I intend to remedy, with your assistance.'

Luca returned the smile. 'I was under the impression that I was paying *you* to assist *me*.'

She chuckled. Their gazes snagged, and Luca could have sworn there was a mutual spark of attraction. Then she dropped her eyes, breaking the connection, and he wondered if he'd imagined it on her part simply because he felt it. Her beauty was almost theatrical in its nature, the contrast of those big eyes in that small face, the black-as-night hair and her pale northern European skin, the sharp cheekbones, the full mouth. There was a sensuality in the way she moved that seemed cultivated and yet guileless. She looked down her small nose in such a haughty manner it made him want to rattle that air of confidence. Yet now he came to look at her again, her hands clasped so tightly together, her shoulders so straight, he had the distinct impression that she was barely holding herself together.

And little wonder! She had scant idea why she was here or what was required of her. What was he thinking, allowing himself to become so distracted when he had been impatiently counting the days and hours waiting for this very moment to arrive? Luca set his empty cup and saucer down on the table. 'To business, Miss Wickes. Or may I call you Rebecca?'

'I much prefer Becky.'

Most decidedly she was nervous and trying desperately not to show it. 'Becky.' He smiled reassuringly. 'It suits you. And you must call me Luca.'

'Luca. Does that mean *lucky*?'

'Actually it means *light*, but I hope that you will bring me luck, Miss Becky Wickes.'

For some reason, his words made her glower. 'Before you say any more, I should tell you what I've already made very clear to The Procurer. I won't play cards, straight or crooked, just to win you a fortune.'

'Did not The Procurer make it very clear that wasn't at all what I required?' Luca asked, taken aback by her vehemence. 'Do I look like a man of meagre means?'

She flinched, for his tone made it clear enough that he'd found her implication offensive, but she did not back down. 'You look like a man of very substantial means,' she said, gazing around the room, 'but I'll play no part in making you even richer.'

'I don't want you to make me rich, Becky. I want you to make another man destitute.'

Some might say it was the same thing. Not this surprising woman. She uncrossed her arms, frowning, leaning forward in her chair, ignoring the glossy curl that fell over her forehead. 'Why on earth would you want to do that?'

'Oh, I have every reason,' Luca said, the familiar wave of anger making his mouth curl into a sneer. 'He killed my father.'

Becky's mouth fell open. She must have misheard him. Or his otherwise excellent English had deserted him. Though the way he had snarled the words made her wonder if he had known exactly what he had said. 'Killed? You don't really mean killed?'

'I mean exactly that. My father was murdered. I intend to make the man responsible pay.'

Becky stared, quite staggered. 'But if it was murder, then surely the law...'

'It is not possible. As far as the law is concerned, no crime has been committed. I cannot rely on the law to deliver justice for my father, I must provide that myself. With your assistance.'

'Bloody hell,' Becky muttered softly under her breath, as much at the transformation in her host as his words. There was a cold fury in his eyes, a bleak set to his mouth. 'When you say justice...'

'I do not mean an eye for an eye,' he replied with a smile that made her shiver. 'This is not a personal vendetta. It is a question of honour, to put right the wrongs inflicted, not only on my father, but on our most beloved city. Also to avenge a betrayal of the very worst kind, for the man who had my father killed was his best friend.'

Becky stared at the man opposite, utterly dumbfounded. Vengeance. Honour. Righting wrongs. 'The Procurer didn't tell me any of this—did she know?'

'*Si*. It is part of her—her terms,' Luca replied. 'What is required and why. She promises complete discretion. I am relieved to discover that she is a woman of her word.'

His Italian accent had become more pronounced. He was upset. His father had been murdered, for heaven's sake, of course he was upset! 'I'm very sorry, perhaps I'm being slow, but I'm afraid I'm none the wiser.'

Across from her, Luca let out a heavy sigh, making an obvious effort to relax. 'It is I who should apologise. It is such a very painful subject, I did not anticipate finding myself so—so affected, talking about it.'

'Would you like another cup of tea?' Becky said, completely at a loss as to how to respond.

Luca gave a snort of laughter. 'Tea. You English think it is the cure for everything. Do not be offended. I am not laughing at you, but you will admit, it is funny.'

'I suppose it is,' Becky said, simply relieved to have lightened the tension in him. 'You don't mind if I have a second cup?'

'Please.'

She could feel his eyes on her as she took her time pouring, adding milk, wondering what the devil she was to make of what he'd told her. She took a sip, and he smiled at her again, a warm smile that made her wonder if she'd imagined that formidable stranger.

'I have been so anxiously waiting your arrival,' he said, 'so eager to execute my plan, that I forget you know nothing at all. Naturally, you want to ask questions.'

'But I've no right to ask them,' Becky said, re-membering this belatedly. 'You don't need to explain yourself, only tell me what it is you require me to do. I'm remembering, don't worry, that the fee you'll pay guarantees my unswerving loyalty.'

Luca got to his feet, leaning his forehead on the glass of one of the tall windows, staring out at the canal. After a few moments' contemplation, he turned back to face her. 'This is probably going to sound foolish, but I'd much prefer that you helped me because you wanted to, than because you were obliged to.'

'But I am obliged to, if I'm to earn my fee.'

He held out his hand, inviting her to join him at the window. Outside, it was growing dark, the light a strange, iridescent silver, so that she couldn't tell what was water and what was sky. 'My plan requires you to play cards against this man for very high stakes. He is a powerful and influential figure in Venice. He has also demonstrated that he is prepared to be ruthless. It is not without risk. Did The Procurer explain this to you?'

'She told me if I didn't like the set-up I could return to England, no questions asked. I won't be caught, if that's what you're concerned about,' Becky said, dismayed to discover that she didn't feel anywhere near as confident as she sounded. If Jack hadn't given the game away, she wouldn't have been discovered, but it seemed none the less that he'd stolen a bit of her confidence as well as her heart.

'You'll be in disguise, of course,' Luca said. 'It is Carnevale.'

'Carnevale?'

'Carnival. You haven't heard of it? It is the only time of the year in Venice when gambling is permitted—or at least, when a blind eye is turned. You'll be wearing a mask and a costume, like everyone else. You will be Regina di Denari, The Queen of Coins, named after one of our Venetian card suits. I thought it was most appropriate, though if you have another suggestion?'

'Regina di Denari…' she repeated, savouring the sound of it in Italian. 'I think it's perfect. So that's the part I'm to play?'

'One of them.'

'One of them!'

He laughed softly. 'It is a very large fee you are to earn, after all.'

'Not large enough, I'm beginning to think,' Becky retorted. 'How many other roles are there?'

'Only one, but it will be quite a contrast to the Queen of Coins.'

'How much of a contrast?'

'As day is to night. Like Venice herself, you will have two faces to show to the world. You will be two very different women. Do you think you can manage that?'

'Of course I can.' She wished he wouldn't smile at her like that. She wished that his smile didn't make her insides churn up. She wished that the view from the window wasn't so strange and beautiful. She couldn't quite believe that she was here, that *here* was even real.

'I can't quite believe you're here,' Luca said, as if he'd read her thoughts. '*Are* you real, Becky Wickes?'

'As real as you are. And I admit, I'm not at all certain that you are. Maybe this is a dream and I've conjured you up.'

'I'm the one who has been dreaming, dreaming of vengeance. Now that you are here, I can finally act.'

'It's me who has to act,' Becky said, attempting to

bring the conversation back to business, trying to ignore the effect the closeness of Luca's body was having on hers. 'You still haven't told me what my other role is.'

'You will play my painfully shy and gauche English cousin.' He reached out to brush her hair back from her forehead. He barely grazed her skin but she shivered, though his fingers weren't in the least bit cold. 'You are just arrived in Venice,' Luca continued. 'Here to acquire a sprinkling of our city's sophistication, and to provide my mother with some company from her homeland—my mother is English, you know.'

'It's one of the few things I do know.' Becky's head was whirling. 'You want me to play a lady?'

'A young, beautiful lady, who looks out at the world through those big violet eyes with such charming innocence, who understands none of the intrigue going on around her. Venice is a city full of spies, secret societies, informers. Your arrival will have already been noted, so I must plausibly explain your presence, Cousin Rebecca.'

Was he aware that his hand was still resting on her shoulder? Their toes were almost touching. She could see the bluish hint of growth on his cheeks where he had shaved close to his narrow beard. Was this some sort of audition for the part she was to play? But which part? 'In England, if I really were your cousin, you would keep your distance. Are things so very different here?' Their gazes were locked. This was the oddest conversation she'd ever had. Saying one thing. Thinking something else. At least she was, and she was fairly certain he was too. 'The way you're looking at me, it's not at all cousinly, you know.'

He flinched, immediately stepping back. '*Mi scusi.* You must not think I assume because I pay for you to come here that you must…'

'I don't.' It hadn't even occurred to her, though perhaps it should have? But even though she'd only just met him, Becky didn't think that Luca del Pietro was the type of man to take advantage. Not that she'd any intention of allowing him to.

Her head really was whirling. She needed time to think, to try to make sense of all that Luca had told her, and to work out what the many gaps were in his story. She needed time to adjust to her surroundings. She was in a foreign country in a floating palace, for heaven's sake, with a count who wanted to avenge himself on the man who had killed his father. 'This whole situation is very strange,' Becky said.

'Of course it is, and I have not made a very good job of explaining it. I suspect you would benefit from a rest. I will have you shown to your room.'

'Thank you.'

'It will be just the two of us dining tonight. My mother…' Luca hesitated. 'I thought it prudent for her to be otherwise engaged. I was not sure, you see, until I met you…'

'Whether I would pass muster,' Becky said. 'Does this mean that I have?'

'You have, and with flying colours, I am delighted to say, because I don't know what I'd have done if you had not. I think that we will work very well together. And before you say it, I know that I have not explained what it is I want you to do or even why, not properly, but I will. Tomorrow, I promise. You will stay, won't you? You will help me?'

He wasn't pleading, exactly, but he wasn't at all sure of her answer. He wanted her, Becky Wickes, to help him, the Conte del Pietro. More than that. He needed her. It made her feel good. 'Of course I will,' Becky said. 'I've come all this way, haven't I? You think I'd turn my back on the small fortune you're going to pay me?'

'The money means a great deal to you? No, don't answer that, it's a stupid question. You would not be here otherwise, would you?'

'That sort of money, to a woman like me, it's life-changing,' Becky said, using The Procurer's words.

'I have never met a woman like you, but I'm very glad you are here. I think we are going to make an alliance most *formidabile*.'

He lifted her hand to his lips. Still holding her gaze, he pressed a kiss to the back of her hand. The rough brush of his beard, the softness of his lips, was like everything else since she'd arrived, an odd, exciting contrast. Her insides were churning, but Becky managed a cool smile. 'If you'll excuse me,' she said. 'I don't want to be late for dinner, especially since I'm meeting my cousin for the first time.'

Chapter Two

A maid showed Becky to her bedchamber on the next floor of the *palazzo*. As the double doors were flung open, she was about to say that there must have been some mistake, before remembering just in time that she was supposed to be Luca's well-born cousin. She supposed the servants had been informed of this, and wondered what on earth they'd make of the shabby wardrobe of clothes she'd brought with her. Lucky for her that she spoke no Italian. It was best not to know.

'*Signorina?*'

She followed the maid into the room, abandoning any pretence of being at home amid such grandeur as she gazed around her, almost dancing with delight. The vast bedchamber was painted turquoise blue, the same colour seemingly everywhere, making her feel as if she was underwater. Pale blue silk rugs. Blue hangings at the huge windows. They were drawn shut, but Becky guessed they must look out on to the canal. The view would be spectacular in the morning. For now, the room was lit by another of those massive glittering chandeliers. The bed was a four-poster, and bigger than the room in the rookeries she called home. It was so high, so thick with blankets and luxurious quilts, that she reckoned she'd need a step to climb into it. The bed hangings matched the curtains. She couldn't resist smoothing her hand over them. Damask, embroidered with silk. Would there be silk sheets? She was willing to wager that there would be. Never mind playing Luca's cousin, this room was worthy of a princess.

What wasn't blue was gold—no, gilt, that was the word. Little chairs that looked too dainty to be sat upon. A marble-topped washstand. And a mirror. Catching sight of her reflection brought Becky crashing back to earth. She'd bought her dress in a London street market, second-hand but barely worn, using a chunk of the sum The Procurer had given her to cover her expenses. She'd thought it a good buy, but now even the chambermaid looked better dressed. What must Luca have thought? And what on earth did Luca expect her to change into for dinner, which now she thought about it, was bound to be an ordeal. The opportunities to embarrass herself when it came to etiquette were endless. She owned one evening gown, but it had been bought with the gaming hells of St James's in mind. Her card sharp's costume, revealing far more than it concealed, was designed to divert players' attention from her hands. It was totally inappropriate for dinner with Luca. His demure, innocent English cousin would not own, far less wear, such a provocative garment. Thank the stars she hadn't packed it.

There was a copper bath placed in front of a roaring fire. The maid was erecting screens around it, laying out towels to warm. Becky hadn't expected to be living in the lap of luxury like this. Mind you, it was a double-edged sword, for even as she was relishing her surroundings, she was on tenterhooks, terrified she'd make some terrible gaffe that would give her away. If only she could dismiss the maid, she could explore properly, throw herself down on to that huge bed and see if it was as soft as it looked, take off her boots and her stockings and curl her toes into the rugs. There would be time enough, she supposed, when everyone was in bed. Her stay here was going to be short-lived, so she should make the most of it while she could. Though she was definitely not about to permit the woman to undress her. Let her think it was an English peculiarity. She was more than capable of undoing her own stays and garters.

'*No, grazie,*' she said, shaking her head decidedly, slipping behind the screens. Now she could enjoy some privacy, and she wouldn't have to watch the maid's face as she surveyed Becky's meagre wardrobe, searching in vain for evening wear. Quickly ridding herself of her travelling clothes, she sank into the steaming water with a contented sigh. Were these rose petals? And on the little table, beside another jug of hot water, perfumed soap and some sort of oil.

She closed her eyes, allowing the heat to relax her tense limbs and soothe her jangling nerves. She tried to imagine herself playing the lady, all simpering blushes and saucer-eyed wonder. It would be much more of a challenge than the other part she was to play. The Queen of Coins. '*Regina di Denari,*' she mouthed silently. It sounded much better in Italian. Imperious. Seductive. Like this city. And like Luca, a handsome devil, with a smile that ought to be outlawed.

It wasn't like her to be having such thoughts. Perhaps she had become infected by Venice's mystique, the magic in the misty air. She had never been free with her favours—quite the contrary—until Jack came along and stole her heart. It made her cringe now, remembering the way her heart fluttered when he smiled at her, the way she'd gaze at him all starry-eyed, only happy when he was happy, miserable when he was not. She'd loved him, there was no denying it. Their kisses had been lovers' kisses—or so she'd thought. At any rate, they were the only kisses she had shared in all of her twenty-two years, and the only ones she'd been interested in, until now. Luca's kisses, she was willing to bet, would be very different.

Becky's eyes opened with a snap. She was *not* interested in kissing Luca. She was going to stop wallowing in this bath, indulging in idle speculation and slowly turning into a prune. Panicking that she would be late for dinner, she sat up, sending water splashing on to the surrounding mats, and picked up the soap.

'Signorina Wickes, Conte del Pietro.'

Luca, who had been carefully twisting the cork to open a bottle of Prosecco, turned as the library doors closed on the servant.

'Must they announce me every time?' Becky asked, hovering in the doorway.

'I'm afraid formality is the order of the day in palace life. Though I must admit that every time they call me Conte del Pietro, I look over my shoulder expecting to see my father. Are you coming in, or do you plan to have your dinner delivered to you in the doorway?'

'It's just that you're all dressed up and I'm not.'

Becky held out the skirts of her gown. 'I don't have any evening clothes. Sorry.'

She was smiling and glowering at the same time. Embarrassed. Luca cursed his own stupidity for having donned the knee breeches and coat that was the custom for dinner at the *palazzo*. 'It is I who should apologise. This,' he said, indicating his apparel, 'is what my father would have considered appropriate, and my mother still does. Neither are here, for very different reasons. Please, come in. To me you look perfectly lovely.'

'It's the servants' opinions I'm more concerned about,' Becky muttered. 'I didn't know I'd be living in a palace.'

'Venice is a city of many palaces.' Which was true, but hardly the point, Becky was clearly thinking, though she refrained from saying so. As the cork popped from the bottle with a sigh, Luca set it down, torn. The Procurer's terms forbade him from asking any questions. Cursing her strict rules of engagement, he poured two crystal flutes of the cold sparkling wine and held one out to Becky. 'Prosecco,' he said. 'Our Italian version of champagne. Personally, I consider it to be superior. *Salute*,' he added, clinking glasses. 'Here is to your arrival in Venice.'

'*Salute*,' Becky repeated in a perfect imitation of his Venetian accent, taking a cautious sip, screwing up her face in surprise as the bubbles burst on her tongue.

'You've never tasted champagne, I take it?' Luca asked.

'No.' She took another sip. 'But I like this. Have you told the servants that I am your cousin?'

'Yes, of course.'

'What were you going to tell them if you'd decided I wouldn't suit?'

Luca grimaced. 'I have no idea, I preferred not to consider such an outcome. A sudden family illness back in England forcing you to return, I suppose. But you do suit, so fortunately I don't have to tell them anything.'

'Except maybe explain why the cousin of one of the richest families in Venice has the wardrobe of one of the poorest families in England.'

She tilted her chin at him, there was a flash of defiance in her eyes, yet he was certain now that she was embarrassed. 'I'm sorry,' Luca said. 'I simply didn't think. It is easily remedied. *Mia madre*, my mother, she will arrange it.' He shook his head as Becky made to protest. 'We will say that your luggage was lost in transit, or that your parents wished you to be attired on the Continent, since it is well known,' he added with a sly smile, 'that the English know nothing of couture.'

'Yes, but, Luca, I don't have any money.'

'Luckily, I have an surfeit of it. Think of the outfits as your stage costumes. Therefore the expense is my responsibility.'

'Yes, that makes sense,' Becky said, looking extremely relieved. 'Though I don't imagine your mother will be very pleased to hear— Luca, does she *know* why I'm here?'

'*Si.*'

'And what does she think of your plan to avenge your father's—my goodness, her husband's death?'

'She understands that it is a matter of honour, why it is so important to me to see some sort of justice served. It is the least I can do for him.'

All of which was true. It should have been sufficient, but Becky was not fooled. 'You mean she understands but doesn't necessarily agree?'

Shrewd, that was the English word to describe Becky Wickes. Or one of them. An admirable quality in a card sharp, but they weren't playing cards, and Luca was not accustomed to having his motives questioned. In fact he wasn't accustomed to being questioned about anything. 'My mother's opinion should not concern you, since she is not the one paying your fee.' He regretted it immediately, as Becky's expression stiffened.

'I'm sorry. I didn't mean…'

'No, you were right to remind me that it's none of my business.'

She took her time finishing her Prosecco and setting the glass back down on the silver tray before making for one of the bookcases, running her finger over Italian titles which she couldn't possibly understand. Irked by his own arrogance, Luca poured them both another glass of Prosecco and joined her. 'I'm afraid I don't react particularly well to being questioned,' he said. 'But I am capable of admitting to being wrong.'

She took the glass he offered her, touching it to his before taking a sip. 'Not that it happens often, I imagine.'

He laughed reluctantly. 'More often than I'd like. I have always been—headstrong? I think that is the word. Acting before thinking, you know?'

'Not a wise move in my game.'

What was her game, precisely? Where had she come from? What had she left behind? He longed to ask. He hadn't thought that the terms of their contract would be so constraining. He hadn't expected to be so curious. But perhaps if he was a little more honest with her, she would come to trust him. 'My mother does not approve of my plans,' Luca said, 'you were right about that. My father's death was such a terrible shock, she wants to draw a line under the whole ghastly business.'

'When did it happen?'

'In April this year. I was in Scotland, and did not make it back to Venice in time for the funeral.'

'I'm so sorry.'

'*Grazie.*'

'Was there an enquiry? If he had been murdered, there must have been—I don't know how the law works here. Do you have the equivalent of Bow Street Runners?'

'There was no enquiry, my father's death was deemed to be a tragic accident.' Luca drained his glass, glancing at the clock which was chiming the hour, and on cue Brunetti appeared to announce that dinner was served.

'We can discuss it in the morning, every detail, I promise you,' he said, offering Becky his arm, 'and then I'll introduce you to my mother. She should be home by midday. For tonight, let's take the opportunity to get to know each other a little better.'

The major-domo led them in a stately procession to the room next door. The dining room was another huge chamber, grand to the point of being overwhelming, with a woodland scene painted on the ceiling. Becky made out strange beasts which were half-man and half-wolf or goat, with naked torsos, horned heads, leering down at her, drinking from flagons of wine or playing the pipes. It was enough to put anyone off their dinner, so she decided not to look again.

The table looked as if it could accommodate at least thirty diners. Two places were set at the far end of the polished expanse of mahogany. Torn between awe and amusement, Becky knew enough to allow Luca to help her into her seat, but one look at the array of silverware and glasses in front of her wiped the smile from her face. She watched with growing dismay as Luca sipped and swirled the wine presented to him before his nod of approval prompted the major-domo to fill her glass. Two servants arrived, carrying a silver platter between them. She presumed the major-domo was reciting the contents of the platter. Completely intimidated, Becky simply stared, first at the platter, where she recognised not a single dish, then at the major-domo and then finally at Luca.

Whatever it was he'd noted in her expression, he rapped out a command to the servants. The platter was placed on the table. The major-domo and his consorts trod haughtily out, and Becky heaved a huge sigh of relief. 'What did you tell them?'

'That my English cousin is quite ignorant of our splendid Venetian cuisine, and so I would take it upon myself to make a selection for you. Thus educating your vastly inferior English palate.'

'Thank you.' She was blushing, she could feel the heat spreading up her throat to her cheeks, but there was no point in pretending, it was far too important that she learn while she could. 'You'll need to educate my poor English manners as well as my palate I'm afraid,' Becky said, keeping her eyes on the delicate porcelain plate in front of her. 'I not only have no idea what's on that platter, but I couldn't hazard a guess at what implement I'm supposed to use to eat it.'

'It is the same for all the English who visit Italy you know,' Luca said, getting to his feet. 'Our food, it confuses them. It will be my pleasure to introduce you to it.'

He was being kind, Becky knew that, but she was grateful for it all the same, and extremely grateful that he'd dismissed all the witnesses to her ignorance. As he presented the platter to her, she managed a smile. 'It does look lovely.'

'But of course. The first step to enjoying food is to find it pleasing to the eye. Now, these are *carciofe alla romana*, which is to say braised artichokes prepared in the Roman style—because, just between us, though Venetian cooking is obviously far superior to anything served in England, in Italy, I regret to say that we Venetians are considered to be culinary peasants.' He set a strange off-white chunk of something that looked nothing like the big blowsy green artichokes they sold at the Covent Garden fruit market on her plate.

'Grazie,' Becky said dubiously.

'Now, these are *ambretti all'olio e limone*, which is simply prawns and lemon. Would you like some?'

'They smell delicious. Yes, please.'

'Ostriche alla tarantina.'

'Oysters. I recognise these, though I've never had them hot like this.'

'You'll like them. This is octopus. Try it. And these are *biancheti*.'

'Whitebait,' Becky exclaimed triumphantly after a brief study of the little fish. 'I'll have some of those too, please, unless— Am I supposed to try only one dish?'

'No. This is *antipasti*, the whole point is to sample a little of everything.' Luca sat back down, filling his own plate. 'Use your fingers, then rinse them when you're done. That's what the bowl at the side of your plate is for, see, with the slice of lemon floating in it.'

'Well, I'm glad you told me that or I might have drunk it, thinking it lemon soup!'

'You mustn't worry, Becky. People will expect you to be confused by our customs here. They're very different.'

'Were you the same, when you first went to England? When was that?' She rolled her eyes. 'Sorry, I forgot. No questions.'

'I'm willing to waive that rule if you are.'

Becky examined the chunk of octopus on her plate, then popped it into her mouth. She'd expected it to be chewy, fishy, but it was neither, melting on her tongue, tasting of wine and lemon and parsley. Luca was waiting on an answer, but he could wait. She took a sip of wine. Also delicious. It wasn't that she was ashamed of her humble background, but it was like night and day to all this. Would Luca think less of her for it? In one way it didn't matter, since he'd already committed to her staying.

She picked up an oyster shell, tipping the contents into her mouth, giving a little sigh of pleasure as this too melted on her tongue, soft and sweet, nothing like the briny ones served from barrels back home. Yes, of course it mattered. They were going to be spending a lot of time together. She had warmed to Luca immediately and she wanted him to like her in return. She

certainly didn't want him looking down his aristocratic nose at her, but if she didn't reveal a little of her
humble origins, he wouldn't know just how much help
she was going to need to learn how to be convincing
in her role as his cousin. If she had to learn, and make
any number of mistakes in the process, she'd rather
it was from him, in front of him, and not in public.
And there was the fact that she wanted to know more
about him too.

'Go on, then,' Becky said, 'let's agree to forget
the rule for now. But you first. What took you to England?'

'The Royal Navy,' he said promptly. 'When I was
twelve, my father sent me as an ensign. When I resigned my commission four years ago, I was a captain.'

'I knew it!' Becky exclaimed. 'When I first set eyes
on you, I thought you looked liked a pirate.'

'I think the Admiralty might have something to say
about that description,' he answered, grinning, 'though
there were times when it was accurate enough.'

Becky pushed her empty plate to one side. 'Have
you been all over the world? I can picture you, leaping from deck to deck, cutlass in hand, confiscating
chests of gold from the Spanish.'

'You forgot to mention the parrot on my shoulder.
And my peg leg.'

'And the lovely wench, swooning in your arms because you rescued her from a rival pirate, who we
know must be the evil one, because he's wearing an
eyepatch.'

Luca threw back his head and laughed. 'You've
watched too many plays.'

'Not watched, but acted in them,' Becky admitted,

smiling at the surprise registered on his face. 'And not any of the kind of roles you're imagining either.'

'What do you think I'm imagining?'

'Breeches roles. Not that I wasn't asked, and not that I bother about showing off my ankles or playing the man, but…' Becky's smile faded. 'It's the assumption associated with those particular roles that I resented. I haven't been on the stage for— Oh, five years now. Since I was seventeen,' she added, 'in case you're curious and too polite to ask my age.'

'It's not the thing in England,' Luca agreed, 'to discuss age or money. But you'll find attitudes differ here in Venice.'

Brunetti, the major-domo, entered the dining room at this point, followed by his minions bearing more dishes, and Luca busied himself with serving her the next course. Risotto, he called it, rice with wild mushrooms, to be eaten with a spoon. It was creamy but not sweet, and though it looked like a pudding it tasted nothing like.

'I think you might be right about Italian cooking, compared to English,' Becky said. 'Not that I'm exactly qualified to compare, mind you. I've never had a dinner like this. All this food just for two people, it seems an awful lot. We didn't even finish the— What did you call it?'

'Antipasti. It will doubtless be finished in the kitchen. Palace staff eat better than most. What kind of food do you like to eat, Becky?'

'Whatever I can lay my hands on, usually. Beggars can't be choosers.' She spoke flippantly. What she'd meant was, *I don't want to talk about it.* Then she remembered that she'd agreed to talk, and that Luca had talked, and it was her turn. 'I don't have a kitchen, never mind a cook. I eat from pie shops. Whatever's cheap at the market at the end of the day, bread—ordinary food, you know?'

He didn't, she could see from his face. 'But you seem... Not comfortable, but you don't seem to be *uncomfortable* with all this,' Luca said, waving his hand at the room, frowning.

'Well, that's a relief to know. The only time I've ever sat at a table anything like this was on the stage, where the food was made from plaster and cardboard. I'm a good actress. Luckily for me, The Procurer spotted that.'

'She saw you onstage?'

Becky shook her head. 'I told you, I've not been on the stage for five years, and The Procurer is...' She bit her tongue, mortified. 'Now, that is one subject I'm not at liberty to discuss.'

'Then tell me instead, what you meant when you said that you resented the connotations of— What did you call them, breeches roles?'

'That's when a girl plays a boy on the stage.' Becky studied him over her wine glass. 'You know perfectly well what I meant. That a girl who flaunts her legs on the stage is reckoned to be willing to open them offstage,' she said bluntly. 'It's what draws most denizens of the pit, with good reason in many cases. But I wanted none of it, and it was easier to remove myself from harm's way than to keep fending them off.'

'Surely whoever was in charge—the theatre manager?—would have protected you.'

Becky laughed harshly. 'Then he would have needed to protect me from himself. He was the worst of the lot. A perk of the job is how he viewed it,' she said sardonically. 'Play nice, you get the best parts. Refuse to let him paw you with his grubby little hands, the work dries up. I decided to take the decision out of his hands by quitting. There are many actresses who are happy to exploit their good looks to their advantage, and good luck to them, but I, for one, refused to. They are the ones being exploited, in my view.'

She was surprised to see that Luca seemed genuinely shocked. 'Which makes you rather remarkable, I think,' he said. 'Was there no one else to look out for you?'

'I was seventeen, hardly a child. You grow up quickly, in that game. If you mean my parents, I never knew my father. As for my mother, she was an actress herself. She lived long enough to put me on the stage alongside her. I was six, maybe seven when she died.' Becky finished her risotto and drained her wine glass, and decided to put an end to this conversation too. She wasn't used to talking about herself. 'I never went to school, but I didn't need to, not with the stage to educate me. Reading. Writing. Manners. Plays of all sorts, from bawdy nonsense to Shakespeare, who can be quite bawdy himself. Anyway, that's quite enough about me for now. I'm much more interested in hearing about you and your life on the ocean wave.'

To her relief, Luca obliged. He was a natural story-teller, transporting her from the dreary dockyards of Plymouth and the grey seas of England, to the azure blue of the Mediterranean, the sultry sun of Egypt, the mayhem of Lisbon and the vast expanse of the New World. There were naval battles, but he glossed over those in ~~v~~ that she could see disguised pain, suffering, the darker side of human nature. And though he made little of his own role in war at sea, it was clear enough it had been a significant one, that he was not one of those officers who hid behind his men.

'And then, when Napoleon was defeated at Waterloo, it was obvious that there would be no more wars, and therefore no need for a vast naval fleet. The prospect of sitting behind a desk in the Admiralty filled me with dread,' Luca said, 'and so I resigned my commission. Yes,' he added over his shoulder to his major-domo, who had appeared once more, 'we're quite finished.'

Becky looked down at her empty plate. There were fish bones. She hardly recalled being served any fish. Her wine glass was half-full of red, not white. How long had Luca been talking, answering her eager questions? But she wasn't nearly satisfied. 'Why the navy though? And why the English navy?'

'British. Because Venice no longer possesses one. Because I would never countenance serving our usurpers any more than my father would have, whether French or Austrian. Because my mother's family have a proud seafaring tradition. Admirals, and pirates too,' Luca said with a wicked smile.

Shaking her head at the offer of coffee, Becky sat back in her seat with a contented sigh. She'd eaten so much she was sleepy. 'What have you been doing for the last years, then?'

'Learning how to build ships, not sail them,' Luca retorted. 'I spent some time in Glasgow. The Scots are even better ship makers than we Venetians used to be, though it pains me to say it. My father, to my surprise, heartily endorsed my desire to become a shipwright.'

'But why? Noble families like yours don't tend to dirty their hands by becoming involved in trade.'

'We are Venetians,' Luca said. 'We invented trade.'

Becky bit back a smile. He puffed up with pride whenever he mentioned his beloved Venice. 'I'm surprised you ever left the city if you love it so much.'

'We once had a great navy. Our merchant ships travelled the world. But all that was lost as other seafaring nations supplanted us. Venice's reputation these days is based on its notoriety for vice and excess, a city devoted to pleasure. Always, when people talk of her, it is Carnival and nothing else. It is because I am determined to contribute somehow to making this city great again that I left her.'

'But how? Aren't you— Don't the Austrians rule here?'

His mouth tightened. 'For now. Building new ships to re-establish trading routes. That is my dream. Though for the moment, I keep it to myself.' Luca put a finger to his mouth, making a show of peering over his shoulder. 'There is one thing you must never forget about Venice,' he said in a stage whisper. 'There are spies everywhere.'

'I hope you don't ever plan to tread the boards. You're a terrible actor.'

But Luca's expression became serious. 'I mean it. Within these walls it is safe to speak your mind, but in public you must keep your counsel. Intrigue is a way of life and Venice can be a dangerous city for the unwary.'

'How can somewhere so beautiful be so menacing?'

'Because Venice is a city of contrasts. Light and shadow. Beauty and decay. Stone and water.'

'You make it sound fascinating. I look forward to exploring it.'

'It will be my pleasure to be your guide.'

He smiled at her, and she forgot what she was about to say. Sightseeing, she reminded herself, that was what they were talking about, but her eyes were locked on his, and all she could do was stare, mesmerised. She wondered what it would feel like to be kissed by him, and he must have read her thoughts, because there was a gleam in his eyes that made her think he wanted to kiss her too.

The table was in the way, but she was on her feet now, and so was he. He had closed the gap between them. She was lifting her face to his. And then he muttered something, shook his head, stepped back, and at the same time she regained her senses and moved away.

'In the morning, after breakfast,' Luca said, his voice gruff, 'we will draw up a plan of action.'

'In the morning,' Becky repeated, trying to regulate her breathing, 'I will assume the role of your demure cousin Rebecca.'

He looked as relieved as she felt. She wondered if he was thinking the same as her, that it was for the best, since cousins couldn't kiss.

'But in the meantime, you must be tired,' he said.

'Yes,' she agreed gratefully. 'Very tired. I will bid you goodnight.'

He took her hand, bowing over it with a mocking little smile, pressing the lightest of kisses to her fingertips. '*Buona notte*, Becky.'

'Goodnight?' A slight nod, and she repeated the words, enjoying the soft, sensual sound of them. '*Buona notte*, Luca.'

Chapter Three

Becky woke with a start. Completely disoriented by the comforting, heavy weight of the bedclothes, the softness of the mattress, the serene silence, it took her a moment to realise she wasn't in her cramped garret in the rookeries. The room was cool, but nothing like the bone-chilling cold of a London winter morning. There was an ember still smouldering in the fireplace that would take only a moment to relight. Picking up some kindling from the basket on the hearth, it occurred to her that this would be the maid's task, so she put it back.

A narrow shaft of light slanted through the gap in the curtains, but it was enough to allow her to get to the window from the fireplace without bumping into any of the clutter of chairs and occasional tables that littered the room. Gazing out, the canal was shrouded in a blanket of silvery-grey mist. She caught her breath at the sheer beauty of the scene, leaning over the little Juliet balcony to get a better view of the rows of gondolas bobbing gently on the canal banks, to breathe in the salty air, to drink in the utter stillness of the scene, like a painting or a world where she was the only person alive.

Nothing had prepared her for this. In London, no matter the time of day, there was noise, there were people, there was constant bustle. London was a city painted in shades of grey most of the time, the air tasting of the smoke which formed a grimy hem around the cleanest of petticoats. In London, the sky didn't change colour dramatically like this, clearing and lightening to the palest of blue as the sun rose. The fast-running Thames was a muddy brown colour. Before her eyes, the Grand Canal was becoming bluer and bluer, the sunlight painting bright strips of gold on top of the turquoise. It was magical, there was no other word for it.

She watched, fascinated, as the canal came to life, the first gondolas with a lantern in the prow cutting elegantly through the waters, the oar of the gondoliers barely stirring the surface. Only when a man appeared on a balcony opposite hers and blew an extravagant kiss did she recall that she was wearing a nightgown, that her hair was down, that she was displaying herself on the balcony of the Palazzo Pietro like— Well, not like Luca's demure English relative.

Closing the windows, but leaving the curtains drawn back, Becky retreated back into the warm, luxurious nest of her four-poster bed. She had no idea whether she should ring for the maid. No idea whether breakfast would be brought to her, or whether she should seek it out. Reality, long overdue, came crashing down on her. She truly was in another world, one in which she felt completely and utterly out of her depth. Yet she had to convince everyone, from the army of staff at the *palazzo*, to everyone in 'society', whatever Luca meant by that, that she was Cousin Rebecca, born and bred to all this.

Flopping back on to the pillows, Becky tried to calm the rising tide of panic welling up inside her. She'd been on the stage almost before she could walk, and she was an accomplished actress. Cousin Rebecca was just another role she had to play. She could master it if she worked hard enough. So what, if she was living in a palace and not just acting in front of a painted back-drop, acting was acting, wasn't it? And if she thought about it, which she had better do right now, wasn't confidence the key to her success with her card tricks? People only see what they want to see. She'd said some-thing of the sort to The Procurer, and it was true. There was no reason, none at all, why the servants here would look at her and see a card sharp or even just a com-mon Londoner.

She wasn't common; she was extraordinary. Luca had said so. Of course, she wasn't really, it was just that he'd never met anyone like her. She wasn't extraordinary, she was simply different, beyond his ken, as he was beyond hers. It would certainly explain the most unexpected end to the evening last night. Becky burrowed deeper under the covers, pulling the sheet over her burning face. What on earth had possessed her! Her only con-solation was that Luca had seemed to be as shocked as she was by that inexplicable almost kiss. He could eas-ily have taken advantage. She would not have resisted him, she was ashamed to admit. Thank heavens the pair of them had come to their senses in time. It must be that strangeness which drew them, two opposites attracted to each other like magnets. She'd simply have to work harder to resist, because the very last thing she wanted was to get burnt again.

Pushing back the bedcovers, Becky sat up to face the cold light of day. She'd learnt a bitter lesson with Jack. She'd given her soppy heart to Jack. Looking back, she couldn't believe she'd been so gullible. All these years fending for herself, and she'd not once been tempted by any of the offers that came her way— though they'd been of the crude sort, and hardly tempting, she was forced to admit. While Jack—well, Jack was a charmer. He didn't proposition her, he—yes, she could admit it, even if it made her toes curl—he had wooed her. Seduced her with compliments and promises, gradually taking more and more advantage as she fell for his weasel words and his false declarations of love. Only then, when she'd handed him her heart on a plate, did he start to use her for his own ends, so subtly she didn't notice until it was too late. It made her blood boil, thinking of the fiasco at Crockford's that might have resulted in the loss of her liberty, if not her life. There was a moment, when it was all tumbling down like a house of cards, when she'd turned to Jack, pleading with her eyes for him to rescue her. Instead of which, he'd turned his back on her and fled to save his own skin. Only then did she realise that it had all been a tissue of lies. Even now, thinking about it left a bitter taste in her mouth. What an idiot she'd been.

But look where it had brought her. Becky propped herself up on the mountain of pillows. If Jack could see her now! She tried to imagine his expression if he walked into the room to see her lying like a princess in this huge bed, but she couldn't. She didn't actually want to picture Jack here at all. In fact the very notion of him being in her bedchamber, seeing her in her nightgown, made her feel queasy, even though he'd seen her in her nightgown numerous times, and had been in her bed any number of times too. But she didn't want to remember that either. Or his kisses, which she must have enjoyed at the time, though the idea of them now... Becky screwed up her face in distaste.

Luca now, she could happily imagine Luca standing here at the side of her bed, gazing down at her in that smouldering way of his. So very different from Jack in every way, Luca was. Kissing Luca would be like walking one of those tightropes acrobats used in the piazza at Covent Garden. Dangerous and exciting at the same time. Thrilling, that was what Luca's kisses would be, because he really was from a different world. A world of luxury and sinful decadence, like the food she'd eaten, the silk sheets she was lying on, the paintings hanging on the walls and the dreamlike city outside her window. A world to be savoured, relished, as long as she remembered it could never be her world.

Outside in the corridor, she could hear the sound of servants going about their business. It was time for her to concentrate on hers. She had to transform herself into the Queen of Coins. She was to play the demure cousin. She was to make a man a pauper to avenge the death of Luca's father. She didn't know how he died or why, or if it really was murder in the first place. There were a great many questions needing answers before she could fully understand her various roles. If Luca's father had been murdered, Luca was entitled to justice, wasn't he? She'd be doing a good deed by helping him, and in the process helping herself by earning a substantial fee. With renewed determination, Becky slithered down from the bed and began to get dressed before the maid arrived with unwanted offers of help.

After breakfast they had retired to what Luca called the small parlour, and though to Becky it looked like a very large one, it could, she supposed, be described as small compared to the drawing room, measuring only about a quarter of the acreage. The chamber was situated at the back of the *palazzo* with a view out to a smaller, narrower canal. The walls were ruby red, and the ceiling fresco relatively plain, with just a few romping cupids and a smattering of clouds. The fire burning beneath the huge white marble mantelpiece, the well-cushioned sofa and chairs drawn up beside the hearth, the pot of coffee on the little table between the chairs where she and Luca sat facing one another, gave the room an illusion of cosiness—for a palace, that was.

He poured two cups of coffee. It was very strong, black and sugarless, almost chewy compared to the drink she was used to, and Becky wasn't at all sure that she liked it. Luca, on the other hand, clearly relished the stuff, draining his cup in one gulp. 'Carnival begins in earnest soon, and we have a great deal to do in preparation for it. But before we get down to business, I would like to sincerely apologise for my behaviour last night.'

'Oh, please, there is no need…'

'There is every need. I did not even think to ask if you were married, though I assumed you were not, else you would have mentioned it.'

'And quite rightly too!' Becky said indignantly.

'What kind of wife would I be, to have encouraged you to— Not that I did kiss you, but...'

'You did not encourage me,' Luca interrupted, mercifully cutting her short. 'I don't know what possessed me.'

'No more do I,' Becky replied, her cheeks flaming. 'Fortunately we both came to our senses. Despite appearances, I'm not that sort of woman.'

'That much was obvious given what you told me last night. You left what I am sure could have been a very lucrative career on the stage precisely because you are not that sort of woman. I am extremely sorry if I gave you the impression that I am that sort of man however.' Luca pushed his hair back from his brow, looking deeply uncomfortable. 'You would be forgiven for thinking that I am just like all those others, seeking to take advantage of an innocent...'

'But you didn't, did you? Take advantage, I mean? And you could have,' Becky said painfully. 'The truth is, if you'd kissed me I doubt I'd have stopped you. But you didn't. You're not a bit like them. It didn't even occur to me to compare you to the likes of them.'

'*Grazie.*'

She was touched. He'd clearly been agonising over something that was just as much her fault as his. 'I'm not an innocent, Luca,' Becky said. 'I'm not what you might call a loose woman, far from it, but I'm not a Cousin Rebecca either. I knew what I was doing.'

'That is more than I did.'

She laughed, strangely relieved by this admission. 'Shall we forget it ever happened?'

'Easier said than done.'

'Then why don't we concentrate on the job in hand?'

His expression became immediately serious. 'You are right. I will begin, if I may, with a short history lesson, for our city plays a pivotal role in the story. Venice, you see, was once a great city, one of the world's oldest Republics, and one of the most beautiful. Her treasures were beyond compare.'

He began to pace the room, his hands in the pockets of his breeches, a deep frown drawing his brows together. 'My family have always wielded power here. My father, Conte Guido del Pietro, along with his oldest friend, Don Massimo Sarti, were two of the most respected government officials in 1797 when our city surrendered to Napoleon and the Republic fell. Within a year, Napoleon sold Venice to Austria, but before he left, he ordered the city stripped of every asset. Our treasures, statues, paintings, papers, were torn down, packed away and shipped off to France. It was looting on an unprecedented scale.'

Luca dropped back into his chair, stretching his legs out in front of him. 'But they did not steal everything. My father and Don Sarti acted swiftly to preserve some of our city's heritage. Not the most famous works, that would have drawn unwelcome attention, but some of the oldest, most valuable, most sacred. And papers. The history of our city. All of these, they managed to spirit away before the French even knew they existed, to a hiding place only they knew of. It was a tremendous risk for them to take in order to preserve our city's heritage. In the eyes of our oppressors, their actions would be deemed treasonable, and the penalty for treason is death.'

'In England, the penalty for everything is death,' Becky said, curling her lip. 'Whether you steal a silk handkerchief or plot to kill the King.' Or indeed cheat while unwittingly playing cards with one of the King's relatives.

'My father,' Luca said icily, 'did not commit treason. Quite the reverse. It was a noble act born of patriotism. He preserved what belonged to Venice for Venice.'

Becky was about to point out that, whatever his motives, he had stolen the artefacts, but thought better of it. The man, in his son's eyes at least, was obviously some sort of saint. 'What was he planning on doing with all this treasure,' she asked, 'presuming he didn't plan on keeping it buried for ever?'

'They thought, my father and Don Sarti, that the Republic would be quickly restored, at which point they would return the treasures to the city. Sadly, they were mistaken. France gave Venice to Austria. Austria handed Venice back to France. Now, thanks to Wellington, we have lasting peace in Europe, and it looks like Venice will remain as it is, in the Kingdom of Lombardy–Venetia, part of the Austrian empire once more.

'Bear with me, Becky,' Luca added with a sympathetic smile, 'I can see you are wondering what this has to do with your presence here. All is about to become clear. You see, earlier this year my father came to the conclusion that the political situation was now stable enough to negotiate with the authorities for the restoration of the treasures on a no-questions-asked basis.'

Becky frowned. 'Wouldn't that be risky? Since he

had committed treason, according to the law, I mean. Not that I meant to imply…'

'No, you are right,' Luca agreed. 'It was a risk, but one worth taking, my father believed. For those who rule Venice now, it would be a very popular move, to have a hand in restoring what everyone believed lost. But it had been more than twenty years since the treasure had been hidden. Before he broached the idea with the powers that be, my father visited the hiding place, thinking to make a full inventory, only to find it gone. Stolen by the only other person who knew of its existence,' Luca said grimly. 'Don Sarti, his co-conspirator and best friend!'

'Good heavens! But why? If Don Sarti's motives were as noble as your father's…'

'They were, in the beginning, but it seems Don Sarti is in thrall to something which supersedes all other loyalties. Cards.' Luca dug his hands into the deep pockets of his coat, frowning up at the cupid-strewn ceiling. 'When my father confronted him, he confessed to having sold a few pieces each year to play at the *ridotti*, the private gaming hells which operate only during Carnival, hoping each time to recoup his losses.'

'All gamblers believe their next big win is just a turn of the cards away,' Becky said. 'It is what keeps them coming back to the tables.'

'I don't understand it.' Luca shook his head. 'It is one thing to play with one's own money, but to gamble the heritage of our city—Don Sarti knew he was committing a heinous crime. At first, my father thought that everything was lost, but Don Sarti told him he had only recently sold the bulk of the treasure on the black market with the intention of playing deep at the next Carnival, hoping to win double, treble his total losses. He swore it was his intention to gift his winnings back to the city.'

Luca cursed viciously under his breath. '*Mi scusi*, it is difficult for me to talk about this without becoming enraged. The perfidy of the man! To attempt to *justify* his behaviour, to think that he could atone for the loss of irreplaceable artefacts. My father could not believe he had fallen so low.'

'I think,' Becky said tentatively, 'that he probably believed what he said. I've come across men like Don Sarti. It is a madness that grips them. They will beg, steal or borrow to ensure another turn of the cards, another roll of the dice. As long as they have a stake, they will play.' She had always tried to avoid playing against such pathetic creatures. The memory of her time at the tables in the hells was shameful, tinged as it was with the memory of how she had been persuaded to play there in the first place, but that experience was precisely what Luca was paying for. 'I presume,' she said to him, 'that Don Sarti refused to surrender the money into your father's keeping?'

'You presume correctly. My father informed him in no uncertain terms that he would do everything in his power to stop him, going so far as to say that he would make public the story of what they had done, risking his own freedom and his reputation, if Don Sarti did not hand over his ill-gotten gains. The treasure was gone, but what money was left belonged to Venice. Whether or not he would have carried out his threat I will never know, for Don Sarti decided not to take the risk.'

'That was why he had him killed?' Becky whispered, appalled. 'Oh, Luca, that's dreadful.'

'Si.' He was pale, his eyes dark with pain, his hands clenched so tightly into fists that his knuckles were white. 'Fortunately for me, unfortunately for Don Sarti, my father wrote to me in desperation as soon as he returned home from that fateful interview, urging me to return to Venice as soon as possible.'

'So that's how you know!' Becky exclaimed, 'I did wonder…'

'But no. I didn't receive the letter. Instead, as I told you yesterday, the summons which reached me was from my mother, informing me that my father had died. He had been dead almost two months by the time I arrived in Venice, in June. As far as I knew, my father had drowned, slipping on the steps of the *palazzo* in the early hours. He was the worse for wine, so the gondolier claimed, and there was a thick fog when it happened. Though the alarm was raised, help arrived too late to save him. When his body was finally pulled from the canal, he had been dead for some hours.'

'How tragic,' Becky said, aware of the inadequacy of her words.

Luca nodded grimly. 'The summons my father sent finally reached me here in July, having followed in my wake from Venice to London to Plymouth to Glasgow and back. You can imagine how guilty I felt, knowing that I had arrived far too late. He had never asked me for help before, and I had failed him.'

Becky swallowed a lump in her throat. 'But even if you had received the letter telling you of Don Sarti's treachery…'

'Ah, no, that letter contained no details, save to bid my urgent return. My father would not risk his post being intercepted. I was not exaggerating when I said there are spies everywhere. No, there was but one clue in that letter. My father said that he had acquired a new history of the Royal Navy, and looked forward to my thoughts on the volume. It was there, in that book in the library, that he had placed the papers relating the whole sorry affair, exactly as I have told you.'

'What about your mother?'

'She knew nothing, until I showed her the letter. She was almost as shocked as I. My father had been preoccupied in the weeks before he died, a delicate matter of city business, he told her, but nothing more. She didn't even know he had summoned me home.'

Luca wandered over to the window, to gaze out at the narrow canal. Becky joined him. The houses opposite looked almost close enough to touch. 'It's a big leap,' she said, 'from learning that your father's been betrayed by his best friend, to assuming the best friend has had him killed.'

'It was only when I questioned the palace gondoliers and discovered that both of them had been suddenly taken ill that day, forcing my father to use a hired gondola, that I began to question events. I can find no trace of the gondolier described by Brunetti. And then there was the timing. It was, according to my major-domo, almost three in the morning when the gondolier roused the *palazzo* to tell them my father had fallen in, yet my father left the *palazzo* where he had been dining with friends at just after eleven.'

'So you think that the gondolier waited to make certain that he was drowned?'

'I don't think he was one of our Venetian gondo-liers at all. They are a tight-knit group of men, Becky. Hard-working and honest. If this man who brought my father back had been one of them, they would have known who he was.'

'You think he was actually an assassin hired by Don Sarti and sent to silence your father?'

'My father had threatened to expose him. Don Sarti would have been desperate to avoid that at all costs. Taking account of all the circumstances, I think it is almost certain, don't you?'

'Yes, I'm afraid I do. Is there no way you can bring him to justice?'

'If by that you mean getting the authorities in-volved, then no. I have no tangible proof of murder, and the only evidence that the treasure was hidden is my father's letter which, if it was made public, would destroy his reputation. I have no option but to find some other way to hold Don Sarti to account. If my father had been less honourable, if he had not tried to prevent Don Sarti from losing everything they had tried to protect, then he would still be alive today.' Luca took a shuddering breath. 'If I had received that letter in time, perhaps he would be alive still.'

'You can't think that way,' Becky said fervently. 'Even if you had received the letter earlier, you still wouldn't have returned to Venice in time to prevent your father's murder, would you?' Which was no doubt true, but for Luca, she understood, quite irrelevant. He would continue to torture himself with guilt until he had found a way to atone. Finally, she understood his plan. 'You can't bring him back,' she said, 'but you can prevent Don Sarti squandering Venice's money, just as your father wished, is that it? You want me to win it back?'

'Yes.' Luca let out a long, heartfelt sigh. 'That is my plan exactly. I want to reclaim the money for my city, and I want to see Don Sarti destroyed in the process. I want to use his vice against him. We will turn the tables on him, quite literally. We will indulge this passion of his until he has returned everything he took from the city. I have to do this, Becky. *Per amor del cielo*, I have no choice. Until it is done, my life is not my own.'

That too she could see, in the haunted look in his eyes. 'How much do I have to win?' Becky asked, knowing already that she didn't want to hear the answer.

'I don't know for sure, but I can tell you what my father estimated.'

He did, and the sum he named made her blanch. 'It sounds like a king's ransom.'

'A city's ransom. It is a dangerous game we will play. If the stakes are too high for you, you can, as The Procurer said, return to England.'

And face the threat of the gallows? Not likely, Becky thought. 'We have a saying back home, as well to be hung for a sheep as a lamb. One—what do you call it?—*scudo*, or a thousand or a million, I don't suppose it'll make any difference, it's all the same to me. It's not my money I'll be staking, and as for the winnings—what are you planning to do with your winnings, Luca, assuming you're not going to litter the streets of Venice with gold for people to pick up?'

'I hadn't thought that far ahead. Does this mean that I can rely on you?'

She knew she should consider more carefully, but what was the point! Luca desperately needed help for a very good cause. She desperately wanted to earn that fee, her ticket to freedom from a life of trickery, and to dodge the noose. It was risky, extremely risky, but there were always ways of managing risk, always ways of making fortune work in your favour. 'If there's a way to pull it off, I'll find it,' she said, 'but you need to understand one golden rule about gambling. Even when the deck is stacked, there are no guarantees.'

'I think I would trust you less if you tried to pretend otherwise.' He kissed her hand. 'You come to me under tragic circumstances, but you are a beacon of light at the end of a very dark tunnel.' He pressed another kiss to her fingertips before releasing her. 'I don't know about you, but I am in dire need of some refreshment before we continue. My mother will be home soon, and we still have a great deal to discuss.'

Luca's idea of refreshment was more strong black coffee. It arrived so promptly when he rang the bell that Becky thought they must have an endless supply on tap in the kitchen. Just a few sips, and she felt her heart begin to race.

'Would you prefer tea?' he asked, already on to his second cup as she set hers aside.

'No, thank you. This stuff might be mother's milk to you, but if I have any more I'll have palpitations.'

'Mother's milk, that is what they call gin in London, isn't it?'

'You're thinking of mother's ruin. And that's not my cup of tea either. Shall we continue?'

He nodded. 'I have been thinking,' he said, looking

decidedly uncomfortable, 'about your role as Cousin Rebecca. If you are to play it convincingly, it is not only a matter of wearing the right clothes.'

'You mean manners and etiquette? How to behave in polite society. I know I need some help, but I'm a quick learner, I promise.'

'Then you won't be offended if I ask my mother to give you some pointers?'

'I would be delighted,' Becky said, heartily relieved. 'I would have asked you myself, only I didn't want you to think I'm not up to the role. Are you sure she'll be willing to help me?'

'Certainly, because by helping you she'll be helping me.'

'She won't be used to mingling with the likes of me.'

Luca smiled faintly. 'I've never met the likes of you. I find you a very intriguing mixture, Miss Becky Wickes.'

It didn't sound at all like a compliment, so it was silly of her to be blushing like a school chit. 'You make me sound like a cake batter.'

He laughed. 'My mother will like you, I am sure of it.'

Since it wasn't in her interests to contradict him, Becky decided to hold her tongue. 'It's not just a matter of how I behave when I'm Cousin Rebecca though,' she said. 'It's about…'

'The cards,' Luca said, pre-empting her.

'Well, yes.'

'We use different packs here, and we play different games, if that's what you were going to ask.'

'I was.'

'I can teach you. I'm not an expert, I'll have to rely on you to determine how to—to...'

'Cheat. You might as well call a spade a spade, if you'll forgive the terrible pun. That's my particular field of expertise. But there's more to it than that. This Carnival...'

'There is nothing like it. It is exciting, it is dangerous, it is a time of intrigue and of decadence. The whole city takes part. You don't know if you are dancing with a countess or a laundry maid, or even,' Luca said with a wicked smile, 'a man or a woman.'

'No! You're teasing me. You're not telling me you've danced with a man?'

He laughed. 'No, I'm not. But there are some women who dress as men to gain access to the *ridotti.*'

'Those are the private gaming hells where I will play?'

'It's where the Queen of Coins will play.'

'Against Don Sarti?'

The teasing light faded from his eyes. 'Eventually. There's much more to discuss, and details to be ironed out. I have the bones of a plan, but I need you to help me flesh it out.'

''If I'm to put my neck on the line, then I'd rather have a say in how I go about it.'

'When it comes to the cards, I will be yours to command.'

She smiled at that. 'I'm betting that will be a first, Captain del Pietro.'

'I mean it.'

For some reason, this brought a lump to her throat. Until Jack, she'd always worked alone. When Jack came along, she'd let him call the shots, not because she thought he was right, but because he thought it was how things should be. Now here was this blue-blooded pirate with his noble cause telling her that he'd defer to her. *'Grazie,'* Becky said gruffly.

'It is I who should thank you. You don't know how much this means to me.'

'I certainly do now.' She smiled shyly. 'And I want to help, Luca, because I understand, not just because you're paying me, though it would be a lie to say that doesn't matter. The fee I've been promised, it might be a drop in the ocean compared to what you're wanting me to win, but it's...'

'Life-changing. That's what you said.'

'Did I? Well, it is.'

'How will you set about changing your life, Becky?'

'Nothing too dramatic. A roof over my head away from the city. Perhaps in the country. Perhaps abroad. Unlike you, I've not travelled to the four corners of the globe. Until I came here, I'd never been further than Brighton.'

'And did you bathe in the sea?'

Becky laughed. 'I wasn't there on holiday, I was there to work. London empties in the summer—at least it empties of those who can afford to leave. And they expect to be entertained in Brighton, just as in London.'

'Ah, so it was in your acting days, then?'

'No, after that. I was what you'd call a street performer. Card tricks, sleight of hand. It's how I earned my corn, after I left the theatre, as I told you, mostly in Covent Garden, which is where The Procurer saw me perform, but I spent a few summers in Brighton.'

'You are full of surprises.'

'I like to think so.'

'You can have no idea, but you'd fit in perfectly with the Carnival, where what you call street performers roam every street and every square. In St Mark's especially, there are tumblers and rope walkers, puppet shows, fortune tellers and any number of men happy to relieve you of your money with the type of tricks you describe.'

'But no women?'

'I've never seen any.'

'I like to think I could best any man.'

'I've never seen you at work, but I don't think I'd like to bet against you.' Luca frowned. 'But you have played in gaming hells too, you said? The *ridotti* will not be alien to you?'

'I played,' Becky said tersely, 'after I gave up working the piazza about a year ago. I won't be sorry if I never have to enter another one of these places again, after I leave here.'

'They would not have permitted you to play, a woman alone, would they? You would have needed a male companion, an accomplice.'

Becky hesitated. She was extremely reluctant to allow Jack any part of this conversation, but she was even more uncomfortable with Luca imagining her playing the tables aided and abetted by another sharp, just like a common criminal. 'He wasn't an accomplice,' she said belligerently. 'You could call him my paramour.' Which is what the press had labelled Jack, making it sound like *he* was the one in thrall to her. She glowered at Luca. 'Not any longer. I'm quite unattached, and I've no desire to ever be anything else. Is that clear enough for you?'

'I beg your pardon. I did not mean to upset you.'

'You didn't.' Which was patently untrue. She forced a smile. 'I don't like to talk about my life back in England. It's over, that's all you need to know.'

'And you have a new life waiting at the end of Carnevale, yes? Which will be early February this year, for the celebrations must end at the beginning of Lent. What will you do with your fee?'

'I'll buy a little cottage and a comfy chair, and I'll keep my fire burning day and night. Oh, yes, and I'll have a larder full of food.'

'You have modest ambitions.'

'Modest by your standards, not at all by mine. It's more than I've ever had. What will you do, when this is over and you've paid your debt to your father and to Venice?'

'I intend to build ships, as I mentioned,' Luca said.

'What about your responsibilities as Conte del Pietro? Won't you be expected to fill your father's shoes?'

'Probably. There have been overtures, but like you, I have not really considered the practicalities. There, that is another thing we have in common.'

Becky laughed nervously. 'We've almost nothing in common.'

He studied her, a half-smile playing on his lips. 'Are you thinking that is what attracts us? The strangeness?'

'Well, yes,' she said, taken aback. 'I was thinking that.'

'And then there is the fact that you are my avenging angel,' he said. 'I would be bound to be attracted to my salvation.'

'I hadn't thought of that,' Becky said. Her own attempt at a smile died on her lips as her eyes met his, and she could have sworn that the air between them positively crackled. It didn't matter how attracted he was to her or how attracted she was to him, she told herself, she could not possibly be thinking about kissing him.

A soft tap on the door made them both jump guiltily apart just as the servant appeared. 'My mother has returned,' Luca translated. 'She is anxious to meet her niece.'

Chapter Four

'Now, make your curtsy as if I was the Contessa Albrizzi, Rebecca. No, not so deep. That is better. Now, let me see you take a turn around the room.'

Contessa Isabel del Pietro retired to her favourite chair in the drawing room, the one by the tall window looking out on to the Grand Canal also favoured by her son, and Becky obediently began to parade in front of her. It was almost two weeks since she had arrived in Venice, almost two weeks of what she called her Cousin Rebecca lessons, and the Contessa was a hard taskmistress with an eagle eye. Becky had had no idea that putting one foot in front of the other could be so complicated. *Back straight! Chin up! Shoulders back but still relaxed!* There were times when she felt as if she were on a military parade ground, except that she was expected to combine all these things with the ability to glide, which meant walking with slightly bent knees. What was more, even though her head was to be up, her eyes were to be down, and heaven forfend that any bit of her swayed or jiggled or caused her skirts to swish.

Cousin Rebecca was proving the most taxing role she had ever taken on in her life. She'd never had to rehearse so much and so often. She was surprised there wasn't a path worn in the rugs in her bedchamber, from her practising over and over in the small hours of the morning. Walking. Sitting. Curtsying. Holding a glass. Holding a knife. Drinking coffee. Sipping Prosecco. So many things to learn in such a short time. The nights weren't nearly long enough. It was exhausting and tedious, but it was worth it, if she was to avoid giving herself away. Becky ended her perambulation, sinking carefully on to the chair in the prescribed ladylike manner.

The Contessa smiled approvingly. 'Well done, you've come on leaps and bounds.'

'Which is, ironically, one of the things I'm not permitted to do.'

The Contessa laughed. 'You are a much-needed breath of fresh air. Shall I ring for tea?'

'I'll do it.' Becky jumped to her feet to tug the bell. 'How I am progressing? Honestly, if you please.'

'You are doing splendidly. Unless one was searching for evidence to the contrary, no one would take you for anything other than what we claim you to be, my niece.'

'But if one *was* searching for evidence...'

'I meant to reassure you, Rebecca. You are too much of a perfectionist.'

'There's no such thing, not when the stakes are so high.'

A tiny frown marred the smooth perfection of the Contessa's brow. 'I hope my son's desire for justice is not placing you in any real danger.'

Clearly Luca had not confided the detail of his plans to his mother. Becky was torn. She did not want to lie, but the truth was that they were going to be playing a very dangerous game. Or games.

'Forgive me,' the Contessa said, sparing Becky the necessity of prevaricating. 'I should not have asked, for it places you in a very awkward position. I commend your loyalty to my son. I hope he has earned it.'

'Luca is paying me handsomely, Contessa. Money that will transform my life.'

'Money is not everything.'

'I beg your pardon, but it is when you are obliged to count every penny.'

The faintest tinge of colour appeared in the Contessa's sharp cheekbones. 'I did not mean to patronise you. You are so very confident, so assured, so quick to learn and assimilate everything I say, and I have been enjoying our time together so much that I had almost forgotten that you are not my niece.'

The Contessa took the scrap of lace she called a handkerchief from her pocket, and began to fold and refold it on her lap. Confident, she'd said. Assured. Obviously none of Becky's doubts and fears had shown through. Pride mingled with relief, but looking at the Contessa's troubled expression, she felt a twinge of conscience. 'I practise a lot,' she confessed, 'in my room, at night. It doesn't come as naturally to me as you might imagine.'

This admission gained her a faint smile, but the Contessa's frown deepened. 'Did you go hungry, Becky?'

More times than she cared to remember, back in the days when she'd found herself suddenly motherless. But Becky chose to forget those days. 'I've never been a charity case,' she said with justifiable pride. 'I'm twenty-two years old. I've been looking after myself perfectly well for most of my life.'

The Contessa flinched. 'I didn't mean to pry, I was merely interested in learning about your life in London. It is a treat to converse with a fellow Englishwoman. I apologise if my curiosity has caused me to overstep the mark.' She tucked her kerchief back into her pocket. 'Your new wardrobe will be delivered tomorrow. I was thinking that…'

Becky listened with half an ear as the Contessa mused on Cousin Rebecca's various toilettes. She never talked about herself. No one was ever interested in her history or her opinions. She couldn't even recall Jack asking her what she thought or felt about anything. Now here were two people wanting to know all about her, wanting to understand her, when she wasn't sure she understood herself.

Across from her, the Contessa had moved on to the subject of footwear. Becky could not accustom herself to this elegantly beautiful, intelligent woman taking an interest in her. Like her son, she seemed to have the ability to read minds too accurately for Becky's liking. Those eyes, so like Luca's, seemingly sleepy, heavy-lidded, were anything but. There were no airs and graces about the Contessa, but despite that, there was something compelling about her. She was the type of person all eyes followed when she walked into a room, just like Luca.

The major-domo arrived with his cohorts carrying the tea things. 'I'll see to it, Brunetti,' Becky said in her best Cousin Rebecca accent, eager to demonstrate that she'd learnt another lesson to perfection. Brunetti, she knew now, spoke perfect English.

'Is everything to your satisfaction, *signorina*?'

Becky inspected the table. She lifted the lid of the little silver salver to make sure there was enough lemon. Just to annoy Brunetti, she shifted the sugar tongs fractionally to the left. 'Thank you,' she said, bestowing her newly acquired demure smile.

The doors closed, and the Contessa chuckled. 'Very good, Rebecca.'

'Becky, if you please. When we're alone and I'm not in character.' She poured the tea, adding a lemon slice to the Contessa's cup, milk to her own, tinkling the spoon against the china in that irritating manner which was apparently *de rigueur*.

The olive branch was noted. The Contessa smiled. 'Then you must call me Isabel. I was telling you that your clothes are being delivered tomorrow. You must be quite sick of being cooped up here in the *palazzo*, with me drilling you for most of the day in etiquette, then playing cards with Luca all evening.'

'Drilling.' Becky grinned. 'I was just thinking to myself that's exactly what it feels like sometimes, being on an army parade ground when I'm with you.'

'Am I a terrible taskmaster?'

'Yes, but that's exactly what I need. Luca's eager to take Cousin Rebecca out into the world, so I need to be ready.'

Isabel sipped daintily at her tea. 'How are you getting on with my son?'

'He's a demanding taskmaster, just like you,' Becky said warily.

'Though neither of us is as hard on you as you are on yourself.'

'I've no intention of picking up a Venetian deck to play for money until I know I can make the cards do exactly what I want them to. I'm very good, but even I need to practise.'

Isabel set her teacup down with a sigh. 'My apologies. I am interfering, and I promised my son I would not.' To Becky's surprise, she reached over to touch her hand lightly. 'I suspect it's because you've given me a purpose, something to focus on since Guido died.'

'I'm sorry. I sometimes forget that it's not just Luca who lost his father. You lost your husband.'

'I find myself with too much time on my hands, but you must not be thinking that my heart is broken.' Isabel's sardonic smile was very like her son's. 'I was fond enough of Guido, but we were never close and had little in common. Our marriage was arranged. Once I'd given birth to Luca, and the lustiest, healthiest of babies he was too, my husband ceased his visits to my bedchamber. It is the custom here, you see, for the eldest son to inherit everything, the Venetian nobility's way of preserving their vast wealth. If I'd had a second son, he would be expected to remain a single man, and as to daughters— Well, dowries for daughters also dilute a family's wealth.'

'But you're not a Venetian,' Becky exclaimed, aghast, 'and the del Pietro family must be far too wealthy to worry about diluting anything. Did you know this when you married him? Didn't you want more children?'

'I would very much have liked the companionship

of a daughter, though I suppose it is a selfish thing to wish.' Isabel smiled sadly. 'In any event, I was not given the choice. Perhaps if I'd explained my wishes to Guido. But, no, that's preposterous, he would not have listened, and I was much too young to make any demands of my husband. Besides, these Venetian traditions, they are very much entrenched. I was expected to be by his side at all times, apart from in his bed. Would you mind pouring me another cup of tea, please? No, no more lemon. Thank you.'

The polite smile was back, making it clear that the subject was closed. Cousin Rebecca wouldn't dream of doing anything but follow her aunt's lead, but Becky was done with Cousin Rebecca for the moment. 'You must have missed him terribly. Luca, I mean, when he was sent off to England at such a young age.'

'Oh, I would not have dreamed of keeping Luca here in Venice kicking his heels. He was bored rigid by school. He has a very restless nature. He reminds me so much of my own brother. A born sailor, is Mathew, and Luca is too. Though, of course,' Isabel added ruefully, 'Guido always attributed every one of Luca's qualities to his own bloodline. Though he is half-English, as far as Guido was concerned, his son could only ever be wholly Venetian.'

'What does Luca think?'

'Come, Becky, you know the answer to that perfectly well. Luca is a Venetian to his core. Why else would he be so set on this complex plan he is embarking on?'

'Don't you wish for justice? Even if you weren't close, your husband was murdered.'

'And I do most sincerely mourn him, but I fail to

see how humiliating Don Sarti will make me feel any better.'

'It's not about humiliation. Luca wants—' Becky cut herself short. It wasn't her place to argue Luca's case with his mother. 'He feels he has no choice,' she compromised. 'I mean, a letter like the one his father left him, from beyond the grave, it's not exactly something he could ignore.'

'I suppose not. And at least it has brought you into my life. I very much enjoy your company. You will see for yourself when you go out in society, that Venice is not a city which invites intimacy of that kind. Confidences can be sold. Secrets can be betrayed. One must always be on one's guard.'

'Luca's forever telling me that. I thought he was being overcautious.'

'I doubt that is possible. It is a relief to be able to talk frankly as we do. I know you are not truly my niece, but I hope you consider me a friend?'

What Isabel had told her of her life, her marriage, made Becky realise she'd assumed an awful lot and been wrong on every count. That a countess living in a palace could be lonely! That she could have let her husband deprive her of children, pack her only son off to England and then deprive her even of being able to claim any of that son's qualities for her own. It took her breath away. 'You know my stay here is a short one,' Becky said. 'By the time Carnival is over at the latest, I'll be gone.'

'And my son, I hope, will finally be able to stop looking over his shoulder to the past, and look forward to the future. Are you worried that I'll become over-fond of you, Becky?'

She was startled into laughter. 'I'm worried that I'll get too fond of you!'

'Then we'd better make the most of each other's company while we can.' Isabel got to her feet, shaking out her skirts. 'To work, Rebecca. Let us take a turn around the room together, as two genteel ladies are wont to do, and talk about fashion.'

Becky had mastered the games of Primero and Ombre easily enough, but Trappola was a harder nut to crack. The name meant to cheat or to deceive, Luca had told her. Trappola was unique to Venice, he claimed, and Becky could understand why. She picked up the special deck of cards reserved for the game. Swords, Cups, Coins and Batons. *Spade*, she said to herself as she dealt them out in their suites. *Coppe. Denari. Bastoni.* Each suite had three face cards: the Knave or Foot Soldier, the Knight or Cavalier, and the King. For this particular game, there was no three, four, five or six. And no Queen. When she played Trappola at Carnevale she would be the only Queen of Coins.

Becky shuffled expertly and began to practise her dealing, setting herself more and more complex hands to achieve: dealing from the bottom; dealing herself two cards; making false cuts. This was the easy part, the foundation of all the tricks she had played in her Covent Garden days, and the secret to her winning streaks in the gaming hells. Working with a different pack made little difference to the techniques required.

Bored, she began to build a house of cards. Luca had been called away during dinner by the arrival of an old acquaintance of his father's, newly returned to Venice after a long absence, and anxious to pay his condolences. Becky had assumed that he would join her in the small drawing room as usual when he was free, but it had been an hour since she and Isabel had risen from the dinner table. She should probably go to bed. Isabel was right—she was exhausted between learning to be Cousin Rebecca and practising to be the Queen of Coins. Becky had also been working relentlessly on each role and on the lingo, acutely aware of the clock inexorably moving towards the time when she must make her debut, the weight of responsibility making it almost impossible to sleep when she could be honing her skills.

It was almost ten o'clock, according to the huge clock which ticked quietly in the far corner of the room. The card house was complete. Becky toppled it and began to build another, adding in a second pack of cards. She really should go to bed. The days were beginning to blur one into the other. Had she and Luca really almost kissed in this very room? Maybe she'd imagined it. Certainly, Luca gave no sign of remembering when they sat here, night after night. He was all business. Cards and vocabulary. Vocabulary and cards. The Procurer had been right in predicting that Becky would find the lingo easy. Italian was a lovely melodic language, though the Venetian accent was much harsher. Like cockney compared to the King's English, she thought when she heard the servants speak it amongst themselves, though she wouldn't dream of saying so to Luca.

Another card house was complete. Becky studied it carefully and began to dismantle it, card by card. It was a child's trick, one of the first she'd learnt, but it still made her smile. A question of balance. And of building it just right, of course. There came a point when this card or maybe the next would prove one card too many. A point just before that when it looked impossible, as if the cards on each layer were floating. And then…

She slid the next card out, knowing what would happen, watching with satisfaction as it collapsed in an orderly fashion.

'Brava.'

Becky jumped. Luca was standing in the doorway. 'How long have you been there?'

'Long enough to be fascinated.' He walked towards her, pulling out the chair beside her at the card table. 'I take it that you must construct it in such a way that you know which cards are the supporting ones?'

'Something like that.'

'Who taught you to do it?'

'A magician called The Wonderful Waldo. He was a warm-up act in the early days when I was onstage. He wasn't very good, to be honest, but he taught me the basics of card tricks.'

'I'm sorry that I kept you waiting so long. Don Carcolli wished to reminisce of Venice in the old days before Napoleon, when he and my father and Don Sarti more or less ran the city. I thought I might hear something of interest regarding Don Sarti, but like everyone else, Don Carcolli thinks the man a pillar of society.'

'Doesn't anyone know that he plays deep?'

Luca shrugged. 'If they do, they do not speak of it.' He picked up the cards with little enthusiasm. 'We should practise.'

'Yes, we should. Here, give them to me. I've mixed

two packs up.' Becky reached for the cards. Luca's hand covered hers, and she froze. Lifting her eyes to meet his, she could see that he was thinking along similar lines. Not playing cards, but indulging in illicit kisses.

And then he gave himself an almost imperceptible shake before removing his hand. 'Trappola?'

It was a relief to know that he was as determined as she not to be distracted. Except that now she was. 'Trappola,' Becky muttered, preparing to deal, then immediately changing her mind. 'I hope you won't take offence, but I need to pit myself against a more skilled player. Honestly, Luca, speaking as someone who knows, you'll never make a gambler.'

'Am I really that bad?'

She squirmed. 'It's not that you're so very bad, it's just that I'm…'

'An expert. Which is why you and not I will play Don Sarti,' Luca said with a mocking little bow. 'I hadn't considered the need for you to play for real before Carnevale, but I should have. I will think on it. But in the meantime, since I am not worthy to pit my wits against you, will you demonstrate some of your card tricks? Just for fun, mind you. I want you to fleece Don Sarti, not me!'

'I'm already relieving you of a small fortune for my services,' Becky said, more than happy to indulge in a different sort of distraction. 'You can have this for free. So watch carefully.' She shuffled. 'I always started with the flashy stuff. Producing a card from behind someone's ear, that kind of thing,' she said, doing just that, and bursting into a peal of laughter at Luca's astonished expression. 'The aim is to draw an audience, then you can go through your repertoire. The best tricks are the ones that everyone thinks they can see through. Like this one.'

She spread an array of cards on the table. 'Pick one,' she said. 'Now, look at it, and don't let me see. Now, put it back anywhere in the pack.' She performed a complex shuffle, the cards cascading through the air from one hand to the other. One escaped and fluttered on to the table.

'I thought you said you were an expert,' Luca said.

Becky smiled. 'Turn it over.'

'It's my card! That must just be a coincidence.'

Becky arched her brow, then repeated the trick. And then repeated it again. 'You see, you're sure that all it takes is for you to watch me more and more closely,' she said, 'then you'll catch me out.' She turned over the card he thought he had selected freely once again. 'But you won't. And the crowd never did either. At the end, I would pass round a hat. People threw in a few coins, depending on how much I'd entertained them, and how much they could afford to give.'

'If you'd permitted them to bet against you, you could have made a great deal more money.'

'That wouldn't sit well with me.'

'I know, and I very much admire you for that.' Luca caught her wrist as she made to shuffle again. 'Whatever happens, you cannot go back to that life.'

Completely taken aback, Becky let the cards fall. 'If I fail here, I might have no choice.'

His gaze dropped to her hand, where his fingers circled her wrist. He stared at it for some moments, his heavy lids covering his eyes, allowing her no clue to his thoughts. Then he lifted her hand to his mouth, pressing a kiss to her wrist. 'Then we will simply have to ensure that we do not fail,' he said, smiling. 'Show me another trick. This time I am determined to spot how you do it.'

She was unsettled, though she wasn't sure why. Her time in Venice so far, though brief, had been all-consuming. She'd conveniently forgotten it would come to an end and she'd have to consider her future. But there really was no point in worrying about it just at the moment, when what she should be doing was concentrating on earning the money that would at least offer her choices.

She picked up the cards, slipped back into her Covent Garden role and expertly riffled the deck. 'This time, you pick the card and hold on to it. Look at it, remember what it is, then place it face down on the table.' Shuffling—nice, showy shuffling—was required here, to hold his attention. 'The card you selected is the Ace of Cups.'

'How on earth do you know?'

'Because I have it here,' Becky said triumphantly, turning the top card over to reveal the Ace.

'You can't have because I...'

'You have the Knave of Swords.' The way his face fell as he turned over the card made her burst into a peal of laughter.

'How on earth did you do that?'

'Magic.'

'Show me some more,' he said eagerly.

'This one's called Find the Lady,' she said, beginning to enjoy herself as she set out the cards. 'But since we've no Queen of Hearts we'll use the King of Coins, see here? Ready? Now, what you have to do is...'

* * *

'Tricked again!' Luca threw down the card he'd picked in mock disgust. He grinned, pushing back his hair from his eyes. 'Don't explain how you do it, I prefer to believe it really is magic. I would have liked to see you perform in front of an audience. You have a presence—is that the word?—like the best actresses when they come on to the stage, you know?'

'I do, though I think you're flattering me.'

'Not at all. I mean it.' He studied her as she sorted them into their separate suits and packs with speed and dexterity without seeming to look. She was a different person when she worked her tricks, managing to draw him in, making him feel as if she was wholly absorbed in him, only in him, and at the same time creating a barrier between them, as if she were untouchable. He couldn't explain it, he couldn't have said what it was that changed in her expression or her voice or her manner, only that now, as she set the cards aside, it was gone, and she was Becky again. Or the person he knew as Becky, which was different from the one who played Cousin Rebecca so exhaustively during the day and throughout every meal. Was this the real one? He had no way of knowing.

How hard he had worked to stop himself from imagining showering her with kisses as they sat here night after night playing cards. His desire for justice burned ever more fiercely as Carnevale approached, but his desire for the woman who would help him achieve it kept pace with it. It was because she was so very different from any other woman he had desired. It was because he had ruled her out of bounds that he wanted so desperately to break his own rules. It was because she was his avenging angel. He understood all these things, but they did not make his attraction to her any less real.

Becky closed the lacquered box which held the cards. She met his eyes and read his thoughts instantly. He watched, fascinated, as his desire kindled hers. Her eyes became lambent, and her mouth softened, becoming sensuous. Was he imagining it? No, he was sure he was not, and his resolve crumbled.

He pulled her to her feet, wrapping his arms tightly around her. 'I have tried so hard not to think about this.' If she resisted, he would let her go. Sophistry. He knew she would not resist. Her hair had escaped its daytime pinning, forming a cloud of curls around her face. She had such a delightful curve to her bottom that it was impossible to resist the temptation to flatten his hands over it, relishing the little puff of breath that escaped her mouth as he pulled her closer.

It wasn't a good kiss—it was too awkward. She was too small, and he was too tall. They weren't adjusted. They were far too eager. They had waited too long. He lifted his head, saw his confusion reflected in her eyes, wondering how something that should have been so perfect could be so disappointing. Now was the time to stop, Luca told himself, but she made no move to free herself and he was already beyond logic.

Their lips met again. He kissed her slowly, resisting the urge to devour her, sensing the same urge and the same restraint in her. Already he was on fire with wanting her, already afraid that he would lose control. He ran his fingers through her hair, tugging it free of restraining pins so that it cascaded down her back. The skin at the nape of her neck was hot. She watched him, violet eyes under heavy lids, both imperious and sultry. He kissed her again, and she gave a little moan as his mouth found hers, that both reassured and aroused. This was what fire would taste like, feel like, enveloping them both as their mouths opened to each other, as their tongues touched, danced, teased.

He ran his hand down her spine. A perfect curve. She arched her back, pressing herself urgently against him, and their kisses became wild. Her hands tugged at his coat. He shrugged himself out of it and she ran her fingers down his back, clutching at his buttocks, pulling him tighter against her. He managed to steer them both to a sofa, just enough room for him to lie half on her, half by her side, still kissing. Her gown was too high at the neck, but beneath it her breasts were soft handfuls, her corsets barely in evidence. He teased her nipples, watching with a potent pleasure as she moaned, as they tightened, but it was a double-edged sword, for it only served to rouse him to new heights of yearning.

What the devil was he doing? Appalled at his lack of control, and even more appalled at how easily he could have lost control all together, Luca released her, cursing under his breath. '*Mi scusi.* I did not mean...' He stopped short, unwilling to lie, for he had meant, all of it and more. 'I had no right to take such liberties,' he finished lamely.

Becky pushed herself upright, her colour high, gathering up the hair pins that he had scattered so carelessly. 'You didn't take anything, Luca. If I'd asked, you would have stopped.' She took the pin he had found on the sofa, sticking it carelessly into her hair. 'I don't know why I didn't,' she said, shamefaced. 'You won't believe me now, but I…'

'Am not that sort of woman,' he finished for her wryly. 'But I do know that, and it made no difference, though it should have. You are a respectable woman.'

She laughed drily. 'Hardly. I'm a card sharp.'

'One with principles, who does not take *amore* lightly, I think. While I—I have always taken it very lightly.' Luca shook his head. 'We should not find it so very difficult to restrain ourselves.'

She flinched. 'Well, you did in the end, didn't you? I should thank you.'

'I wish I could say you are welcome. By morning, perhaps I will have persuaded myself it was the right thing to do.'

He was rewarded with a mocking little smile. 'Then there's no point in my bidding you to sleep well?'

'None at all.'

'Try the cards,' Becky said, nodding at the box which sat on the table. 'That will take your mind off anything else.'

'Is that what you'll be doing?'

'Tonight, as I do every night. This one is no different.'

The door closed softly behind her. Luca caught sight of himself in the huge mirror above the mantel and grimaced. His hair was a bird's nest, his cravat a tangled knot and his cheeks flushed. Had a servant walked in on them…

He cursed, pouring himself a small glass of grappa. He took a sip of the potent *digestivo*, closing his eyes as it burned its way down his throat, settling in a warm glow in his belly. What had he been thinking to take such an unnecessary risk when so much was at stake? Another sip, and Luca sank down on to the chair at the card table. He hadn't been thinking; that was the point.

They had not been caught, and he couldn't pretend that he regretted it, though it was true, what he'd said to her. Card sharp or no, Becky was a respectable woman with principles and Luca never dallied with respectable women. He enjoyed women's company. He enjoyed making love, though he had never, contrary to what his friends and fellow officers assumed, been the kind of man who took his pleasures whenever and wherever he could. His Italian blood made him passionate, not indiscriminate.

He finished his grappa. He opened the card box and took out a deck, attempting to shuffle as Becky had, but the cards flew from his hand, scattering on to the floor. She was right—he was no match for her, but how to find someone suitable, without giving their game away? Frowning, Luca retrieved the cards and began to sort them into suits.

Looking back over the nights when they'd sat here playing, he realised that though she talked freely enough of what she called her Covent Garden days, she'd revealed little of her most recent history. He knew that she had plied her trade in gaming hells. He guessed, from the way she talked, that she had loathed it. Why then had she given up street entertainment which, if tonight was anything to judge by, she thoroughly enjoyed? The obvious answer was money, but there was nothing obvious about Becky. She did not play to become rich. So why play the hells at all? Was it the man who had been at her side in those hells? A protector, in more ways than one perhaps, and one she had been happy to leave behind, by the sounds of it.

What had made her take the bold step of coming here to Italy at the behest of The Procurer? Again, money was the obvious answer. Yet her needs were modest. A home, a fire, a full larder were the extent of her ambition. It touched him strangely that she should aim so low, pained him that such an extraordinary woman should dream of such a humble life.

Humble to him, but extraordinary to Becky, Luca reminded himself. Who was he to condemn such a choice, to dare to think it unworthy? She would be offended, and rightly so, if she were privy to his thoughts, but still he couldn't help thinking that she deserved so much more. He had never met a woman like her. Perhaps it wasn't very surprising after all that he found her so fascinating and so irresistible. Even though he knew he was playing with fire.

Luca placed the cards back in the box. Tomorrow night, Becky was to make her debut as Cousin Rebecca. In a few weeks, she'd be making her first appearance as the Queen of Coins. The first steps on the path to seeing justice done for his father, the money returned to Venice, its rightful owner. He poured himself another small measure of grappa and turned his mind to ensuring that happened.

Chapter Five

Becky turned the brass handle on the heavy door at the top of the winding flight of stairs, stepped out on to the roof of the Palazzo Pietro and marvelled at the view laid out before her. Roof after roof of red terracotta tiles topped buildings huddled even more closely together than in the worst of London's rookeries, though they looked decidedly prettier. She made her way to the parapet, leaning over to gaze down at the Grand Canal. From this height, she could make out the twists and turns of the channel as it flowed below bridges before meeting the deep blue waters of the lagoon on which Venice floated. Beyond that, a long strip of land which must be the Lido, and clusters of islands. She'd no idea there were so many.

It was a clear day. The sky was pale blue, for once distinguishable from the turquoise waters below. It was Isabel who'd told her about the rooftop garden, accessed by climbing many staircases, past the servants' quarters to the entrance in the attics. Looking around her, Becky didn't think it much of a garden. There were no plants, no greenery at all, just a couple of benches and a table. A waste, she thought. There were any number of other rooftop gardens visible, real gardens, some with small trees, pots, wooden trellises. It would be lovely up here in the summer.

The view was already lovely. There seemed to be hundreds of churches in the city. The huge one, right on the edge of the lagoon with its vast piazza, she knew was San Marco. It reminded her a little bit of St Paul's, but everywhere she looked she could see others, the bell towers marking their locations. The myriad of canals looked like streets from here, winding through the tightly packed houses, some intersecting, some coming to dead ends, the colours dazzling, changing from shades of blue to green to brown, depending on how narrow they were, how high the buildings lining them and the colour of the painted stone. Becky leaned far over the parapet. She'd never seen buildings painted in such bright colours. Golden yellow. Soft pink. Burnt orange. Sparkling white. Though many, when she peered more closely, seemed to be simply stone, and quite decrepit and crumbling at that. Venice, the city of contrasts, was, when it came to rich and poor, not much different from London. There were so very few open spaces though—no parks, only the piazzas, which she now knew to call *campos*.

She was wearing one of her new gowns. A day dress, Isabel called it. White muslin, printed with broad vertical stripes in shades of buff and blue, the skirt hung straight from the fashionable empire-line bodice. The three-quarter-length sleeves were narrow, fitted tight to her wrists. It looked simple enough, but what a palaver it had been to get into it, with all the buttons and loops and ribbons. A soft breeze ruffled the flimsy fabric, which would have been completely transparent, were it not for the many layers of under-clothes which Becky had donned. Chemises and pet-ticoats and a corset laced so tight she'd protested that she couldn't breathe. It certainly helped make sure she sat up straight. She could now appreciate the need for a lady's maid. You'd have to be an octopus to get yourself dressed without help. Perhaps that explained why young ladies like Cousin Rebecca held on to their innocence for so long, it would be too much effort for any man to get through all those barricades. Perhaps if she had been wearing these clothes last night...

Even though she was completely alone, Becky could feel her cheeks flushing. Just as she'd told Luca she would, she had practised cards into the night, fall-ing into an exhausted sleep which left no room for reflections. Then Cousin Rebecca's wardrobe had ar-rived first thing this morning. There had been an em-barrassing amount of clothes to be unpacked. Far too many for one person's needs, though Isabel had as-sured her otherwise. Day dresses and walking dresses, which seemed completely unnecessary since no one could possibly walk any distance in this city without falling into a canal. There were half dresses and half pelisses and half-boots too, though strangely noth-ing called a whole dress or a quarter-boot. Yards of petticoats. Countless pairs of silk stockings so sheer they could pass through a wedding ring. Nightgowns, dressing gowns, evening gowns. Silk and satin and lace, ribbons and buttons.

'What about this one for your introduction into society tonight?' Isabel had asked, holding up a pretty rose-pink gown. 'Or what about this one? Or this?'

White, lemon, sky blue, mint green, the colours worn by a young unmarried girl, Becky now knew. They were all beautiful, but none of them were really hers. She felt a fraud, looking in the mirror just before she came up on to the roof. Now she was in costume, a dress rehearsal for tonight, so to speak, she was overcome with nerves, utterly certain she was going to falter. Isabel, who already knew her far too well for comfort, had seen all of this in her face, and sent her up here to get her equilibrium back, as if she was a set of scales out of balance when what she was, was a girl from the rookeries, a fish from a very small pond, suddenly cast into a huge ocean. And she was floundering.

She scanned the view, but not even the beauty of Venice could distract her. Last night, in the small parlour, for heaven's sake, when any servant could have walked in on them, she had abandoned herself to passion. She had never before behaved in such a wanton way, had never before lost all sense of her surroundings, lost all sense of herself, been so consumed with one and only one desire. She simply couldn't understand it. Luca was nothing to her.

No, that wasn't true. Becky paced to the other side of the roof, gazing sightlessly down at the network of narrow canals. Luca was a very attractive man, there was no doubt about that, and she could happily admit that his particular combination of good looks and devil-may-care air appealed to her on a visceral level. This plan he had concocted, it was bold and it was risky and it was outrageous, as well as honourable. She might be dreading her debut tonight, but she was relishing the fact that she was vital to him—or rather to his cause. He made her feel powerful. She enjoyed being his avenging angel. After the disaster at Crockford's and Jack's betrayals, Luca's cause and Luca himself were very welcome balms to her shattered confidence.

So it was hardly surprising he aroused such passion in her, Becky reasoned. Indifference would have been more surprising. She smiled to herself at the very idea. Such a potent combination of extraordinary man and extraordinary circumstances, it was no wonder at all that she had lost control last night. In fact it was a perfectly natural consequence, and nothing at all to be ashamed of. Or worried about either, she decided. It wasn't as if she was in any danger of falling in love with Luca. She'd tried love on for size and it wasn't for her. Besides, there could not be two more different men than Luca and Jack. Becky wrinkled her nose in disgust.

A shout from the window of one of the houses on the far side of the roof attracted her attention. Another shout, and then another, saw her pick her way across the roof in search of the source. There were people hanging out the windows on both sides of the narrow canal beneath, shouting abuse and encouragement at the two groups of men and boys clustered on either side of the bridge. She couldn't make out a word of the Venetian dialect, probably because none of the words were polite enough for Luca to have taught her, but it was obvious enough what was going on. Her own early experience had taught her that the less people owned, the more stoutly they defended their turf.

'Becky, come away from the edge.' Luca grabbed her by the waist, pulling her back. 'If you fell, you would be killed.'

'I won't fall, I've a good head for heights,' she said, determinedly ignoring the little surge of excitement she felt at the sight of him. 'Look down there. It's like the Montagues and the Capulets. I wonder if one of the women screeching like a banshee from the windows is the Juliet they're fighting over.'

The fight had died down, with both sides retreating back across the bridge to their own territory. Catcalls and jeers came from the windows. Then as quickly as it had started, it was over. 'It's lovely up here,' Becky said, allowing Luca to steer her away from the edge. 'It's a shame you don't make more of it. If I had a sanctuary like this, I'd want to be up here all the time.'

Luca scanned the rooftop, a slight frown making a groove between his brows. 'How did you acquire your head for heights? In the theatre perhaps?'

'No, by scrambling about on the roofs of buildings when I was a kid. They were our playground, our secret space.'

'There are any number of parks in London.'

'With an army of park-keepers determined to keep ragamuffins out. I was born into the slums, Luca.'

'The rookeries, yes?' His face wrinkled with distaste. 'I had worked that much out for myself.'

'It wasn't that bad, you know.'

'I think it must have been a great deal worse than you would ever admit. How did someone as extraordinary as you survive such a terrible life? And not only survive but—I don't know how to say it without insulting you—but you are so…'

'Assured is what your mother called me.'

'Did she?' He steered her over to the wooden bench, sitting down beside her. 'You certainly can appear to be most assured. It fooled me for a while. That first day, before I knew better, for example, it would not have occurred to me for one minute that this woman was born and bred in the slums of London.'

'What gave me away?'

He shook his head, smiling thoughtfully. 'You are a very good actress, but I— Ah, I admit, I have been studying you very closely. It is in the eyes, I think. There are times when you make me think of a captain readying a warship for battle. He is focused on giving orders, issuing battle plans, organising flags, cannons, ammunition, thinking only of what is to come, thinking only of victory, and then he sees one of his men offering up a prayer and it is a jolt, like a shot across the bows, a reminder of the reality of war. In that instant, just for an instant, he is afraid.'

She'd dreaded seeing pity in his eyes. What she saw instead was that Luca had bared a little bit of his own soul to show her that he understood. It brought a lump to her throat. She reached for his hand, pressing her lips to his fingertips. 'I've never had to face what you've just described. I could never be so brave.'

'You displayed bravery every day, by resisting the temptation to exploit your card skills.'

'It's not a temptation when you know it would be wrong. I'm not brave, Luca.'

'Remarkable, then, if you prefer. What I'm trying to say is that you could be anything you want, Becky.'

'Thank you,' she said awkwardly, because he looked as if he really meant it, and she didn't know what on earth to make of that. 'What I want right now, is to make a success of my debut as Cousin Rebecca.'

'Are you nervous? You've no need to be. My mother has been singing your praises.'

'She's biased, since I'm the product of all her training.'

'You are the product of all your own hard work. I have no doubt you will make a most demure Cousin Rebecca, and a most intimidating and unbeatable Queen of Coins. From the stage of Drury Lane, through the piazza of Covent Garden, the gaming hells of St James's to the salons of Venice and Carnival, Miss Becky Wickes will be a resounding success in every role she plays.' Luca eyed her quizzically. 'There seems to be no end to the masks you wear. One would think you'd been born a Venetian.'

'Since you compare me to your precious Venice, I suppose I should be honoured.'

'You don't like compliments much, do you?'

'In my experience, people only pay compliments to get on your good side, so you'll do what they want.'

'But you're already doing what I want.'

Becky studied her hands. 'You've no need to pay me compliments, then, have you?'

'I wasn't complimenting you, I was telling you the truth.' Luca shifted on the bench, stretching his legs out in front of him. 'I've never met a woman like you.'

'I've never met a man like you.'

'Different worlds. A unique situation. That is what I told myself last night. That is why I don't recognise my behaviour.'

'That's what I told myself too,' Becky said, surprised into a strange little laugh. 'Perhaps it's the truth.'

'Perhaps it is. I tried to take your advice, but I am afraid that cards could not hold my attention,' Luca said ruefully. 'So I spent much of the night thinking about how to find a way for you to play against an opponent.'

'And were you successful?'

'I'm afraid not. I don't think there is any way it can be done safely. Cards are played outside Carnevale at the Contessa Benzon's *palazzo*, I have heard, but Cousin Rebecca could not possibly play, and we could not invite one of the more experienced players here, for we cannot risk anyone knowing of the connection between Cousin Rebecca and the Queen of Coins.'

Becky pondered this disappointing news. 'Would it be permissible for Cousin Rebecca to watch rather than play?'

'Would that help?' When she nodded, Luca brightened. 'I am sure we can arrange that.'

'Excellent, though first I have to get through tonight.'

'One role at a time. Did I tell you that you are extraordinary, Miss Becky Wickes?'

'So often that I'm beginning to believe you after all.'

'I hope so.' Luca reached across to push her hair back from her brow. 'Because it is the truth.'

His lashes were thick and sooty, far too long for a man. In the sunlight, there were streaks of chestnut brown in his hair. Her stomach was fluttering at his nearness. She couldn't break free of his gaze, the heat flaring in his eyes waking a craving for his mouth on hers. He was so close. She only had to move the tiniest bit towards him and he'd know what she wanted, and he'd kiss her. But it was broad daylight. And she was dressed in Cousin Rebecca's costume. Confused, Becky jumped to her feet. 'You haven't told me what you think of my gown, Cousin Luca.'

She waited, eyes lowered demurely, hands clasped in front of her, praying that he would take his cue. And at last he did, getting to his feet, making a bow. 'It suits you perfectly, Cousin Rebecca.'

For her debut in Venetian society, Cousin Rebecca wore white. A silk underdress, an overdress of sarsenet, white silk stockings and white silk slippers. A white shawl of the softest cashmere was draped around her shoulders. Her long gloves where white kid. Chiara, her maid, had powdered her face and shoulders under Isabel's strict supervision, and fixed her unruly hair back into such a tight chignon, using so many pins that Becky's head ached. A white gardenia was threaded on a ribbon around her neck.

'I look like a ghost,' she told Isabel.

'It is a pity that your eyes are such a striking colour' was all that the Contessa ventured. 'You must make every effort to keep them lowered.'

Her nerves, slowly building since this morning, made her stomach roil. As the hour of her public debut drew near, Becky's confidence began to falter. A terror of spattering food on her gloves prevented her from eating much at dinner, though she supposed that was in keeping for the role she was playing. A girl this pale must surely be starving. She wondered what Brunetti would make of her sudden loss of appetite, or indeed what the rest of the servants hovering about the dining room would make of her sudden loss of conversation.

'My cousin Rebecca is a little nervous,' Luca said as the major-domo removed her untouched melting lemon sorbet, as if he'd read her thoughts. 'She is to attend the salon of Contessa Albrizzi tonight.'

'A most formidable woman,' Brunetti said. 'But I am sure Signorina Wickes will make a favourable impression.'

Signorina Wickes was on the verge of losing her nerve completely as she prepared for the short journey, waiting in the reception area in her all-enveloping evening cloak for the gondola to be readied. The Contessa, in a magnificent black gown of silk and lace, her head covered in a veil, looked both remote and terrifying. Even Luca, in his formal evening dress of black silk breeches and coat, silk stockings and shoes rather than boots, his hair slicked back from his high brow, seemed every inch the Count, and several miles in status above her. The gondola, with a light gleaming on the gold-toothed prow, looked even more like a floating coffin than usual.

Climbing into it with Luca's aid, Becky repressed a shudder. There was room only for the two women in the cabin. Venice in the dark was a different place, all looming, sinister shadows and murky waters. She clutched her hands together and sat tensely, mentally rehearsing her role. The gondola glided silently along, and too soon for Becky's peace of mind, came to dock. She felt quite sick now. She was sure that if she tried to stand, her legs would give way.

'Rebecca, are you ready?' the Contessa asked.

Her cue. She remembered then; she couldn't think why she'd forgotten, that it had always been like this before a performance. Every single time. And she remembered too, that the moment she took the first step into the glare of the lights, her stage fright disappeared, and she lost herself in whatever part it was she had to play.

'I am ready, Aunt Isabel.' She got to her feet, wrapping her cloak around her. 'Thank you, Cousin Luca,' she whispered as he helped her ashore. Lights blazed from the first floor of the *palazzo*. Braziers burned on both sides of the doors, which stood open. Luca offered his arm to his mother, casting Becky a worried glance. She saw it, but did not respond, following demurely in their wake, back straight, shoulders back, head up, eyes down.

Contessa Albrizzi was known as the Madame de Staël of Venice. Having had the presence of mind to have her first, unhappy marriage annulled, thus freeing her to marry into one of the city's oldest and noblest of families, she had established herself as a passionate patron of the arts and of artists. Rather too passionate, some said, but as a widow of six years' standing, she was free to bestow her favours as she saw fit. Rumour had it, Luca's mother had informed him, that the English poet Byron had been a recipient, but he took this information with a pinch of salt. Lord Byron's name had been linked with almost every woman in Venice. It was fortunate the man had seen fit to finally quit the city after a mammoth bout of debauchery, rumour had it, at the last Carnevale.

'Contessa.' Luca bowed low over the extended hand. 'You know my mother, obviously.'

'Isabel. It is good to see you out in company again. We have missed you.'

The two women curtsied, and Luca's mother indicated that Becky come forward. 'May I present my niece, Rebecca Wickes, come to us from England to acquire a little of our Italian gloss.'

Luca watched anxiously as Becky made a deep curtsy. 'Contessa Albrizzi, it is a great honour to be permitted to attend your salon. I have heard that the *conversazione* is the most sophisticated and well informed in Venice.' Cousin Rebecca smiled shyly. 'I am neither witty nor sophisticated, but I hope to acquire a little of both in such illustrious company.'

'No doubt Contessa del Pietro will be introducing you to Venice's other *salonista*, Contessa Benzon. You will find good *conversazione* there too, Signorina Wickes.'

'Indeed, I believe that we do plan to attend one of the Contessa Benzon's salons, but I must confess...' Here, Cousin Rebecca seemed to blush, dropping her gaze to her gloved hands, a little intake of breath giving her the courage to look back up. 'I must confess, Contessa Albrizzi, that it is this salon I have been most eagerly anticipating.'

Contessa Albrizzi preened at the compliment, forcing Luca to bite back a smile. He had heard his mother's acid remarks on the rivalry between the two *salonistas*. He placed a small bet with himself that Cousin Rebecca would pay the same compliment in reverse to Contessa Benzon.

'Well, now,' Contessa Albrizzi said, surveying the room, 'let me see who I can introduce you to, Signorina Wickes, to begin your education in the art of *conversazione*. You should be aware that political discussions of any sort are frowned upon.' Cousin Rebecca was treated to a condescending smile. 'Though I doubt very much that politics would interest a chit like you. Ah! Signor Antonio Canova is with us tonight, one of our greatest living sculptors. I will have him show you the bust of Helen of Troy, which he carved especially for me. Signor Canova, if you please.'

The introduction was made. The sculptor was only too pleased to have the opportunity to describe his work in lavish detail to a beautiful young English-woman, placing Cousin Rebecca's hand on his arm and steering her away. Luca's mother was surrounded by a clutch of women all anxious to discover whether her English niece had arrived in Venice with a fortune. 'If you will excuse me, Contessa Albrizzi,' Luca said, 'I should accompany my cousin for propriety's sake.'

'Nonsense. Signor Canova is passionate about marble, not flesh and blood. Though I must say, Conte del Pietro, that if your cousin stood still long enough, one could easily mistake her for being a statue. So cold, these English. It is the climate, I suppose, there is no heat, either in their sun or their blood, if you know what I mean. While we Venetian women— Ah, you must be very glad to be home, though, of course, we would all wish it had been under happier circumstances. Your dear father is much missed. I know that everyone will agree with me when I say that Conte Guido del Pietro was a pillar of Venetian society.'

'*Grazie*, Contessa Albrizzi, but I believe that honour was shared with Don Massimo Sarti. I had hoped to see him here tonight.'

'His wife has a fever. Nothing to worry about I am sure, but Don Sarti is such an attentive husband—provided it is not Carnevale, of course, but then Carnevale excuses us all from our conjugal duties. And on that subject, Luca— May I call you Luca?' Receiving a nod, Contessa Albrizzi smiled winsomely up at him. 'You are the last of our real Venetian men. A seafarer who has seen the world. A man who has only to walk into a room for all eyes to be upon him. And it is not only your very attractive person, but a certain air you possess. Ah, do not attempt to be modest, I am sure that I am not the first woman to tell you so.'

'You flatter me, Contessa Albrizzi.' Luca cast his eyes anxiously around the salon. There was no sign of Becky, and his mother had her back turned to him. 'I fear you must excuse me...'

'But, no, I have not quite finished with you yet.' The Contessa's grip on his arm was surprisingly strong. 'Now that your dear mother has come out of mourning, she will be turning her thoughts to providing you with a suitable wife. I do hope that milksop niece of hers is not in the running? You need a Venetian woman, with fire in her heart to match your own passions. If I were but five years younger, I would offer for you myself. But alas, a widow such as I, though rich in worldly goods and lineage, will not serve for the grand del Pietro name. We must find you a pretty virgin, and I have one such in mind.'

'You are very kind, Contessa Albrizzi, but I believe the honour of choosing my bride rests with my mother, now that my father is no longer with us.'

'Indeed, indeed,' the Contessa agreed. 'I will discuss the matter with her. It does you great credit, Luca, that you honour the traditions. But you have not answered my question. This cousin of yours, I am right in thinking that she is too close in blood to be deemed a suitable bride? Though if your mother had her mind set upon the match, the blood ties can easily be over-looked by a purse of gold passed in the right direction.'

'My cousin is here for a few weeks only, Contessa Albrizzi, to acquire a little polish, just as my mother informed you. Her marriage prospects are no concern of mine.'

'I am very relieved to hear this. My own protégée—but I will speak to your mother, as you suggested. You are anxious to rejoin your cousin, I can see. I suggest you try the second salon on the right, where my Helen of Troy is situated, but before you go, Luca...' the Contessa fluttered her eyelashes '...a lusty man such as you has appetites which cannot await the marriage bed. I think you will find that a woman such as I, of a certain age and experience, would leave you more than satisfied.'

'Of that I have no doubt, Contessa Albrizzi, but I fear you do me too great an honour. Now I really must go. Cousin Rebecca will be thinking I have abandoned her. *Scusi.*'

Thinking that, on this evidence, the rumours about the Contessa Albrizzi and Lord Byron were proba-bly accurate, Luca was too concerned about Becky to feel anything other than faint astonishment at the brazen offer he had just received. Weaving his way through the crowded salon with scant apologies to those who tried to waylay him, he found her, as the Contessa had predicted, standing beside the bust of Helen of Troy listening to its creator's flamboyant description of the lengths to which he had gone to select the perfect piece of marble. Canova, with his back to the doorway, was speaking in impassioned

Italian far too rapid for Becky's developing grasp of the language. Luca watched with amusement as, despite having little or no idea of what was being said to her, she nodded sagely, murmuring, *'Si, assolutamente...capisco perfettamente,'* in a serious, awed tone. He wanted to applaud her, shout *brava* and have her take a bow. Instead, he assumed his role of concerned escort.

'Signor Canova, I must thank you for taking such excellent care of my cousin.'

'Conte del Pietro.' The sculptor bowed with a flourish. 'I must commend you on your relative,' he said, reverting to English. 'For an Englishwoman, and so young, she shows great understanding of our arts. I hope you intend to show her some of our beautiful city's other treasures?'

'Starting tomorrow, *signor.*'

'I am sure I have already seen one of the most beautiful,' Cousin Rebecca said. 'I am honoured to have heard the history of your Helen of Troy, *signor.* It is something I shall never forget. *Grazie mille.*' She dropped into a low curtsy, flashing the artist a smile which made him blink, frown and peer more closely at her, but Becky's face was once more a mask as bland as Helen of Troy's.

'Cousin,' Luca said, struggling not to laugh at Canova's confusion. 'My mother wishes to introduce you to her friends.'

With a huge inner sigh of relief, Becky tucked her hand into Luca's arm and allowed him to lead Cousin Rebecca from the room. 'Thank you. I am not sure how much longer I could have fooled Signor Canova into thinking I understood more than one word in twenty of what he was saying.'

'It seemed to me that you were Signor Canova's perfect audience, Cousin Rebecca,' Luca replied, his eyes twinkling with merriment. 'Awestruck by his genius, and struck too dumb to interrupt the flow of his self-aggrandisement.' He stopped short of the double doors which led to the main salon. 'Your performance as Cousin Rebecca is extremely impressive. Contessa Albrizzi was so taken in, she worries that my mother intends you for my bride.'

'Your bride!' Becky gave a most unladylike snort of laughter. 'If only she knew.'

'I suppose it was an obvious leap to make.'

'Good heavens, why?'

Luca shrugged. 'While my father was alive, there was no urgent need for me to marry. Now that I am the Conte del Pietro, it is my responsibility to ensure that there is another to follow me. I need a son, therefore I require my mother to find me a wife.'

Becky eyed him in astonishment. 'You don't think you would make a better match if you picked your own wife?'

'It is the way it is done here, for parents to select a suitable bride, particularly for the eldest son. My parents' marriage was one of contentment. I trust my mother to find me a bride who will suit me equally well.'

Isabel had said as much to Becky only yesterday morning, but the very notion of someone as decided as Luca permitting anyone to make such an important decision for him was unbelievable. What was more, it didn't sound as if Isabel's marriage had been particularly contented. She opened her mouth to say as much to Luca, then closed it again. Isabel had confided in her as a friend. Besides, Luca's marriage—Luca's future beyond Carnival—was nothing to do with her. 'We should return to the salon, unless you wish people to speculate further about the possibility of you making a match with your Cousin Rebecca.'

'You're right, that would be one complication too many,' Luca said wryly. 'Once we have brought Don Sarti to justice, then I will turn my mind to marriage, but until then, I cannot afford to be distracted.'

He had no sooner opened the door than Isabel, who was clearly getting anxious, signalled them to join her. 'Aunt,' Cousin Rebecca said contritely, 'I am so very sorry to have deserted you, but Signor Canova was so fascinating I found it difficult to tear myself away.'

'He must have been extremely fascinating,' Isabel replied tartly. 'It is quite twenty minutes since Luca went in search of you.'

'Cousin Rebecca was so enthralled, I could not bring myself to cut short her enjoyment. I do beg your pardon, *signore*,' Luca said, addressing his mother's coterie.

'Ladies,' Isabel said, 'may I present my niece. Rebecca my dear, make your curtsy.' She waited as Becky did so. 'My friends have been accusing me of keeping your existence a secret, Rebecca.'

'Indeed, Signorina Wickes, we were most surprised by your arrival. I am Signora Fabbiano, incidentally.'

Becky dropped another curtsy, murmuring that she was delighted to make her acquaintance.

'Contessa del Pietro has spoken often of her brother's children.'

'No doubt because I wrote to her often of them,' Luca said. 'If I have called anywhere home while serving in the Royal Navy, it has been with my uncle, the Admiral, and his family. Indeed, one of my cousins actually served aboard the same ship as me, as my first officer.'

'This we know,' Signora Fabbiano said. 'But of Signorina Wickes…'

'My sister's daughter,' Isabel said. 'I must say, I find it incredible that I have never mentioned her, but perhaps it is because I so rarely hear from my dear sister, for she lives such a secluded life in the wilds of Wiltshire.'

Which was Becky's cue to chime in. 'Dear Papa is a country vicar, and Mama is very much occupied with assisting him in running the parish. She has little time for anything other than good works.'

'So you are the daughter of a man of the cloth?' Signora Fabbiano looked suitably unimpressed. 'You will excuse my asking, Signorina Wickes, but here in Venice we like to understand such matters, it prevents confusion, you see. Your father, then, he is not a rich man?'

'We are poor as church mice,' Cousin Rebecca replied, with a shy smile. 'Were it not for my Aunt Isabel's overwhelming generosity, I would not even own a gown fit to wear this evening.'

'Poor as church mice,' Signora Fabbiano repeated, shaking her head. 'Poor little Signorina Wickes, you must be finding the luxury of the Palazzo Pietro a real treat.'

'It is beyond anything I could have imagined,' Becky replied truthfully.

'Your aunt was telling us that it is your mother's intention to find you a husband when you return to England?'

If I returned to England, Becky thought, I'd be much more likely to find myself in the arms of the law than a suitor. If only she could tell Signora Fabbiano this interesting fact, there would be no need for the tale she was instead about to spout. Isabel had warned her that she would be subject to this kind of inquisition, but she hadn't really believed her. Now she was extremely grateful for her foresight. 'If I could find a man as wonderful as dear Papa I would be very happy,' Becky said soulfully.

'You aspire no higher than a mere clergyman?'

'It was good enough for Mama,' Cousin Rebecca said, trying not to grit her teeth, for Signora Fabbiano could not keep the disdain from her voice. 'I can think of no better example.'

'You will have no cause to wear such a gown as the Contessa del Pietro has provided you with, in the wilds of… Where did you say it was?'

'Wiltshire, *signora*. Perhaps not,' Cousin Rebecca said, 'but I am sure I can cut it down to make the most beautiful christening robe.' Apparently covered in maidenly confusion at having made so immodest a remark, Cousin Rebecca buried her face in her kerchief. Becky was struggling to stay in character. She had no time for these people, they were everything she was not, but it didn't feel right, deceiving them. They had welcomed her into their company, when, if they knew the truth, they'd cross the road—or the canal— to avoid being contaminated by her.

'Well, Contessa del Pietro, and what do you make

of that? To have brought the chit all this way, to our most sophisticated city. Any spit and polish you apply, which is, I believe, the correct English term, will be quite wasted.'

'Perhaps,' Isabel said smoothly, 'but I will have had the pleasure of my niece's company while she acquires it. Rebecca is the closest thing I have to a daughter of my own,' she added.

The warm smile which accompanied this remark served only to make Becky bury her face further in her kerchief, her embarrassment now quite real. Isabel thought she knew her, but she had no idea she was harbouring a gallows cheat. Of course, it was ludicrous to imagine that Isabel could ever think of her as a daughter, but she did think of her as a friend. Which they couldn't be, Becky should have known that. Their friendship, like Cousin Rebecca, was simply an illusion.

'*Si, si...*' Signora Fabianno was nodding. 'Now I understand. A son, even one so handsome as yours, my dear Isabel, is no substitute for a woman's company. So you make a long visit to the Contessa, Signorina Wickes?'

'Cousin Rebecca is with us only until the end of Carnevale,' Luca intervened, to Becky's relief. 'It will be my pleasure to show her our beautiful city, and to rediscover it for myself, through fresh eyes.'

'Though you will not wish such fresh, innocent eyes, to see too much of Carnevale, Conte del Pietro?'

'Indeed not,' Luca said, seemingly quite affronted.

'And you will not, I hope, devote yourself exclusively to your cousin. Charming as you are I am sure, Signorina Wickes, you will understand that the Conte del Pietro requires more worldly company. And there is plenty to be had of it at Carnevale, is that not so, *signor*?'

'Signora Fabianno! If you please, no more in front of my niece.'

'Your pardon, Isabel. Perhaps your niece would like to meet Aurora? My eldest daughter,' she added, smiling at Luca, 'and I must say, without prejudice, one of the most beautiful of Venice's maidens. I am sure she would be delighted to join you on some of your sightseeing trips. You will find her most agreeable, Conte del Pietro.'

Chapter Six

The next morning, Luca informed Becky that he intended to make good on his promise to take her sightseeing. It was a beautiful winter's day, with a bright sun shining in a cloudless sky. Happy to permit Chiara to select an appropriate outfit, Becky wore a white muslin day gown with long sleeves and a small plain collar. Three layers of petticoats, the maid insisted, would provide the necessary protection against the cold, and Becky knew better than to disagree. The dusky-pink velvet half pelisse had a double row of buttons, a military-style cap, half-boots and gloves to match. With her hair gathered at her nape in a deceptively simple chignon, and a pretty but most impractical reticule that was big enough only to hold her kerchief dangling from her wrist, Becky barely recognised herself.

'The colour suits Signorina Wickes very well,' Chiara said, angling the cap at a jauntier angle. 'You look as if you belong here.'

'*Grazie,*' Becky said, smiling to herself. 'That is a bigger compliment than you realise.'

Luca was waiting for her on the small quay outside the *palazzo*, looking very piratical in a short black cloak, black breeches and highly polished black boots, his hair blowing about his face in the breeze, for he wore no hat. 'Cousin Rebecca,' he said with a formal bow, 'I am delighted that you could join me.'

She was surprised to see that this gondola had no cabin, and was therefore completely open to the elements. Following him on to the bobbing craft, Becky was even more surprised when Luca picked up the long oar and took up position at the stern.

'I told the gondolier that his services were not required. Do not fear,' he said, untying the ropes and beginning to row them out on to the Grand Canal. 'I ended my naval career as the captain of a frigate, but I discovered my love of the sea here in Venice. I have been piloting gondolas since I was a boy.'

'I'm simply glad that I don't have to play Cousin Rebecca, since we are alone.' She had to twist her neck to speak to him, seated as she was at the rear of the gondola, facing in the direction in which Luca was rowing. Clutching the side of the narrow boat, Becky clambered over to the other seat, facing Luca. 'Speaking of being alone, I hope you are not planning to take Signora Fabianno up on her offer to foist her daughter on us, not if she is anything like her mother.'

Luca laughed. 'Were you as shocked as Cousin Rebecca appeared to be, by Signora Fabianno's questions? I warned you that we Venetians do not find the subjects of money or marital prospects vulgar.'

''I think we made it perfectly clear that Cousin Rebecca is not a contender for the position of Contessa del Pietro at any rate.'

Luca smiled wryly, concentrating on steering their gondola further out into the canal. 'My mother tells me that she has already received any number of social invitations which include you.'

'Do I have to go, Luca? I know it's what we agreed, but last night, it felt wrong deceiving all those people.'

'Wrong? A necessary but harmless deception which cost them nothing.'

She frowned down at her hands, as if they could help her divine how much to say without giving herself away. 'If they knew me, the real me, I mean, they wouldn't allow me to step over their thresholds. I'm not your cousin.'

'But it did not occur to any of them that you are not. You played the part to perfection.'

'People see what they want to see, Luca.'

'Accept the compliment, Becky. I could not have imagined a more accomplished performance.'

'Thank you.'

'Are you really so unhappy playing that part?'

Yes was the straight answer. But she'd accepted The Procurer's offer, she couldn't renege on it now. Besides, it wasn't only a case of her fee. Luca had not mentioned his father's murder since the day after her arrival, when he'd told her the story behind his plan, but the pain must lurk, just beneath the surface, carefully tethered. Did he let it loose when he was alone? Did he cry out as she had done, in the days after she'd discovered Jack's perfidy? She couldn't imagine it, somehow. Recalling her own bitter tears now made her cringe inwardly. Jack had hurt her, but how much deeper was the hurt Luca nursed deep within him?

How little she knew of him despite the many hours they'd spent together.

'Forget I mentioned it,' Becky said. 'What matters is that we've taken the first step. I know how much it means to you.'

His face tightened. *'Grazie,'* he said, and the simple word quashed all her qualms.

He had pushed his cloak back over one shoulder, where it fluttered behind him in the breeze. Balanced on the narrow stern, his booted legs braced, both hands on the oar, using an almost circular motion to propel and steer the craft seemingly effortlessly, she could only imagine the strength of his shoulders and arms, the muscles rippling with the effort. The sunlight flickered over the chestnut highlights in his hair. The air smelt so sweet, the motion of the boat was soothing.

'Who taught you how to— Is it called rowing when there is only the one oar?'

'Si. It was one of my father's gondoliers who taught me when I was perhaps seven or eight. Not in a gondola like this, but in a much smaller one, and not so grand. There is no other way to get around in Venice, so many of the footpaths end in blind alleys, or they are flooded at high tide.'

'What about your father, could he row?'

'Yes, but it was beneath the dignity of the Conte del Pietro to break sweat.'

'You are the Conte del Pietro now.'

Luca grinned. 'Not today. Today, I am simply a Venetian showing his beautiful city to a beautiful lady. And there on the left is one of our most beautiful *palazzos* and one of the oldest. It is known as the Ca' d'Oro.'

'The Golden House?' Becky hazarded, though she could see no trace of gold on the ornate exterior.

Luca nodded. 'Home to the Contorini family until the Republic fell. They were the pre-eminent family in Venice until then. Even more powerful than my own. The doge of Venice was effectively the city's prince. You will see his palace facing out to the Lido, where the Grand Canal enters the lagoon.'

Becky gazed around her in wonder. 'Are all these buildings *palazzos*?'

'Not all of them are so grand inside as out,' Luca replied. 'Many are falling into ruin and some even into the canal. And not all are so comfortable to live in as the Palazzo Pietro either. Many of the most venerable Venetian families have become too poor to maintain them.'

'Though they look so very beautiful from here.'

'But as you very well know, appearances, especially here in Venice, can be deceptive. This is the Ponte de Rialto we are passing under.'

The elaborate, covered stone bridge spanned the canal at a sharp bend, rows of shops lining the arches. They travelled on, following another bend in the canal, and the waters changed from turquoise to sea green as the canal became wider and the breeze stronger. Becky listened as Luca pointed out churches and palaces, but there were so many of them, each more awe-inspiring than the next, that she felt quite dazed. Finally, the gondola came to the end of the Grand Canal and the vista opened to one of islands, the Lido in the distance and the sparkling blue of the lagoon. She shifted to the forward-facing seat at Luca's feet to better drink in the view.

'The Giardini Reali,' Luca said, pointing to the first large green space that she had seen in the city, gondolas vying for berthing spaces on the jetty which faced it. 'Built by Napoleon, to compensate us for all that he looted, perhaps.'

But Becky's gaze had already moved on to the elegant tower of the Campanile San Marco, which she had seen from the rooftop of the Palazzo Pietro, and the spectacle of Venice's most splendid square.

'The *piazetta*,' Luca told her, holding the gondola steady to allow her a better view. 'The Doge's Palace is there on the other side, and the Piazza San Marco leads off the *piazetta*, with the church…'

'I can see the domes. My goodness, there are so many people here.'

'Wait until Carnevale. This is nothing. I think our street theatre will put anything you have experienced in London or Brighton to shame. The *volo della colombina*, for example, the flight of the dove, where a man dressed as an angel sails down a rope from the campanile to the palace.'

'I would love to see that.'

'You shall. Though Cousin Rebecca cannot risk her innocence at Carnevale under cover of darkness, it would be cruel to deny her the delights to be offered at San Marco in the daylight. Do you wish me to tie up here so you can have a closer look?'

Becky eyed the crowds with little relish. 'We would most likely encounter acquaintances of yours, wouldn't we?'

'I have been away from Venice for so long I doubt

it, but friends of my parents, almost certainly. Would you prefer to go for a stroll somewhere away from the crowds, with no need to play Cousin Rebecca?'

'I'd love to, though I can't imagine where. I thought London was crowded. I've never seen so many buildings crammed into such a small space. No wonder there are so many gardens on the roofs, there's nowhere else to put them.'

'But we do have a beach,' Luca said, turning the gondola away from the view of San Marco, towards the long narrow spit of land known as the Lido. 'The English poet Lord Byron won a swimming race from the Lido to here, I am told. Not content with winning though, he swam the length of the Grand Canal too.'

'Why on earth would he do such a thing?'

Luca shrugged. 'For certain individuals, being notorious is a vocation.'

The breeze freshened and the gondola bobbed on the waves. By the time Luca helped her ashore, Becky was glad to feel solid ground beneath her feet. Though she could see no sign of a beach, the open space, the trees and the absence of crowded buildings were refreshing.

Luca took her arm, leading her along a narrow path directly to the coast which faced out to the Adriatic Sea, and there was the beach. Becky stopped short on the edge of the long strip of golden sand. There were two horse riders galloping away from them in the distance, a clutch of the distinctively shaped fishing boats bobbing on the horizon, but not another soul around. She lifted her face to the breeze, breathing deep of the stinging briny air, pulling off her hat, relishing the way the wind ruffled her hair, tugged at her skirts, making her realise how very constrained she'd been feeling. 'The sand looks so soft, but I don't want to spoil my boots walking on it. Do you think I would be beyond the pale if I took them off?'

'Why not? Though you will find the sand very cold on your feet,' Luca said as Becky perched on a rock and began to grapple with the buttons of her pink boots.

Her hair was escaping its pins, falling in a tangle of ringlets over her face. Her cheeks were pink, her eyes sparkling with anticipation as she set the boots down, wriggling her stocking-clad toes, her smile mischievous as she met his eyes. 'Turn your back,' she said.

He did, most reluctantly, wondering what on earth she could be doing, rewarded, when she caught his arm, with a glimpse of her naked feet, toes curling into the sand. She had closed her eyes, her face tilted up to the weak sun. When she opened them again, her smile was one of pure delight. 'That feels absolutely wonderful.'

She looked so delectable, so innocently joyful, that his heart lifted at the sight of her. He was not conscious of the burden he had carried with him since reading his father's letter, until it lifted momentarily as he smiled down at her, and the world narrowed, so that all that mattered was this moment, this beach, this woman, and the wide expanse of the Adriatic in front of him. The sea had always drawn him. It drew him now, as he caught Becky's hand in his and began to run with her, headlong along the beach, laughing as they stumbled in the soft sand, laughing at her squeal of surprise as it darkened and firmed towards the water's edge, where he stopped short, but Becky did not, picking up her skirts and jumping over a wavelet into the sea.

She yelped. 'It's freezing.'

'I did warn you.'

Another wave caught the back of her legs, making her stagger forward, lifting her skirts higher. Her legs were very pale and very shapely. Luca eyed them appreciatively. 'Don't go any further out. The sand shelves so steeply...'

But it was too late, Becky had already taken another step, which took the water well above her knees. He sprang forward, grabbing her just before she fell.

'Your boots, they'll be ruined,' she said breathlessly as he pulled her back on to the shore.

'I have other boots, but only one Becky.'

Balancing on his arm, she inspected one of her feet. 'I'm covered in sand.'

'You would have been covered in a great deal more than sand if you had fallen in.'

'My hero.' She clasped her hands dramatically to her breast, her eyes dancing with merriment. 'How can I ever thank you, kind sir?'

For answer, he scooped her up into his arms, holding her high against his chest as she wriggled in mock outrage, then clung to his neck as he began to march back across the sands to the shelter of the small dune where she had left her stockings and boots.

'Put me down, sir, put me down at once,' Becky said, in her best outraged-fair-maiden voice, gasping in surprise when he did, letting her slide down to her feet, unfastening his cloak and wrapping it around her shoulders. 'I don't need…' she protested.

'*I* can't afford for you to catch a chill,' Luca said, pushing her hair back from her face. He smiled down at her, quite beguiled. He knew that her life had been a constant struggle. He knew that she must be old beyond her years in many ways, having lived amid so much poverty and suffering, yet she seemed so carefree, took such innocent delight in a walk on a beach. He couldn't bear the notion of her ever returning to that life, though he knew better than to say so.

'What are you thinking, Luca?'

Her smile was dazzling. He stopped thinking. He pulled her tight up against him. He could have sworn the wind dropped as her eyes met his, and the waves grew silent as she slid her arms around his neck, and then there was a rushing, roaring in his ears as their lips met, and they kissed.

She tasted of salt. He licked into the corner of her mouth, relishing the way it made her shiver against him. He slid his hands down her back, beneath his cloak. Her new clothes came with undergarments that deprived his senses of her soft curves, until his hands came to rest on her bottom and blood rushed to his groin in response and his tongue sought hers. Their mouths fitted perfectly, matching kiss for kiss as they stumbled in the sand and then sank on to it, their mouths still clinging as Becky lay back, his cloak spread out on the sand, and he covered her body with his and she gave a soft sigh, pulling him closer.

He dragged his mouth away for the pleasure of looking at her, eyes dark with the passion he knew was reflected in his own, her lips slightly parted. He ran his hand up her flank, past the dip in her waist, seeking the swell of her breast, but encountered only the buttons of her jacket, and beneath that the boning of her corsets.

His frustration must have shown on his face, for she gave a throaty little chuckle. 'The attire of young ladies,' she said, 'is designed to frustrate all but the most persistent.'

Luca groaned. 'It is certainly designed to frustrate.'

'Both parties.' She pulled his mouth back to hers, kissing him fiercely. He felt himself spinning out of control. Their legs were tangled in her petticoats and the skirts of his coat. He wanted to touch skin and soft flesh, but there seemed to be thick folds of cloth between them. Their mouths clung as he rolled over on to his back, taking Becky with him, and he gave a startled cry as the movement freed her to sit astride him, the aching length of his erection between her legs, though still with far too much material between them. He muttered her name, eyes screwed shut at the pleasure, the astounding pleasure, of just having her there, and then flying open as she leaned forward to kiss him again, and the movement made him throb.

He felt such a gut-wrenching desire to be inside her, it was almost overwhelming. When Becky ended the kiss, sliding on to the sand at his side, he was lost for words, breathing heavily.

Beside him, she too seemed to be struggling for breath and control. 'I think it's safe to say that I now have sand almost everywhere.'

He pushed himself upright, shaking the sand from his hair. 'You are not the only one. On the bright side, at least we need not worry about one of my servants discovering us.'

Becky's smile was perfunctory. She busied herself brushing the sand off her feet, and he made a pretence of looking away as she put her stockings back on. 'Is the danger of discovery part of the thrill, Luca?'

'No!' He whirled back around to face her. 'The thrill, as you call it, is you, and nothing else.' Luca picked up a handful of golden sand, letting the grains trickle through his fingers. 'At the risk of repeating myself, I find you extraordinary. And fascinating. And irresistible.'

'You haven't said that I'm irresistible before.'

'But I've proved it, twice in the space of two days.'

'I'm not a hussy, Luca.'

'*Basta!* You think I don't know that? Why would you say such a thing?'

'People assume that women like me, from my background— They think that we're too poor to afford morals.'

Luca opened his mouth to protest, then closed it again. She held his gaze, such a mixture of defiance and pride in her expression that his heart contracted. 'Unfortunately some are,' he said heavily. 'I cannot claim ignorance of such women. I've seen them gathering on the docks as our ship tied up in ports across the world. They do not seek pleasure, such women, they seek money for food, for clothes, for their children. I have never taken advantage of what they offer, and I did not, for one second, think that you were one such, if that is what you are asking.'

Her lip wobbled. 'It would be a natural assumption to make. Let's face it, if I'd really been Cousin

Rebecca and not Becky Wickes, you wouldn't have kissed my hand, never mind…'

'Wanting to kiss you all over?' Luca shuffled closer, covering her hands with his. 'It has nothing to do with where you come from, and everything to do with who you are, can't you see that? I don't think of you as a hussy or a virgin or anything in between. I think of you only as Becky. Unique. And to me, irresistible.'

Slipping her hand from Luca's, Becky leaned back on her elbows, tilting her face up to the watery sun. 'I've never in my life behaved like this before. You've turned me into a wanton.'

'You have had exactly the same effect on me, you know.'

She stole a shy glance at him. 'In a few weeks I'll be gone and we'll never see each other again, and I expect all this will seem like a dream, won't it? Though actually, it seems like a dream to me most of the time already. And when I go, your life will return to normal. Perhaps you'll marry the fair Aurora.'

Luca shrugged. 'Perhaps.'

She eyed him curiously, unable to believe that he was so indifferent to such a momentous event as he appeared. 'You can't truly believe that a wife chosen in such a manner would make either of you happy.'

'Matrimony here is a matter of convenience,' Luca said impatiently. 'I thought I had explained.'

'You did, but— I don't know, it sounds such a cold, calculated arrangement, and you are neither cold nor calculating.'

'*Grazie.* You know, marriage such as the one which will be arranged for me, it will be much more successful than those which are made for love. We will have much in common, my wife and I. Shared heritage. Shared traditions. Shared society. Once we have a son, we will both be free to take a lover. After duty is done, then there can be passion. And when that passion has burned itself out, then there are other lovers to be had.'

He spoke prosaically. His logic, his tone implied, was impeccable. It most likely was, but Becky was repelled. 'Children aren't a commodity, Luca, and nor should wives be. How can you be so sure that when the woman who has borne you a son decides to warm another man's bed, you won't care?'

'You don't understand.'

'No, I don't.' Becky crossed her arms. 'I don't understand why it is you must take a virgin bride, but the moment she's done her duty by you, the chastity that meant so much is completely irrelevant. What happened to the promise to forsake all others, or don't you make that one in Italy?'

'In my experience,' Luca retorted, 'marriages in England are conducted in exactly the same way. The difference being you don't admit it.'

'That may be the case for those with property and bloodlines to worry about, but for most people, marriage is about love. Having a family, not just a son. Being happy with one person, and not taking a string of lovers.'

'For most people, but not for Becky Wickes?'

'What do you mean?'

'You are very determined that marriage forms no part of your future.'

Taken aback at having the tables turned on her, Becky glowered. 'We were talking about you.'

'And now we are talking about you. Love. Marriage. A family. If that makes for such happiness as you declare, why don't you want it for yourself?'

Becky frowned. Surely that was not what she'd said? She had dreamed of exactly that with Jack, it was the reason she'd gone along with his lies for so long, thinking that it might eventually lead her to a happy ending. Aware of Luca's scrutiny, she sought some flippant riposte, but the words wouldn't come. She'd learnt her lesson, but she wouldn't allow Jack to make a cynic of her. 'I'm happier on my own,' she said gruffly.

'Though it was not always so, no? This man, your paramour…'

'Proved just that,' Becky said hastily. 'That I was better off on my own.' She didn't want to talk to Luca about Jack. She was sick of thinking about Jack, and the very notion of him as the loving husband and father she'd once dreamed he would be was ludicrous. Absolutely ludicrous.

She stared at Luca, a smile beginning to dawn. So many times she'd told herself that she was well rid of him, but until now she hadn't believed it. *'Meno male,'* she said, because it sounded so much better in Italian than English. Goodness, it really was true!

'What is it? What are you thinking?'

Becky shook her head, still smiling, as much at Luca's confusion as her own thoughts. 'We should get going, or we'll be crossing the lagoon in the pitch dark.'

'I have done so many times, I could do it blindfold,'

Luca said, though he followed her lead, getting to his feet, shaking out sand from his coat and cloak again, frowning out over the sea as she set about putting on her boots.

He remained silent, pensive, as they retraced their steps back along the narrow path to the other side of the Lido. The lagoon was a darker blue now, the sun beginning to sink. Luca lit the lamp in the prow of the gondola, but as she made to clamber on board, he caught her arm. 'It is different for me. I am not callous but I have no choice but to marry.'

'I do understand that.' She pressed his hand to her cheek. His skin was warm, hers cold. 'It's funny to think, isn't it, that here you are, one of the richest men in Venice, from one of the noblest families, and you don't have a choice in the matter, while I, who don't even know who my father was, can do as I please.'

This time he made no move to prevent her as she climbed into the gondola, leaping lightly in after her, unfastening the rope from the jetty and fitting the oar into the rowlock. The waters were still, the air at that stage between day and dusk where it seemed to be holding its breath. Becky—in the seat facing towards the city, where the lights were beginning to appear—shivered.

'Take this. I don't need it, the rowing will keep me warm.'

His cloak fluttered on to her knees. After a moment's hesitation, she wrapped herself in it, twisting around in the seat to look up at him. *'Grazie.'*

He shrugged, clearly still brooding on their previous conversation. 'For centuries, the Venetian nobility have been arranging successful marriages in the traditional way. Why should I be an exception?'

Her questions had unsettled him. What right had she to question his life, his future? 'It's none of my business, Luca. My only wish is for you to be happy.'

'Why shouldn't I be?'

Why indeed? And why should she care! But she did. Becky sighed, turning her back on him. 'I fervently hope that you will be, Luca.'

Chapter Seven

For her first visit to the opera, Cousin Rebecca wore a rose-pink satin evening gown with an overdress of white muslin embroidered with leaves and flowers. A chemisette made of the same muslin, worn under the gown's low-cut décolleté, covered every inch of flesh at her bosom and protected her maidenly modesty. Becky's hair was pinned so tightly back that it made her feel as if her forehead was being stretched, but she could not deny that the coiffure, along with the face powder, transformed her. And the resultant headache ensured that she did not forget she was in costume.

La Fenice, as the opera house was known, was a short gondola trip along some of the minor canals, which became crowded as they approached the *campo* which fronted the theatre, obliging their gondolier to jockey for position to gain a berth. Becky's stage career had not included the opera, so this was her first experience and she was looking forward to it, having been assured by Isabel that it was perfectly acceptable for Cousin Rebecca to do so.

'The Venetians' claim that their opera is the best in

the world is, unlike some of their other superlatives, most probably true,' the Contessa said, slanting a teasing glance at her son as she took her seat in their private box.

'That, even the English do not dispute,' Luca said to Becky, who was sitting between them. 'My mother's brother, Admiral Riddell, is a connoisseur of the opera. He has been only once to La Fenice, but he still talks of it.'

'In 1792, the year after your birth, and the opening season of the new theatre,' Isabel said. 'I remember it well, though it must be coming up for thirty years ago now.'

'And you have not seen your brother since?' Becky asked.

'Oh, he has visited on a couple of occasions since, but in the summer, outside the opera season.'

'Haven't you ever returned to England since you married?'

'My uncle invited you to visit him several times, to coincide with my ship being docked in Plymouth,' Luca reminded his mother when she hesitated. 'You were apparently unable to oblige because my father insisted he needed you by his side in Venice.'

'Regretfully, that is true,' Isabel replied.

'Didn't you want to see your son and your family?'

Isabel's clear-eyed gaze faltered under Luca's scrutiny. 'You think your father cared that I missed you? He cared only for his position of influence, his precious reputation, and, of course, above all his devotion to his precious Venice. I was a vital appendage, and so in his eyes I could not be spared.' She drew in a sharp breath, immediately contrite. 'I beg your pardon. I should not have spoken in such blunt terms. I do not know what came over me.'

Stuck between mother and son, Becky hardly dared to breathe. Luca, far from angry, seemed thunderstruck. 'Was my father so devoted to Venice as to be completely selfish and intransigent?'

Isabel shook her head. 'He did not see it that way. If I had made more of a fuss—insisted, perhaps—but I did not. I regret it. Of late, there have been several things I have realised that I regret,' she said with a sad little smile aimed at Becky. 'But what is the point in regrets? They change nothing. The future is what matters. Now that I am no longer tied to your father's side, perhaps I will visit England. But for now,' she continued brightly, 'I think we should tell Rebecca the story of Rossini's *Tancredi*, for she may not be able to follow it when it starts. It was the first opera performed here when the theatre opened, and...'

'Were you unhappy, Mama?'

'Oh, Luca, what kind of question is that to ask me?'

'Perhaps one I should have asked long before now.'

Becky sensed Isabel stiffening. 'I spoke to you in confidence,' the Contessa said to her. 'I thought you understood that.'

'I did. I...'

'You are mistaken if you think I'm asking you because Becky has betrayed a confidence,' Luca interrupted. 'I see now though, why she is so very antagonistic towards our Venetian marital customs.'

'We are embarrassing her,' Isabel said tersely. 'And in danger of spoiling the opera for her too.'

'You are right.' Luca made a visible effort to relax as

the orchestra started to tune up. 'Quickly, then, before the curtain comes up, let me outline the plot of *Tancredi*.'

It was, as ever, a bravura excellent performance, but Luca could not concentrate. Beside him, Becky sat leaning forward, unlike him, completely immersed in the opera. It was a rare chance to study her unobserved. Though garbed as Cousin Rebecca, in her fascination with the stage, she was wholly Becky. Emotions flickered across her face, reflecting the mood of the music. Her wide-eyed gaze missed nothing, neither on the stage nor in the wings, somehow anticipating the changes of scenery before the faint grinding of wheels and pulleys began. Very early on, she noticed that the singers took their cues from the conductor, her ear so acutely attuned that she frowned when the chorus came in a fraction too late, making him smile as she nodded her approval when one of the male leads manoeuvred the diva, in the middle of an aria, out of the way of an oncoming prop.

His mother was staring at the stage, but he could tell from her carefully blank expression that she wasn't watching the opera. She had become very fond of Becky. She had confided in Becky what he hadn't even guessed. Had his mother felt her marriage a prison? Had his father been her jailer? An exaggeration, surely? He'd forgotten how hurt he had been, all those years ago, when she had refused the Admiral's first invitation. The second refusal. Yes, he had minded that less. From the first time he set foot on the deck of a Royal Naval frigate, his heart had been given to that life. Venice, his mother, his father, they would always be there, waiting, while the world was his to explore there and then. Duty and desire were serendipitously one, he'd thought, but had he simply been selfish?

A ripple of applause signalled the end of an aria. The first act was nearing an end. Those standing in the pit began to shuffle restlessly. In the tiers of boxes, thoughts were turning to the interval Prosecco, the turning of opera glasses from the stage to the audience. Luca uncrossed his legs. He knew so little of his parents' lives, and it was almost entirely his own fault. He had never asked, never been curious, as absorbed in his own life as his father had apparently been in his.

Did he intend to fill his father's shoes, Becky had asked him. He remembered giving some vague reply about not having considered it, when the truth was he had no idea what it would entail. He had always been so proud of his father, but for the first time that pride sat ill with him.

The singing was reaching a crescendo. Casting an idle glance around the theatre as the curtain came down, Luca tensed. The box next to theirs, in the same coveted position at the centre of the horseshoe facing the stage, had been empty for the first act. His mother had noticed, but chosen not to comment. He had been both disappointed and relieved. With a sense of dread and cold fury, he watched the servant, standing sentinel by the open door, make way for the owners of the box to enter.

'What is it, Cousin Luca?'

Becky was looking up at him anxiously. His feelings must have been writ large on his face. He unclenched his jaw, forcing a rigid smile as he got to his feet. 'Don Sarti and his family have arrived, Cousin Rebecca. His wife must have recovered from her indisposition. Unfortunately we have not time for formal introductions, but I think we ought to make our bows.'

The morning after the opera, Aunt Isabel was confined to her bed with a headache and Cousin Luca had left the *palazzo* at first light, leaving Becky to take a solitary breakfast—if taking coffee and a buttered roll in the company of Brunetti and two other footmen could be called solitary. She went up to the roof afterwards, the only place in the *palazzo* where she ever felt truly alone. It was another bright, sunny winter's day. Simply breathing in the salty air, looking out at the glinting turquoise of the lagoon and the deeper blue of the Adriatic beyond made Becky feel a little better. She had not slept last night, and for once it was not because she had been rehearsing.

The opera had been magical. It wasn't only the music, it was the combination of singing and acting, the complex interaction between the huge chorus and the principals, the dramatic nature of the story, the way that the music enhanced every emotion. For Becky, opera had always been tainted by the bawdy reputation of opera dancers, the notoriety of the green room and the ogling bucks who frequented it. Seeing it from front of house rather than backstage was a revelation. On one level, she couldn't help but be aware of the moving props, the stage directions, the greasepaint and the gaudy costumes, but on anther level she had given herself up to the illusion, lost herself in the story, stirred to her soul by the music.

And then Don Sarti and his family had arrived, and a very different drama began to unfold. It had not been Luca's first encounter with the Don, but it had been his first since concluding that his father's best friend had ordered his father's murder. What had astounded Becky was that he was so unprepared. She herself had felt quite sick, looking at the man that the Queen of Coins was to destroy, thankful for Cousin Rebecca's face powder, and even more thankful that only a curtsy had been required of her. Isabel had appeared the least affected, Becky had thought at the time. Her headache this morning told a different story. Isabel, she knew, had had several encounters with the Sarti family since her husband's death, enough to deaden the blow but not to blunt the impact.

But Luca! If ever Becky needed proof of how much this plan of his meant to him, last night provided it. Barely contained anger had emanated from him in waves for the remainder of the opera, so palpably that Becky fancied Don Sarti must sense it. He held himself so rigidly, she wondered he did not break a bone or grind a tooth to dust. His eyes burned with a fervour that was frightening. Remembering it made her shiver. This was not a game they were playing. In the day-to-day effort to play Cousin Rebecca, she had not lost sight of the Queen of Coins, but she had relegated her to the supporting cast. Soon, Luca's avenging angel was to take centre stage, and Becky had better make bloody sure she didn't fail.

She'd brought the cards up on to the roof with her. Knowing how fond she was of the space, Luca had equipped it with a table, more comfortable chairs and cushions too. One of the *palazzo*'s army of staff must have brought those in at night, for they were never damp. She dealt herself two hands of Trappola and began to pit her wits against herself, but it was no good. Cousin Rebecca would attend the Contessa Benzon's salon tomorrow, her first opportunity to watch others play. It would reduce the risk when the Queen of Coins made her debut, but not enough for Becky's peace of mind.

She was flicking through her sketches for the Queen of Coins's costume when the door to the roof opened, and Luca appeared. He was dressed in long boots and leather breeches, his black hair a wild tangle from the wind, his cheeks bright. To her relief, he was smiling. To her annoyance, his smile set off that distracting fluttering in her belly. 'You missed breakfast, Cousin Luca,' she said, assuming her demure smile.

'I went riding on the Lido. I keep several horses there. It cleared the cobwebs.' He kicked the door firmly shut and strode towards her, ignoring her Cousin Rebecca smile, swept her into his arms and kissed her.

His lips were warm against hers. She closed her eyes, momentarily giving herself up to the delight of their kisses, before dragging her mouth from his. 'Cousin Luca!' Becky said in mock outrage. 'How dare you!'

He tightened his hold, a teasing smile playing on his lips. 'That,' he said softly, his mouth against her ear, 'was most decidedly not a Cousin Rebecca kiss.'

'That is because Cousin Rebecca does not know how to kiss,' Becky said primly.

He nibbled her earlobe. She bit back a tiny moan. His mouth travelled down her throat, stopping at the ruffled neck of her gown. 'On the other hand, Becky most certainly knows how to kiss. In fact I'd go so far as to say that Becky's kisses are the most delightful kisses I have ever enjoyed.'

Her heart was fluttering wildly. Her pulses were racing. Her hands had found their way around his neck. 'High praise indeed, when you must have enjoyed a great many kisses in your time, Captain del Pietro.'

'Not nearly as many as you imagine. In any case, when I look into those big violet eyes of yours, I forget every one of them, and crave only yours.'

It was no use. It was over a week since they had last kissed at the Lido. Telling herself that she'd never be able to concentrate on anything else until she satisfied her own craving, Becky pulled him towards her and claimed his mouth. Dear heavens, but it was sublime. She could drown in their kisses, lose herself in the heady delight of them, her lips clinging to his, relishing the sweep of his tongue, the whisper of his breath, the taste of him. Relishing the way his hands shaped her body, tugging her tight against him. His hair was like silk. His cheeks were rough with stubble, yet his beard was surprisingly soft. They kissed until they were breathless, and when they dragged their mouths apart they stood, locked in one another's arms, gazing dazed into one another's eyes.

And then the grating sound of the door opening made them spring apart. Luca cursed. 'I ordered tea for you. I forgot.'

Becky hastily turned her back, pretending to admire the view as two footmen began to set out the tea things and the inevitable pot of coffee for Luca. Brunetti had decided not to make the arduous climb, she was relieved to note. The major-domo would not have failed to notice Cousin Rebecca's flushed countenance.

'Grazie,' Luca said, as the door closed with a creak.

'How did you know I'd be up here?' Becky asked, sitting down to make the tea.

'You feel at home here,' he said simply, helping himself to coffee.

'You find it strange that I should prefer a rooftop to a palace?' She poured herself a cup of tea, adding milk and three sugar lumps since Isabel wasn't there to disapprove. 'There are times when I can't quite believe that I'm staying in an actual palace. I've been here almost three weeks and I don't think I've been in half of the rooms.'

Luca was already pouring his second coffee. 'Would you like a tour?'

'Only if you are sure we wouldn't get lost.'

He grinned. 'It's an alluring prospect, to lose myself with you in an attic somewhere, or in one of the secret rooms behind the panelling in the library.'

'Are there secret rooms behind the panelling in the library?'

'Two. I have no idea what their original use was, presumably to hide valuables.'

'Talking of which…'

'Ah. That is your let-us-turn-our-minds-to-business voice.'

'We have a great deal of business to discuss, Luca.'

'Si. Last night, seeing that man…' His mouth tightened. 'Brazenly sitting there in his opera box, waving to the great and the good of the city, his wife and his daughter by his side. It made me feel sick.'

Don Sarti had looked every bit the contented spouse and father, Becky thought. She had imagined a stage villain. Don Massimo Sarti was in fact a handsome man past his prime, with grizzled grey curls, a broad, intelligent brow, a benevolent smile and a quiet yet definite air of authority. This was the inveterate gambler that the Queen of Coins was to bring to his knees. She found it difficult to believe. 'I'm glad he will be in disguise,' Becky said. 'I presume you know *what* disguise?'

'You must not be taken in by the man's appearance. Never forget that he is a thief and a murderer.'

'And a man who, when he has a hand of cards, is in the grips of a compulsion. I understand that, Luca. I am not getting cold feet, it's simply that seeing him with his family last night made what I have to do suddenly very real.'

'And it brought home to me how determined I am that it will be done.' Luca set his cup down on the tray. 'We cannot fail.'

'No, I've been thinking about that.' Becky took a breath to pluck up her courage, but Luca spoke first.

'So have I. It is not enough that you observe the game being played, you must practise by taking part.'

'Yes. That's exactly what I was thinking. But you said…'

'That there is no play, save of the kind you will see tonight, before Carnevale.'

'And since Cousin Rebecca cannot play in the Contessa Benzon's salon…'

'Nor can the Queen of Coins make an appearance there, amusing as that prospect may be.'

'The Queen of Coins cannot make any appearance until she has a suitable disguise to wear. I have some sketches…'

'In a moment.' Luca turned towards her on the

bench. 'Carnevale peaks in the first six weeks of the new year. That is when we will bring Don Sarti to justice. But before then, in December, Carnevale begins, and sport may be found by those who care to seek it out. I have learnt that some *ridotti* will open their doors discreetly some time in the next week or so. The stakes are modest. Like every aspect of Carnevale, the wildness and debauchery escalates as Lent approaches.'

'And you think that the Queen of Coins will be able to gain entry to these places? Who told you of them?'

'My mother. Last night, after you went to bed.'

Becky clattered her teacup into her saucer. 'Isabel! What does she know of such matters?'

'I admit I was surprised. But as we saw last night at the opera, she is more than capable of surprising me.' Luca smiled crookedly. 'You have been here for less than three weeks, and you know my mother better than I do.'

'No, that's not true.'

But he shook his head. 'Perhaps it is because you are both English that you understand each other. My mother freely admitted to me last night that if she had been Venetian, and therefore willing to abide by our marital conventions, she would have been happier in her marriage. But she was neither. I think it was a mistake for my father to choose an English bride. If my mother had been able to bring herself to take a *cavaliere servante*, an established lover, then perhaps things might have been different. I know you heartily disapprove of the way my marriage will be arranged, but at least my wife will be content in a way that my mother was not.'

'Perhaps you're right,' Becky said, though she remained unconvinced. 'Perhaps I simply don't understand how things are arranged here. It is so alien to me, and still is, by the sounds of it, to your mother in some ways. Do you think she will visit her family in England now, as she suggested she might?'

'I have already encouraged her to do so.'

After Carnevale no doubt, Becky thought. After she had brought the husband and father she had seen at the opera last night to his knees. A notion that was beginning to sit a little uncomfortably with her. 'You haven't told me what Don Sartie's Carnival disguise is,' she reminded him.

'You prefer to think of him in character, yes?' Luca asked, proving once again that he saw a great deal more than she would like. 'Very well, it matters not to me how you view him, as long as you win. He wears what is known as a *bauta* mask. It is most commonly white, but a few are gilded. The *bauta* covers the entire face, with only the wearer's eyes on show. Traditionally, there is no mouth, but the lower part of the mask is pointed out, like this,' Luca said, demonstrating, 'so that the wearer can speak, drink, even eat.'

'It sounds grotesque.'

'It is meant to be. The intention behind many of the masks is to frighten as well as disguise identity. The *bauta* disguises the voice to an extent, as well as the face, because of the shape.'

'Why does Don Sarti wear this particular style?'

Luca laughed sardonically. 'In the days of the Republic, the *bauta* and a certain type of black hat, the *tricorno*, and a red or black cloak were worn by all citizens entitled to vote, in order to keep ballots secret. Don Sarti's Carnevale costume is his little jibe at our oppressors.'

'But if many wear that style, how will we know we have our man?'

'We will have to make sure that the Queen of Coins is an irresistible challenge for him. He likes to play deep. We will have to ensure that the stakes are suitably high.'

'Luca, I've been thinking about that. If what you said about the *ridotti* opening in a week's time is true, then the Queen of Coins, by starting small, can build a significant stake and accumulate some experience at the same time.'

'That is a very good idea.'

'It is.' Becky beamed. 'And it gets better. She'll not only be building her experience, but something even more important. A reputation for being unbeatable.'

Luca clapped his hands together. 'Of course! Don Sarti will be unable to resist such a challenge!'

'And when of the Queen of Coins defeats him, what will keep him coming back for more?'

'His arrogance,' Luca said, whistling. 'And the more he loses, the more recklessly he will gamble. We will uses his weakness to relieve him of the money that rightly belongs to Venice. I think you might be a genius.'

'Let's not get too carried away yet. It's a good plan, but before we can get our fish on the hook, we not only have to establish the Queen of Coins as a player, we have to get Don Sarti interested. Society needs to talk, in Don Sarti's hearing, of the invincible card player, a woman no less, who has never been defeated.'

'My mother could help us with this. Thanks to my father, she is extremely well connected.'

'I think that would be a mistake,' Becky said after a moment's hesitation, for Isabel would indeed be ideally placed to help them. 'You know that she doesn't approve of what you are doing. She'd help you, because you're her son and she'd do anything you asked of her but…'

'You think I would be putting her in an invidious position?'

'I do.'

He considered this, frowning down at his hand, which was drumming a tattoo on his thigh. 'I don't understand her reservations, but I know she has them. It would be unfair of me. You're right.'

'I am?'

'Astonishingly, since it means that I must therefore be wrong.'

Becky chuckled. 'I promise, it will be our secret.'

'Che bella,' Luca muttered. 'Do you have any idea what you do to me when you laugh like that?' He leaned over, brushing her hair away from her cheek. 'But I must remind myself that there are any number of rooftops overlooking this one, and that it is almost December and that cold such as this is not conducive to lovemaking.' He kissed her softly, then he released her with a theatrical sigh. 'Tell me instead your thoughts on your disguise as the Queen of Coins. I think you said you had some preliminary sketches?'

'I did. I do.' Becky floundered about for her sketchbook. It had fallen on to the ground. She bent to retrieve it, taking the opportunity to take a couple of deep, calming breaths. Save that they didn't calm her.

It was as well that Luca had demonstrated restraint, as she wasn't sure how she would have reacted had he not. She was strung tight as a bow as she sat back down, her fingers fumbling with the pages of the little book. 'The Queen of Coins,' she said, forcing herself to focus on the first, tentative drawing, turning the page for Luca to see. 'My starting point was the way she's depicted on the cards, obviously, but then I began to think. What is it that we want people to see, what is it that makes her stand out—because we want her to be distinctive, don't we?'

It was working. As she turned the page to the next sketch, she could see that she'd caught Luca's interest. 'We want her to be everything that Cousin Rebecca isn't. Arrogant. Regal. Seductive. But the one thing she has in common with Cousin Rebecca is that no one dare touch her.' She turned the page to the final sketch, watching with satisfaction as Luca's smile dawned. 'What do you think?'

'I cannot imagine anything more perfect.'

Cousin Rebecca accompanied her aunt to Contessa Benzon's salon the following evening. As they entered the room, which was stifling hot and bustling, Becky was assailed by a wave of boredom. Most of the faces looked familiar, some from Contessa Albrizzi's salon, but most from the many calls Rebecca had paid with her aunt Isabel in the intervening ten days. Calls when she had drunk endless cups of insipid tea, for the Venetians could not understand that the leaves must be given time to infuse. She had smiled endless vapid smiles, listening to endless tedious conversations. She tried, when she returned from these excursions, to recall what had been discussed, but it was all a jumble of who was wearing what and tittle-tattle. None of Isabel's acquaintances seemed to *do* anything, save pay calls and gossip endlessly. This life of leisure and luxury, which would have been beyond her own wildest dreams only a month ago, Becky was finding not only wearisome but inexplicable.

'Don't they mind that they serve no purpose?' she'd asked Isabel earlier, as Chiara pattered to and fro with a selection of gowns for Cousin Rebecca to choose from for the coming evening.

Isabel's brittle laugh made her realise how insulting she had been. 'I didn't mean you,' Becky had added swiftly.

'But you make a valid point, Rebecca. Another thing I shall endeavour to change when you are no longer with me.'

Which had brought a lump to Becky's throat. When she was with the Contessa, she increasingly forgot her own sordid history and felt herself truly to be Isabel's friend. She was deluding herself. Though the regal woman in whose wake she was currently trailing was not her friend Isabel, but Contessa del Pietro. 'Contessa Benzon, it has been too long,' she was saying to the statuesque woman who must be their hostess. 'May I introduce you to my niece from England, Signorina Rebecca Wickes.'

Contessa Maria Querini Benzon had once been a famous beauty renowned for courting scandal. She had, Isabel had informed Becky earlier, danced virtually naked around the Tree of Liberty, wearing only a brief Roman-style tunic during the fall of the Republic. A song inspired by this outrageous act was still a favourite with the gondoliers twenty years later. Her latest scandal had been to marry her lover after thirty years together, but her notoriety had more to do with her passion for food than for her husband. The Contessa, a true Venetian, loved polenta so much that she would not leave her *palazzo* without a slice of it tucked into her bosom. The gondoliers called her The Steaming Lady.

As the introductions were made, it struck Becky yet again what a topsy-turvy tangle were the rules and the morals by which these upper-class Venetians lived. A bride must be a virgin, yet a wife was expected to take a lover. Fidelity, that most fundamental virtue in her eyes, meant nothing here. She, who had been true in every way to the man she'd thought she loved, would be perceived as a fallen women by these people, simply because she'd given herself without a formal blessing. Making Cousin Rebecca's curtsy, Becky felt more than ever that she did not belong here.

'I have heard a great deal about you, Signorina Wickes,' Contessa Benzon said with an engaging and refreshingly genuine smile which made Becky's prepared platitudes die on her lips. 'Isabel's little English niece, who dreams of marrying a man of the church just like her papa, do I have that right?'

'Perfectly,' Cousin Rebecca replied, disappointed to see no giveaway trail of steam rising from her hostess's gown. Was that scepticism in the Contessa's voice, or the more usual scorn?

'I confess, Isabel, I was most surprised to hear this story. A niece of yours to marry a man of the cloth! When one would have thought her a perfect match for your son. Oh, I know you will say that she is too close in blood, but we all know that is a rule which can be waived when it is convenient.'

'Rebecca has very modest ambitions,' Isabel replied. 'I would not dream of trying to redirect them.'

'Wisely said, Isabel, but there is one who I think could do so easily, if he chose? What do you say to that, Conte del Pietro?'

'My cousin's mind is quite made-up on the matter.'

'Such a modest young woman, with such modest ambitions, yet she has a will of iron it seems,' Contessa Benzon mused. 'For I find it very difficult to believe she could be immune to your charms, Conte del Pietro. Perhaps he has not tried hard enough. What do you say, Signorina Wickes?'

Thinking sardonically that Luca had barely had to try at all, Becky was forced to look up. 'I do not aspire to such lofty heights,' she said drily.

'But you would like to, no? Who would not?'

Contessa Benzon fluttered her eyelashes meaningfully at Luca, whose manful struggle to conceal his shock at the very obvious suggestion was too much for Becky. She gave a snort of laughter, and though she quickly turned it into a cough, her hostess was not fooled.

'I advise you to look a little more closely at your cousin, Conte del Pietro,' she said with a gleeful smile. 'Appearances can be most deceptive. But I have detained you enough,' she continued, sparing any of them the need to respond. 'Isabel, I see your coterie have gathered over in the corner, you will wish to join them with your niece. Conte del Pietro, my salon is at your disposal. You will excuse me, I have newly arrived guests to greet.'

* * *

The evening continued as all such evenings did, Luca was discovering, with the conversation largely consisting of veiled hints as to his matrimonial prospects, discreet scrutiny of the chances of him following his father into the heart of the city's administration and subtle probing from some as to his inclinations to attend their various societies and clubs. Politics could not be discussed overtly, that much he understood, for the Austrians had spies everywhere, but he was beginning to find the Venetian habit of making an unnecessary mystery of every subject tedious.

Luca had never been much interested in politics, preferring action to words. It was why the navy had suited him, and why he wanted to build ships. What he would do with his fleet was another matter. He had assumed that he would sail with them, but all of Venice expected Conte del Pietro to remain in the city, not absent himself for months, possibly years at a time. He had always known he belonged to Venice, it was in the del Pietro blood that he serve his city, but until his father's life was taken, the date had always been deferred to some mythical point in the future. That was another crime to add to the list committed by Don Sarti. He had stolen Luca's freedom from him.

The man with whom he had been conversing was looking at him expectantly. Luca couldn't even remember his name, let alone what they'd been talking about. Spotting Becky out of the corner of his eye, seated beside his mother and looking as bored as he felt, he made his bow and an apology. '*Mi scusi, signor*, I think my cousin wishes to speak to me.'

He had to suppress a smile, for Becky almost forgot she was Cousin Rebecca in her hurry to get to her feet when he suggested they get some fresh air. '*Grazie*, Cousin Luca,' she said, 'it is true, I am suffocating. From the heat, that is, of course, not from the company, which is as diverting and delightful as always. *Meno male*,' she added for his ears alone as he led her away. 'I thought you would never come and rescue me. Didn't you promise to find a way to let me watch some card playing?'

'It is taking place in another room. We can use the terrace to observe the game. Try looking a little less happy to escape and a little more as if you are about to faint.'

She responded to her cue immediately, and with no questions. Luca watched, fascinated, as Cousin Rebecca's already pale complexion seemed to go grey. Her lids drooped. Her knees began to give way. 'Cousin Luca,' she whispered in a perfect stage aside, 'I fear I am quite overcome.'

She took a tottering step towards the window and Luca, waving aside an offer to help, put a cousinly arm around her waist. 'Some air, that is all she needs.'

'Oh, yes, thank you, just a little air,' Cousin Rebecca said plaintively. The curtain was obligingly held aside, the tall windows on to the terrace opened. 'I am so embarrassed, please excuse— My cousin will take care of me,' Cousin Rebecca implored, and the concerned guest obligingly retreated.

As soon as the curtains fell back together, Becky straightened up. 'Which way? Oh, Luca, what if the curtains to the room are drawn?'

'They are not. They were, but I remedied that.'

'Excellent. Are you sure we won't be spotted from inside?'

'If anyone looks up, you can faint into my arms.'

'Magari,' Becky said with an impish grin, using one of Chiara's favourite words. 'I wish!'

'Not as much as I do,' Luca muttered under his breath, following in her wake as she crept light-footed along the narrow balcony, past the second set of windows belonging to Contessa Benzon's grand drawing room, to the light streaming from the card room, where she stopped short.

'This is perfect,' she whispered as he stopped beside her. 'Both tables closest to the window are playing Trappola. You don't have to watch. Just keep a lookout for me, and be prepared to catch me if required.'

She turned her attention back to the room, and was immediately rapt with concentration. Two floors below, Luca could hear the rush of the waters of the Grand Canal that told him the tide was on the turn. He would not build his ships at the old docks, he would build a new dockyard, modelled on the one on the River Clyde in Glasgow, where they constricted ocean-going clippers, faster than any other. He would send his fleet across the world to trade in silks and in tea, in spices and tobacco, bringing trade back to his city and much-needed work. In the cool night of the last days of November, Luca leaned on the low edge of the balcony and gazed out to sea, indulging himself in his dreams.

'I hope you employed someone more attentive to act as lookout when you were at sea.' Becky's voice in his ear startled him from his reverie. 'Don't worry,' she said, flashing him a smile, 'no one has come in search of us, but I think we'd better return to the drawing room before they do.'

'Was it helpful, even though they were playing for pleasure, not money?'

'Yes. The two ladies in particular were very skilful players. Do you think you can persuade your mother to leave now? I don't think I can bear...'

'Not yet,' Luca said curtly, ushering her through the still-open window. 'Look over there. Don Sarti has arrived with his family.'

'Luca...'

'I am more prepared this time,' he told her with a grim smile. As he propelled Cousin Rebecca towards the Sarti family, his stomach was clenched in a tight ball, but his fists were determinedly unfurled, even though every instinct urged him to grab the man by the throat and throttle the life out of him.

'Luca.' Don Sarti held out his hand. 'I was saying to my wife, when we saw you at the opera the other night, how good it was to see your mother back in circulation. I believe the credit belongs to this young lady, her niece?'

'Allow me to introduce Signorina Wickes,' Luca said, discovering that he was loathe to do so.

'Signorina Wickes, it is a pleasure. I confess, I was not aware of your existence until you arrived in Venice. May I introduce you to my wife, and to my daughter, Beatrice.'

'I hope your aunt will bring you to tea, Signorina Wickes,' Donna Sarti said, after Becky made her curtsy. 'Beatrice will be happy to have a new acquaintance, won't you, my dear?'

'Indeed, Mama,' her daughter murmured, looking,

to Luca's eye, every bit as demure and colourless as Cousin Rebecca, and on the face of it, a perfect match.

It was not a friendship he wished to encourage, though he could think of no way to curb it without raising suspicion. He would have a word with his mother about it. He couldn't risk Becky being too much in Don Sarti's company. Only then did it occur to him to wonder how much of Donna Sarti's company his mother usually kept. Were the two women friends? He was about to find out.

'Anna. And Beatrice. How lovely to see you.'

He watched his mother greet both Sarti women warmly, and he had his answer. It surprised him, for his mother had not alluded to any such friendship, though it was natural enough, he supposed, for the wives of two old friends to be on good terms.

'Don Sarti, good evening.'

His mother's greeting was significantly cooler, but the Don didn't appear to consider this unusual. 'Contessa.'

Was Sarti looking ill at ease? Was his conscience bothering him in the slightest? Luca couldn't decide.

'I will leave you to catch up with Isabel,' Don Sarti was saying now to his wife. 'I believe there are cards underway in the other salon. No,' he added swiftly, as his wife's face fell. 'Of course, I am not going to play, my dear. What is the fun in playing without a stake to risk?'

As he excused himself, making for the connecting door, Luca saw Donna Sarti's eyes following her husband, her mouth pursed into a tight line.

Chapter Eight

The sky was gunmetal grey and lowering two days later, when Luca took Cousin Rebecca out on the pretext of another sightseeing trip, though the real reason for their expedition was to visit the mask-maker. Once again, they were in the open gondola with Luca taking the oar himself. Becky, swathed in a woollen hooded cloak, sat once again in the seat facing him rather than the direction in which he was rowing. They headed away from the Grand Canal, through a confusing network of tributary canals which gave her a completely different impression of the city. Although some of the buildings were clad in gaily painted stucco, all were decrepit and in varying states of decay.

The buildings towered high over the canals. It seemed to Becky, craning her neck, that the narrower the strip of water that separated them, the taller they were built, as if reaching desperately for the remote sky. The bridges were not ornate but simple low spans, requiring Luca to duck as they passed underneath. Moss grew thick on the steps, a deep, vibrant green, while the canals themselves reflected the colours of the surrounding buildings—muddy brown and dusky pink and milky grey. Where there were walkways they were precarious and narrow, connected by shallow flights of steps. It would be very easy to lose one's footing on the damp cobblestones, even easier for the unwary to slither down those treacherous little steps and plunge headlong into the murky water.

There were few people visible, yet Becky had an acute sensation of being watched, from behind green shutters, from just around the corner of the warren of passageways. Voices echoed, but they seemed to emanate from far away. Cats sat on the top of the steps leading down into the waters, on the window ledges, in the doorways, watching. It was eerie and beautiful, haunting and frightening. 'I wouldn't like to come here on my own at night,' she said to Luca, keeping her voice low, in tune with her mood.

'I would not advise it, especially not on foot,' he replied. 'Even Venetians can get lost and end up walking around in circles. You can be five minutes from your destination, and it can end up taking you an hour or more.'

Becky shivered. 'I feel like there are eyes everywhere. It's like walking through the rookeries at night. You know the place is overrun with people but you can't see them, not unless you know where to look.'

'I don't like to think of you alone in a place like this, day or night.'

'It's safe enough if you are known,' Becky said. 'Most of the time,' she added with a wry smile. 'When you live there, and you don't know any different, it's not so bad. Now— No, I wouldn't go back even if I could.'

'Could?'

'It's just a saying,' she said hurriedly, cursing herself for the stupid mistake. Trust Luca to notice it! 'What I'm saying is, I don't aspire to live in a *palazzo*, but I don't want to live in a slum.' She leaned back, gazing up at the narrow grey sliver of sky. 'I'm beginning to think that I need to broaden my horizons a bit though. I don't just mean travel, which I *have* been thinking about, thanks to you, but… It was something your mother said, about wanting to be useful.'

'Talking of my mother, I've written to my uncle, asking him to arrange safe passage for Mama to England as soon as he can.'

'Luca!' Becky jumped up, causing the gondola to rock wildly before sitting down again immediately. 'Sorry, I forgot we were on a boat! I was going to hug you.'

'Then far be it from me to stop you.'

'It would be most improper of me to do so,' Becky said primly. 'Have you told Isabel that you've written to her brother?'

'No, I want it to be a surprise. I've forgotten why I came to mention it now.'

'I was talking about wanting to be useful. The problem is that I have no idea what I mean by that. Have you thought about what you're going to do with the money we will win back for the city?'

'I have. In fact, we're nearly at our destination. If you don't mind a short detour, I can show you.'

'Please,' she said, intrigued, since they were in one of the dingiest and most run-down districts of Venice she had seen so far.

Making sure that her hood covered most of her

face, Becky clutched Luca's hand gratefully as she stepped on to the slimy cobblestones. She would have missed the narrow passageway had she been alone, would have fallen in the sudden gloom were it not for his support, and was dazzled when they emerged suddenly into a large *campo* with a bustling market. The stalls were covered in garish canvas awnings, the vegetables and fruit, considering the time of year, ripe and brightly coloured, but it was the plentiful mounds of unfamiliar fish which intrigued Becky. 'I don't think I know what half of these are. What is that horrible thing with the gaping mouth full of sharp teeth?'

'*Coda di rospo*, which means tail of the toad. You don't eat the ugly bit,' Luca said. 'These are all various species of octopus, which you've had in antipasti, but not these little ones, which are called *folpeti* in Venetian.'

'And these... Are they snails?' Becky asked, eyeing the writhing mass of shells.

'Sea snails,' Luca answered, laughing at her expression. 'We call them *bovoleti*.'

'They sound much nicer than they look.' They carried on, past stalls selling bread and wine, and many more fish stalls. 'There's no meat for sale,' Becky observed.

'This is one of Venice's poorest quarters. They can't afford meat,' Luca replied. 'Many here have no work. There was once a charitable school and a hospital, but the funding for both dried up. Now these people are struggling to survive.'

It was horribly familiar, yet it seemed so much worse for such poverty to exist in such beautiful surroundings—and there was beauty everywhere, Becky noted, gazing around her. A portico carved with vine leaves, elaborate latticework in an arched window, coloured glass in a fanlight, a wooden balcony tilting precariously. Venice, even in her pockets of decay, was beautiful. Though beauty provided scant solace to an empty belly or a cold hearth, she knew all too well. 'Do you plan to help them?'

'By restoring the schools and the hospitals which have fallen into disuse, for a start.'

'And more appreciated I'm sure than some old paintings hanging in a gallery.'

'My father's motives were noble but you have a point.'

'Perhaps I will follow your example and use my windfall for a good cause. Establish a school? I have no idea what it would cost. Or I could fund a refuge for young girls. You know, a safe house.'

'The kind of sanctuary which wasn't available to you, Becky?'

She coloured. 'Could I afford that, do you think?'

'Easily, but don't spend it all on other people.'

'Are you worried that I'll get a taste for the high life?'

He laughed. 'Your favourite place in my *palazzo* is the rooftop. You already have a taste for the high life.'

'I think of it as my little kingdom.' They had come to the end of the market. On the far side of the *campo*, three children were throwing a stick for a scrawny dog to fetch. It was starting to rain. 'What people want, in my experience, is not charity, Luca. It's the ability to earn a living. You'll do more for these people by building your dockyard and creating jobs than handing out alms.'

'Or building them a fountain?' he asked with a mocking smile. 'It was one of the things I'd thought of. Beautiful and also practical. Clean drinking water is in scarce supply.'

'Who'd have thought that spending money would be such hard work?' Becky said. 'If you're not careful, it will take over your life and your shipbuilding plans will remain a pipe dream.'

'All of it will be a pipe dream if we don't get the Queen of Coins's costume made. The studio is not far from here.'

It was ironic, Luca thought as he guided Becky the short distance to the mask-maker's studio, that while her horizons were rapidly expanding, his were narrowing alarmingly. Would dispensing all this money become a burden? What was the point in worrying about it now? he thought impatiently. After Carnevale was time enough. Though after Carnevale, the time when his life would begin afresh, was beginning to feel like the time when his freedom would be surrendered completely. The point when he would assume the mantle and the responsibilities of being the Conte del Pietro. Justice would have been done—yes, that was still a most uplifting prospect. But Becky, through whom justice would be served, would be gone.

There were weeks and weeks left before then. They had barely begun. 'This is it,' he said, stopping abruptly in front of a shuttered window.

'There's no sign. It doesn't even look like a shop. Are you sure? And are you absolutely certain that this man can be trusted?'

'The mask-maker knows the identity of every Venetian who wears his creations. In his own way, he is even more powerful than my father was. His family have been creating masks for generations, and for generations have kept the owners' identities secret. I would go as far as to say that if there is one man in Venice who can be trusted, it is he.'

Becky still looked dubious, but from the moment she stepped through the door and into the studio she was, as Luca had known she would be, completely enraptured.

Bartolomeo, the only name the mask-maker was ever known by, locked the door behind them, bowing low. 'Conte del Pietro. It is an honour. I don't believe I have created a mask for you before.'

'I require only a *volto*,' Luca said, pointing at an example of the simple white ghost mask. 'It is the *signorina* who has a more specialised request. Show Bartolomeo your design,' he added in English to Becky.

She did so, and as he had expected, the mask-maker eyed the drawing with delight, exclaiming in a stream of excited Italian which Luca translated for her. 'The *colombina*, a classic half mask extended over the forehead, an excellent choice! The *colombina* should be worn only by the most beautiful women, it will suit the *signorina* to perfection, such a mouth as she has, and a very shapely chin. She must decide whether to fix it with laces, which is what I would recommend, though some do prefer the baton.'

'Laces, please tell him,' Becky said. 'I need to have both hands free.'

But Bartolomeo had already moved on to the particulars of the design, poring over the sketch, making several drawings of his own, then, with a brief *'mi scusi'*, tilting Becky's face this way and that, nodding in satisfaction.

'The *signorina*'s eyes,' Luca translated, 'have a sparkling quality. We will highlight this with the application of crystals of blue like this.'

Becky pored over the redrawn design, entranced by the subtle changes which the mask-maker had made. As he began to position crystals in shades of blue over what she could now see was a template, her belly fluttered with excitement. 'It is wonderful,' she said to Bartolomeo in Italian. 'Absolutely superb.'

'No ostentatious feathers for the *signorina*. Her perfect beauty means she has no need of any further adornment. You agree?'

'What did he say?' Becky asked, after Luca had nodded his agreement.

'He said he was ready to begin your first fitting.'

The mask-maker sat Becky down on a stool. Several heavy clay models were placed over her face, until both Bartolomeo and Becky were happy with the fit and level of comfort. She listened, fascinated, as he explained the process which would follow, with Luca translating. 'This will be the mould. He will then make your mask using layers of special paper and a glue which is the most secret of formulas, to make a very light mask, which will be further shaped and trimmed, then decorated to your design. And it will be delivered in…?'

'For you, Conte del Pietro, and for the very beautiful *signorina*, I will work through the night. The mask will be ready in three days. The delivery will be to yourself at the Palazzo Pietro? And you wish a *volto* for yourself? The most popular mask. I have some already prepared in various sizes. Come, let us see what is the best fit.'

It was late afternoon by the time they left Bartolomeo's studio, for the mask-maker was also liaising with the dressmaker who would fashion the Queen of Coins's costume. The market in the *campo* had long ago been packed up and closed for the day. They crossed the now-empty space, littered with detritus, to reach the passageway which would take them back to the gondola, their footsteps echoing, accompanied only by a small tabby cat. Above them, the sky was still pale blue with wispy clouds, but the waters of the canal were darkening to an inky colour.

'There will be a beautiful sunset in a little while,' Luca said, helping Becky back into the gondola. 'I know a place not far from here where we can watch it if you like.'

'Yes, please, I'd like that very much. I don't want to return to the *palazzo* just yet. I'm enjoying being outside in the fresh air.'

Musing that what he enjoyed was the pleasure of her company, regardless of the location, Luca rowed them to a junction where two canals crossed, then tied the gondola up facing west before joining Becky on the bench. 'The sunsets at this time of year are dramatic but are over very quickly,' he said, risking putting an arm around her to pull her closer, her thigh against his, his arm on the curve of her waist, an exquisite torture.

The canal turned darker as the sun sank, the shadows cast by the overlooking buildings disappearing.

Above, the sky became almost colourless, the air around them cooling abruptly so that their breaths began to cloud, and then the show began. A tinge of pale pink low in the sky streaked with white, turned the canal into a mirror of pewter and silver. On the horizon, pink darkened to violet, and the fast-sinking sun streaked orange and vermilion. As the mantle of night fell, making black hulks of the buildings, the remnants of the setting sun produced blindingly vibrant hues. And then it was over, as dramatically as it had begun.

The air hung heavy and silent, expectant, for why else would a sun set so ravishingly if it was not to encourage a kiss? They were not alone, Luca knew that, but it felt as if they were, and that was all that mattered. His heart began to thump as their lips met. If kisses could speak, this one surely spoke of yearning. Of wanting. Of passion too long pent up. There was so much restraint in their kiss, in the clutch of their hands, in the tensing of their muscles, as if every ounce of effort was needed to suppress something wild. Such longing.

Their kiss came to a reluctant end, leaving them facing each other, their expressions cloaked by the gloom, only their quickened breathing and the gentle rocking of the gondola against its mooring to betray them.

Becky had been on tenterhooks for the last four days, waiting anxiously for Luca to decide the time was right for the Queen of Coins to make her debut appearance. Finally, that time had arrived. As the clock struck eleven, she ceased her anxious pacing. She was already wearing undergarments beneath her dressing gown in preparation. She had piled her hair high on her head, allowing it to trail in wild curls down her back and over one eye. Placing her powder and rouge in her pocket, she quit the room.

The corridor was dark, but years spent creeping back to her lodgings from the theatre at night meant Becky could see as well as a cat in the dark. The staff of the Palazzo Pietro went early to bed. There was only one night porter on duty in the reception hall three floors below. Becky glided silently down from the second to the first floor, making for the library.

Luca was waiting, dressed in his customary black, looking decidedly raffish rather than sombre. 'Everything is prepared,' he said, offering her a fortifying glass of wine, which Becky refused.

'I need to keep my wits about me.'

Butterflies began to flutter in her tummy as Luca pulled a book from the lower shelf of one of the bookcases and twisted a lever to open the door of the secret chamber. 'Your boudoir awaits,' he said.

Becky stepped into the square, windowless room, where a lamp was already lit on the table. It was warm from the huge fire which burned in the adjoining library wall. The costume, swathed in muslin, was laid out on a chaise longue. On the table beside the lamp was her mask. A gilded chair beside the table, and a full-length mirror were the room's only other furnishings.

'There's a handle on your side of the door,' Luca said. 'I'll wait in the library.'

He closed the door. Becky carefully removed the muslin from her gown. With only her sketches to work from and not a single fitting, there was every chance that it would fail to meet her expectations, or fail to fit. But the costume revealed made her gasp with delight. It was as if the dressmaker had been able to read Becky's thoughts. Whoever she was, the woman was a genius.

She cast off her dressing gown and picked up the tunic. Made of cobalt-blue silk, it had been inspired by the costume Becky had once worn to play Queen Guinevere, with long tight-fitting sleeves, a very low neckline and a full skirt. Black lacing was sewn into the waist, like a corset on the outside of the gown. She pulled it tight, pleased to see that the effect was exactly as she'd imagined, making her waist look impossibly small, her cleavage almost too plentiful for the gown, in comparison. The overdress which would serve as a coat was made of black silk lined with cobalt blue, with long pointed sleeves trailing medieval-style almost to the ground. It had a wide hood that would conceal the Queen of Coins's face and protect her from the elements. A broad band of silver embroidery trimmed the overdress, and a wide sash of black silk embroidered with silver sat like a girdle on her hips. Black boots with pointed toes were adorned with crystals which matched those on her mask.

Becky applied a dusting of powder to her neck, throat and bosom, and a coating of rouge to her lips, before she tied her mask in place. Pulling a swathe of her curls over her shoulder to trail provocatively over her cleavage, she fixed the hood in place with some pins, and stepped in front of the mirror.

She barely recognised the creature reflected there. Her eyes, glittering behind the mask, seemed more

blue than violet, picking up the colour of the gown.
The vivid colours—black, blue and silver—were a
stark contrast to the pale lustre of her skin, the vermilion slash of her lips. The Queen of Coins was a
sensual creature, but she was also intimidating. She
was mysterious, regal, remote, yet there was something about the hood and the mask, the shadowed face
and the exposed bosom that beckoned, hinting at intimacy. She was a woman of contrasts, like the city
she was to conquer. If Becky could have imagined
the perfect role for herself, it would be this one. The
costume made her feel strong, powerful even. Luca's
avenging angel. She smiled at herself, a slow, deliberately provocative smile. She was ready.

As she opened to door back into the library Luca
turned quickly, setting the wine glass which had been
raised to his lips quickly down. *'Che meraviglia,'* he
said with a soft whistle. 'I don't know whether to
throw myself at your feet or into your arms.'

Becky couldn't resist giving a little twirl. 'You
like?'

'I like very much,' he said. 'And you, I think, much
prefer to be the Queen of Coins than Cousin Rebecca?'

'Let's just see if the Queen of Coins is successful first.'

'I do not see how you can fail. No man, seeing
you in this most delectable outfit, will be looking at
your hands,' Luca said, quite blatantly eyeing Becky's
breasts. 'I presume that was a deliberate ploy?'

'To distract my opponents, not my protector,' she
said pointedly.

He laughed. *'Mi scusi,* but I am not yet dressed for
the role. One moment.' He threw his long black silk

cloak over his shoulders, fastening the silver buttons at the neck. The *volto* mask was chalk white and completely plain, covering his entire face apart from his chin. The black tricorn hat placed on top made him unrecognisable and slightly intimidating. 'Now,' Luca said, 'we are ready. Tonight, I very much hope, signals the beginning of the end for Don Sarti.'

They left the *palazzo* through a door at the back of the secret room that opened on to a narrow canal. The air grew noticeably colder as they descended a steep flight of steps. Luca held the lantern high, revealing a gondola tied to a rusty iron ring. 'Who left the boat here?' Becky asked.

'One of the gondoliers. I told him I had a lover's tryst.' Luca was already on board, holding his hand out for Becky. 'He won't say anything, don't worry. I think he was surprised that I hadn't asked for the boat before. This secret entrance has always been used to enter or leave the *palazzo* undetected.'

Becky took her usual seat facing him, accustomed now to the gondola's motion. Luca picked up the oar, set it into its lock, untied the rope and kicked the boat out into the canal. It was a dark night, the thin strip of sky visible too dark with clouds for any stars to shine. If there was a moon, it was in another part of the heavens. Luca was a dark, sinister shape on the stern, his *volto* mask eerily pale under the black shadow of his hat. He could be anyone, a complete stranger, as could she, she supposed, in her Queen of Coins costume, hiding behind her mask. Yet the enveloping night encouraged confidences. 'Have you had many lovers, Luca?' she asked.

'None since my return to Venice. Before then, a few, though not so very many. We went our separate ways when passion died, as it always does.'

'Does it?'

He did not answer until he had steered the gondola under one of the low arched bridges, so low that it forced him to duck his head. 'That has always been my experience.'

Becky tilted her head back to search the sullen sky for pinpoints of light, but found none. She had no previous experience of passion. Her desire for Luca burned so persistently that she found it difficult to believe it would die. But then, there had been a time not so very long ago when she'd thought her love would never die, and a time even closer to hand when she'd thought her heart was broken. She'd been wrong about both. Startled, she tested herself, but though the bitterness of that final betrayal which threatened to put a noose around her neck was still every bit as strong, she felt nothing else save a sense of relief that her eyes had been well and truly opened. What an escape she'd had! Were it not for the fact that she was a wanted criminal…

Her eyes flew open as the gondola bumped against a wooden jetty and Luca jumped out to secure it. As she followed him on to dry land, something brushed past her gown, making her jump. 'Where are we? Where is the *ridotto*? I can't see any lights.'

'It is a short walk from here. Are you happy with the plan?'

She ought to be, it was her plan, and they had discussed it often enough. She opened her mouth to reassure him, only to be assailed by a memory of the last time she had played the tables. She screwed her eyes shut, trying to will it away but it persisted. When she had realised what had happened, there had been a moment of shocked disbelief. All eyes were on her, but time seemed to stand still, and her mind was quite frozen. Jack, she'd thought, where was he? Only the scuffle, the shout, as he fled startled her into action, too terrified that the hands reaching for her would catch her to concern herself with the act of betrayal.

'Becky?'

Her mouth was dry. Her knees were like jelly. Sweat trickled down her back. Under the shadow of her hood, impeded by her mask, she tried to take calming breaths. Tonight she would not fail. Tonight, the Queen of Coins would triumph. She would not let Luca down. She checked the strings on her mask. She placed her hand on Luca's arm. *'Andiamo,'* she said. 'Let's go and win some money.'

Chapter Nine

It was still dark when they left the *ridotto*, though dawn was not far-off. Becky felt as if she was floating, as if she had drunk a magnum of Prosecco. She couldn't stop smiling. She jumped down into the gondola, making it rock wildly. 'We did it.'

Luca was unfastening his mask, casting it with his tricorn hat on to the other bench and running his fingers through his flattened hair. 'You did it.'

'*We* did it.' Becky threw herself on to the bench, making the heavy purse containing her winnings clunk against her thigh. 'You selected the opponents, the Queen of Coins vanquished them one by one.'

Luca cast off and began to turn the gondola. 'Though there were moments when it seemed to me that the Queen of Coins was the one about to lose.'

Becky chuckled. 'Oh, that is all part of the act. You have to give your adversary hope. You have to lead him to believe that he can beat you, else he will not be tempted to play on.' Her face fell. 'That sounds very callous.'

'I think you were fair, in the circumstances. You

did not permit the stakes to go anywhere near as high as some of the more reckless gamblers wished.'

'That is true,' she said, brightening. 'Do you think the Queen of Coins is being talked about already?'

'From the minute she walked into the room she was a sensation, and I believe I played my part in stirring up interest. By the end of the night, I had the pleasure of several of my stories regarding the identity of the mysterious Queen of Coins being quoted back to me along with various other speculations not of my devising. The runaway Bulgarian princess was my personal favourite.'

Becky let out a peal of laughter, which echoed around the narrow canal. 'I know we must repeat our success several times over before Carnival starts properly, but we did make an excellent start, didn't we?'

'A dream start.'

'All of this feels like a dream.' She lay back on the bench, watching starry-eyed as Luca rowed the gondola back to the *palazzo*, the sky lightening just enough for her to see his handsome countenance.

He was smiling as he tied the boat up, carefully securing the oar before helping her out and lighting the lamp. 'Are you tired?'

Becky shook her head. 'I feel like I'll never sleep again, though I will be very relieved to take off this mask.' She followed him back up the steps to the door of the secret room, pulling the pins that secured her hood and untying her mask with a happy sigh as Luca locked the door behind them, placing his hat and mask on to the table. 'A nightcap to celebrate, I think,' he said. 'Wait there.'

Becky pulled the purse containing her winnings

from the secret pocket inside her overdress and put it beside the masks. After the cold outside, the room felt warm. She untied the sash and slipped out of the outer dress of her costume, and then sank on to the chaise longue, wriggling her numb toes inside her boots and loosening the laces at the front of her tunic. All her fears were completely unfounded. Not one of her many opponents had suspected foul play for a moment. True, they had none of them been experts, she was already far more skilled than any of them, but it was reassuring all the same. Much more reassuring than she had realised.

'I thought it was time that you tasted grappa.' Luca, now cloakless and coatless, was carrying two small glasses. 'It is distilled from the skin and the seeds of grapes which are leftover from winemaking. Don't screw up your face. It tastes good, I promise.'

He sat down beside her, handing her one of the little glasses. 'To the Queen of Coins. *Salute.*'

'*Salute.*' Becky took a cautious sip, gasping as the fiery liquid hit the back of her throat. 'That is a great deal stronger than wine.'

'It is not to your taste?'

She took a second cautious sip. This time, now that she was prepared for it, she enjoyed the tingling warmth. 'It is good, though I don't think I'd manage more than one glass, it would go straight to my head, and I'm already a little bit drunk on success.'

'Well-deserved success. All your hours of practice have paid off.'

'This is only the first step, Luca.'

'I know, but it is a truly wonderful feeling to have finally taken it, to be one step closer to my goal.' He threw back the rest of his own grappa, turning towards her as he set the glass down on the floor. 'Thanks to you.'

His leg was brushing against hers. A long strand of silky hair fell over his brow. His smile was warm, his brow for once free of even the faintest trace of a frown. It was as intoxicating as grappa, to bask in her success, the relief of it, the outrageousness of it. And now that it was over, the vicarious thrill of it, made all the more thrilling by knowing she was winning for Luca.

'I couldn't have done it without you,' Becky said, reaching up to brush his hair back from his forehead.

He caught her hand, pressing a kiss to her palm, and the warmth of admiration in his eyes changed to a different sort of heat as their gazes clashed and held and Becky's heart began to race with a very different kind of excitement. His mouth lingered on her palm. He licked his way up her thumb and his lips closed around it. She shivered in sheer delight and everything she had been feeling merged, transforming itself into the burning heat of desire.

Yet she couldn't move. Luca's gaze was scorching, transfixed on hers as he licked the tip of her index finger, drawing it into his mouth. She had only to blink to stop him, to pull her hand free from his, but it didn't even occur to her. She was positively smouldering, every lick, every kiss, the sweet dragging of his mouth on her fingers sending sparks of heat through her veins to concentrate in an aching drag of desire low in her belly.

His breath was shallow, his pupils dilated as his mouth closed on her little finger, and Becky shuddered, released from her trance, falling towards him on the chaise longue. He let out a low groan as their lips met, their tongues met, their bodies met in a tangle of wild kisses and feverish hands. She stopped thinking, surrendering herself to the spinning, urgent need for skin to touch skin, plucking at the buttons of Luca's waistcoat, tugging his shirt free from his pantaloons to run her hands up his back, thrilling at the ripple of his muscles beneath her palms and the shudder of delight which coursed through him at her touch.

When he dragged his mouth from hers, her whimper of protest turned into a sigh of delight as he kissed his way down her throat to lick into the valley between her breasts, tugging at the loose fastenings of her tunic enough to slip it down her shoulders. More kisses, on the exposed flesh of her breasts, her nipples hard and aching inside the constraints of her corsets. He was murmuring in Italian, words she didn't recognise, but which sounded like pleas and promises she longed for him to fulfil.

She stood up to wriggle free of her tunic. Luca cast off his waistcoat and then, at her urging, pulled his shirt over his head. His torso was smooth and tanned, his skin gleaming in the lamplight. Entranced, Becky traced the muscles of his shoulders, down the slight swell of his chest to the dip of his belly, relishing the way her touch made him shiver. She pressed her mouth to his skin, tasting salt and soap and heat. His fingers were running through her hair, spreading it out over her naked shoulders, his hands on her back, then on her arms, then on her breasts, cupping them through her corset, making her cry out with delight, arching against him, her mouth desperately seeking his, and finding it in a deep, urgent kiss.

She could feel the distinctive evidence of his arousal pressing between her thighs through the single petticoat she wore over her pantaloons. Mindless, she clutched at the firm flesh of his buttocks. Staggering backwards, she found herself pressed against the door which connected with the library, and still they kissed feverishly. Luca's hand was under her petticoat now, and instinctively she wrapped her leg around his, yanking the thin cambric higher in the process. He muttered her name, one hand braced against the door behind her, the other between her thighs, finding her flesh between the split in her pantaloons, his fingers sliding into her, forcing her to cling frantically to the last remnants of self-control. She was strung so tightly that it would not take much to set her over. She was torn between wanting to fall headlong into her climax, and to cling on, to enjoy and endure for as long as she could.

But Luca gave her no choice. Kisses, his tongue matching his fingers, stroking, thrusting, making her tighten, surrendering herself to the spiralling, twisting tension inside her, arching against him as it took her, making her cry out, cling to him, pulsing and throbbing in complete abandon.

When it was over, she clung limply to him, drained and sated. Luca was still unmistakably aroused, yet he was gently disentangling himself from her. Confused and fast becoming embarrassed by her state of undress and her wanton abandon, Becky grabbed her dressing gown, belting it tightly around her. 'I think the grappa must have gone to our heads, after all,' she said, because she had to say something.

'If anything went to my head, it was you. Now, please, go to bed before I lose what very little is left of my self-control.'

When Becky awoke it was already light. The curtains in her bedchamber had been drawn to show one of those misty days, where the sky and the canals seemed to merge. Sitting up in bed, she saw that the fire was burning brightly in the grate, and even as she peered over at the clock trying to make out the time, Chiara crept into the room, bearing a huge tray.

'*Buongiorno*, Signorina Wickes. It is not like you to oversleep. I have brought you breakfast.'

'The Contessa! I was to accompany her on her morning calls.'

'Conte del Pietro has accompanied her instead. Do you want breakfast in bed or do you wish to sit by the fire?'

'By the fire, I think,' Becky said, appalled by the idea of getting breadcrumbs between her silk sheets. 'Just set it down, Chiara. There is no need for you to stay, thank you.'

Becky wrapped herself in her dressing gown and sat cosily by the fire. In addition to tea things, the tray contained warm bread rolls wrapped in a cloth, butter, apricot and cherry jam, several mouthwatering sweet pastries and the little biscotti filled with raisins which the Venetians called *zaletti*. Her tummy rumbling as she brewed her tea, Becky broke off a piece of pastry and popped it into her mouth, closing her eyes as it melted in buttery flakes on her tongue. A flurry of rain spattered against the window. She curled up on the chair, tucking her bare toes under a velvet cushion. There was something quite delightfully decadent in being inside in front of a blazing fire with a tray of good things to eat while outside the weather turned nasty. When Carnival was over, when she was rich enough to have her own little cottage somewhere, she could probably sit like this all day every day if she wished, getting fat on sugary treats and…

And what! Wishing her life away? Ignoring the world outside, caring nothing for it, as long as she was warm and well fed? Becky wrapped her hands around her teacup in a way that Isabel would deeply disapprove of, and sighed to herself. Her little pipe dream was just that. She'd be bored rigid within a few days—say a week at most. And as for eating herself fat, something she used to dream of when she went to bed ravenous, while buttering a roll and smearing on a dollop of cherry jam was still novel enough to be a real treat, it was no longer the limit of her ambitions.

Becky topped up her tea from the pot, and topped up the pot from the hot-water kettle. It was Luca's fault. He'd opened her eyes to possibilities she could never have envisaged on her own. A world to explore and people in it she could help. Though she still had no idea how to go about such an undertaking. Or even where. Because she was fooling herself, thinking it could ever be in England.

Setting her cup back on the tray along with her empty plate, Becky padded over to the window. Her breath steamed up the cold glass. The rain had settled in, the heavy sky turning the canal below a dull pewter. It was one thing to escape, but another to admit that she couldn't risk going back. And it was one thing to imagine herself free to travel round the world, but to know that she had no home to return to—not that she ever wanted to return to the home she had left.

Despite the rain, Becky opened the tall windows and stepped on to the narrow balcony. She had never been one to indulge in self-pity, and she wasn't about to do it now, especially when she had less reason than ever to do so. She had no ties back in London. Hers had always been a solitary life and she'd liked it that way. Funny, but even at her most besotted, there had always been a part of her that had resented the changes she'd had to make to accommodate Jack. Funny, now she thought about it, how little changes she'd actually made. The trauma of their parting had obscured the fact that she hadn't really missed him. She'd miss Isabel a great deal more. And Luca…

Oh, Luca. Last night, he had been utterly transformed by their success. Last night, she had seen him carefree, lit up, happy. It was an infectious mix. Very infectious. Wrapping her arms around herself, Becky slipped back inside, sinking back down beside the fireside. Her utter abandonment still astonished her, but she was no longer embarrassed, nor could she bring herself to regret it. This extraordinary situation, this extraordinary man, were an all-too-brief departure from the natural order of things. At the end of Carnival they would part, their respective futures taking them in radically different directions. But that was still weeks away.

Becky closed her eyes, letting herself drift into a delightful dream of last night. Passion was such a very different thing to love. A very much more delightful experience, where instinct ruled, and pleasure was the only thing that mattered. It would pass, Luca had said, and she hoped fervently that he was right, at the same time hoping fervently that it would not fade too quickly. He had opened her eyes to a whole new world of gratification last night, a world she was eager to explore.

She'd never taken a lover before Jack wormed his way into her affections, so there had been no one for her to compare him to. Becky winced. She didn't much like the thought of doing so now. Perhaps it was because she had been so anxious to please, that she hadn't been so very satisfied herself back then. That would certainly be one explanation. Another would be that Jack had been as selfish in her bed as he'd been in every other aspect of her life, interested only in what she could provide him with, and giving back in return the bare minimum he could get away with. Now, that, unfortunately, rang very true.

While Luca— Oh, Luca was a very different matter. The next time—Becky smiled to herself, unfurling her legs from beneath her and stretching her toes to the fire, yielding to the temptation of imagining just exactly how the next time might be.

It was late afternoon by the time Luca and his mother arrived back at the *palazzo* in the pouring rain, leaving little time to change for dinner. He had spent most of the day taking tea and making polite conversation, with frustratingly few opportunities to bolster the legend of the Queen of Coins, his mother's friends being far more interested in stakes of the matrimonial kind. Accepting an *aperitivo* from Brunetti, he took his usual seat by the window in the otherwise empty drawing room.

Brunetti hovered, adjusting cushions, tending to the fire, waiting on the ladies' arrival. Luca stared out at the dark sweep of the Grand Canal. A few sleepless hours of contemplation in the early morning had left him baffled by his behaviour last night. Not what had happened, so much as what had not. Becky was entirely beyond his ken. He had no one to compare her to, nor did he wish to. The situation presented them such limited opportunities to indulge their mutual passion, last night's conflagration was inevitable, he had concluded. What confused him was why he had not taken matters to the ultimate conclusion.

Not because of lack of desire, that much was certain. He had never wanted anyone the way he wanted Becky. And she had wanted him every bit as much, he didn't doubt that either. As a result, they were both behaving out of character. She, who was not in the habit of offering, would have given him all, and he, who was in the habit of taking all had demurred. He was, for the first time in his life, uncertain of his own feelings. He didn't doubt what he wanted, but he wasn't sure it would be a good idea for either of them. Familiarity bred not contempt but indifference, had always been his experience. But the more he knew of Becky, the more he wanted her.

Whether their mutual desire would persist or fade was a moot point, however. At the end of Carnevale Becky would leave Venice, and he would take up the reins of his new life in the city, his duty to his father done, justice served. He would build his ships. He would restore the stolen treasures to Venice in a new form. He would step into his father's shoes. It was all he had dreamed of, all he had wanted, since he'd read his father's letter, yet all he could think of was that Becky would play no part in it.

He would miss her! There, he could admit that much. But it would pass—it would have to. And in the meantime, instead of dwelling over Becky's looming departure, what he ought to do was enjoy the time they did have.

The door opened, Brunetti bustled over to greet his mother and her niece, and Luca got to his feet. Becky was dressed in lemon tonight, one of Cousin Rebecca's simple gowns with a demure neckline, though it seemed to him, as she stepped lightly towards him, that it clung in a very far from demure way to the curves he had explored so delightfully last night.

'Good evening, Cousin Luca.'

Her smile was tentative as she made her curtsy. He couldn't resist taking her hand, pressing it fleetingly, smiling into her eyes in a most uncousinly way. 'Cousin Rebecca,' he said, 'as always, it is a pleasure to see you.'

'Your absence was much commented on today, Rebecca. I was forced to make your excuses at every call we made.'

'I am very sorry.' Becky pushed her untouched wine aside. Isabel, who had been rather silent throughout dinner was, now that the servants had departed, sounding decidedly waspish. 'I will ask Chiara to wake me if it ever happens again.'

'Please do. Now that it is widely accepted that I

have a niece, I would rather she did not garner a reputation for being either sickly or unreliable.'

'Mama, that is most unfair of you,' Luca said mildly. 'You must know perfectly well why Becky was so tired.'

'Presumably she was playing at a *ridotto* in her other guise,' Isabel replied tetchily. 'Though why you should imagine that I know this *perfectly well* when you have been at great pains to keep your plans from me, I do not know.'

'I have kept my plans from you because you expressed a desire not to know,' Luca retorted coldly. 'Despite having read my father's letter, despite his desperate plea for justice, you would rather sweep the entire matter under the carpet.'

'For very good reason.' Isabel picked up her napkin and began to pleat it. 'I apologise for my harsh tone, Rebecca.'

'I shouldn't have overslept.'

'Oh, it's not that.' Isabel threw her napkin down and took a sip of her wine. 'Anna Sarti was at the Fabbiano *palazzo* this afternoon. The poor woman is on tenterhooks knowing the start of Carnevale is fast approaching.'

'She knows, then, that her husband is a reckless gambler?' Becky asked with a sinking feeling in the pit of her stomach, though she had suspected as much from a remark made by the Contessa Albrizzi.

'Of course, she knows and dreads the coming weeks, though there is nothing she can do.'

'For which we should be grateful,' Luca said tersely. 'You know that the money he will stake belongs to Venice, not to Sarti.'

'Of course.' Isabel took another sip of wine. 'I also understand your desire to put right a terrible wrong.' She smiled weakly. 'Unfortunately, it is not only Don Sarti who will pay the price.'

'That is a matter for Don Sarti's conscience, not mine.'

Isabel nodded again. Luca poured himself a cup of coffee. Becky's conscience niggled her. Why did Isabel believe Donna Sarti would also pay, if the Queen of Coins took only what the Don had stolen? The winnings would be put to good use too, she reminded herself. Schools and hospitals for the people, Luca had said. If Anna Sarti knew the truth...

'Rebecca, I see from that fierce frown that I have upset you.' Isabel leaned across the table to press her hand. 'I promised not to interfere. I beg your pardon, Luca, you must do as you see fit to honour your father's memory. And when you have, Rebecca will be free to return to England. We will miss you. Do you have plans?'

'Nothing cast in stone,' Becky said vaguely. 'Though I'm not sure I want to go back to England,' she added, which was at least close to the truth.

'Really? But you must have family there?'

'Unfortunately, I don't. I am quite alone in the world.'

'You poor thing! Even though I have not seen my own family for decades, at least I have the consolation of knowing they are alive and well.'

'I'm well used to being on my own. In fact, I prefer it.'

'But you are still very young, with your life stretching out in front of you. Perhaps you'll marry, have a family of your own. Though I would not recommend a country vicar,' Isabel said. 'That may very well suit my niece, but...'

'That is a very poor attempt at a joke. If I wished to marry—which I do not—no man of the cloth would take me. You have no idea—' Becky broke off, appalled, suddenly on the brink of tears.

Isabel flinched. 'You are right, I do not. It was presumptuous of me to put myself in your shoes.'

'Yes, it was. You no more understand my life than I do yours, nor would ever want to. Your life may well be one of privilege, Isabel, but it's also mapped out in advance for you. I may not have much, but I do have the freedom to choose.'

Becky hadn't felt so completely out of place since the first night she'd arrived. After a day so foolishly anticipating seeing Luca again, all she wanted was to be alone. Without waiting for either mother or son to fill the astonished silence, she pushed back her chair and got to her feet. 'I'm here to carry out a specific task. When it's completed, I'll be gone. It will be as if I was never here in the first place. It cannot be any other way and that is for the best, for all of us. *Buona notte.*'

Chapter Ten

It had been raining overnight. The rooftop terrace was damp underfoot, though the sun was making a determined effort to break through the grey cloud. Becky gazed out morosely over the rooftops towards the Lido, where, Isabel had informed her, Luca had gone riding. Her mood, in contrast to the sparkling blue lagoon, was as grey and gloomy as the leaden sky above her.

She had waved away Isabel's attempt to apologise over breakfast. There was nothing to apologise for, after all. They had not quarrelled. Isabel had simply been curious. Becky preferred to keep her plans to herself. If they had really been friends it would be a different matter, but they were not friends. Last night, what Becky had said was a timely reminder for all of them of the real reason for her presence here. She had shocked them both with her vehemence, but it was for the best. She didn't belong here, nor would she ever.

'And I'd better make bloody sure I remember that from now on,' she muttered to herself. The arrival of a tea tray—courtesy of the Contessa, the servant informed her—made her feel like an ungrateful wretch.

Passing on her thanks, pouring a very welcome cup of piping hot tea and adding three sugars, Becky steeled herself. Isabel, she could keep her distance from. Cousin Rebecca was in awe of her aunt anyway. But Luca was another matter.

She curled her fingers around her cup, sitting back on the bench. Only yesterday morning, lolling about in her bedchamber in the aftermath of their lovemaking the night before, she'd been imagining all sorts of passionate couplings between them, quite forgetting the sole purpose of her being here. Nothing mattered more to Luca than his quest for poetic justice. Becky was his means to achieving it, and anything else she was to him was merely a product of this. When Carnevale was over, Luca would have no further need of her. His suggestion that she gaily set off to travel the world, it occurred to her now, reflected his own passion for travel, not hers. She was even entertaining the notion to please him, giving no thought to the practicalities, or the reality of travelling alone as a single woman. Her inexperience, ignorance of the world beyond London coupled with the sense of isolation she would feel, made it a daunting prospect.

But there was an even more scary thought. By his own admission, Luca indulged in dalliances, whose passion always died sooner or later. There wasn't anything wrong with that. It wasn't that she was in danger of falling in love with him, but that didn't mean she was immune to being hurt. In the cold light of day, her behaviour in the secret room behind the library appalled her. It wasn't what she had done, it was why. Because Luca mattered.

She was not as far gone as to be foolishly thinking

there could be any sort of future together for them, nor even to want it. She hated this world he inhabited, the stifling drawing rooms and the conversations where one thing was said and another meant entirely. Masks were not only worn during Carnival. Beneath that rich, sophisticated veneer of polite society, as far as she could see, there were a lot of unhappy people. She didn't understand the Venetian ways, Luca had said, and she never wanted to. She was glad she'd never be anything other than an impostor here. She liked Luca. She admired him and she found him fiercely attractive, but she didn't like his world and she couldn't believe a man like him could ever be happy in it. Though that was for him to discover, long after she'd left.

In the meantime, he was a distraction she really could not afford. Luca wasn't Jack, but if she wasn't careful, history could repeat itself. If the Queen of Coins failed, not only would Becky fail to earn the fee which would change her life, she could lose her life if she were caught manipulating the cards. She needed to concentrate totally on the task at hand, and so did Luca. She had not come to Venice to find a friend in Isabel or a lover in Luca. She'd come here to fund a new life for herself, and that was the thing she'd lost sight of these last few days. Her hard-won freedom depended on it. She was determined she wasn't going to lose sight of that again.

Becky was leaning out over the parapet when the door to the roof terrace creaked open. Before she turned, she already sensed it was Luca. He was looking particularly windswept, his eyes and cheeks glowing with the exercise and fresh air, his hair tangled, and despite herself, she felt a lurch of excitement at the sight of him. 'I hoped you'd find me here,' she said. 'I want to talk to you.'

He muttered something under his breath, striding across the roof to her, and clasped her hands. 'Please, I know what you're going to say, but I beg you not to do anything rash before you hear me out. Last night at dinner, it was clear that my mother's misguided concerns for Donna Sarti were making you uncomfortable. And then her misguided attempt to speculate about your marital prospects appeared to make things worse. But what wasn't clear to me until later, and it should have been,' he said wretchedly, 'was that I was at the root of your strange mood. I got carried away, Becky, and though you too seemed to be more than willing—I should have known you'd think differently in the morning. Please, tell me you're not thinking of leaving. It won't happen again.'

He had reached exactly the same conclusion as she, though via a very different route. She snatched her hands free. 'I didn't think differently in the morning, Luca. Quite the contrary. Heaven help me, I actually dreamed of more.'

She had the satisfaction of seeing him look astonished. 'So did I,' he said with a crooked smile.

If only he hadn't said that. But it made no difference. 'We can't always have what we want,' Becky said brusquely. 'Especially when it gets in the way of what we really want, and that's what's in danger of happening. You're a distraction I don't need, and frankly, I'm a distraction you can't afford. I'm not leaving. I'm staying, but there's too much at stake to risk letting passion cloud our judgement, Luca. You were the very one who pointed out on the first day we met, that we are playing a dangerous game. If I am caught...'

'You won't be.'

'No, I won't, because I'm going to do everything in my power to make sure I'm not. And so are you. I'm not going to fall into the same trap as last time.'

His eyes narrowed. 'Last time? What do you mean?'

Her stomach roiled, her heart felt as if it was in her mouth, but she met his eyes unflinching. 'That's what I want to talk to you about. Perhaps it would be better if we sat down?'

'I have a feeling this requires fresh tea. I am sure that I will need coffee.'

In something of a daze, Luca went inside to summon a servant. Becky wasn't leaving. Becky was staying. Becky thought he was a distraction. Becky didn't want to make the same mistake as last time, whatever that meant.

She was right, he thought with a sinking feeling. They had become distracted. It was a timely reminder that Becky was not here to play Becky, but the Queen of Coins. And a timely reminder that when she was done with that role, she would leave Venice.

Giving his instructions to the servant, Luca found himself wondering how many more times he'd order a pot of tea for Cousin Rebecca along with his own coffee. It was a sobering thought but, for the moment, quite irrelevant. Becky was waiting for him, and whatever she was about to tell him, she was dreading it. The answer to the question of why she had left England, he guessed. An account of what became of the man she referred to as her paramour, he suspected. The past that Becky had been so reluctant to talk about.

Luca paused on the final step to the terrace. He had no idea what to expect, but whatever she wanted from him, he needed to be able to provide it. He had come too far to give up now.

He opened the door, crossing to the bench, handing Becky the cloak he'd asked the servant to bring. 'I know you say you never feel the cold, but I have a feeling we're going to be here for a while.'

'Grazie.'

She wrapped herself in the voluminous garment, sitting on the edge of the bench as if readying herself to fly. Her skin was pale. There were dark circles under her huge violet eyes. The usual strand of glossy black curls had escaped to trail down her cheek. With difficulty, he resisted the familiar impulse to tuck it behind her ear. She looked at the same time both terrified and resolute. He wanted to reassure her, but knew better than to offer empty platitudes, knew that she was in fact quite capable of shocking him. So he kept his counsel until the tea and coffee came, watching the familiar hesitation before she decided to add a third sugar lump, the little smile of satisfaction that always greeted the first sip, the way she held the cup between her hands to warm them. The habit of a woman who had grown up in cold, damp, inadequate accommodation, he finally realised. How little he really knew of her or her life.

Becky took another sip and angled herself towards him, clearly bracing herself. 'My story centres around Jack, though I expect you've guessed that.' She took another sip of tea before setting the cup down with trembling hands. 'My paramour, they called him in the scandal sheets, though I thought of him as my husband. Not that we were really married, but I've never seen the need for a bit of paper to confirm what you already know. Or think you know,' she added with a bitter curl to her lip. 'I was twenty when I met him, and I prided myself on being worldly-wise. It turned out I was wrong.'

The tale she told was sparse on details, for which Luca was grateful. She said enough for him to imagine the charming rogue who had first seduced her, and then used and abused her. He had to work hard not to curl his hands into tight fists as Becky made light of her lover's greed, blaming herself for her own gullibility in not challenging his duplicitous lies as he lured her away from the streets where she had been content to perform her tricks and into the murky gaming hells of St James's.

'He told me that the money was to pay his father's debts,' she said. 'His father was in prison, his mother and brothers left without food, fearing eviction. How could I refuse to help him when I had the ability to do so?'

How indeed, Luca thought, his lip curling. The scurrilous bastard had clearly known Becky well enough to detect the tender heart beneath the gritty veneer. He hated the man for that and was uncomfortably aware that there was also, lurking beneath his contempt, something akin to jealousy.

'I couldn't make enough in the streets for what he claimed he needed,' Becky continued, 'so he taught me how to play the tables—he saw, you see, just how easy it would be to turn my hand, literally—from card tricks to card sharping. But no matter how much I won, it was never enough to satisfy his demands. There was always another debt to be paid, rent, food, clothes to buy and schooling for his brothers and sisters too.'

'It didn't occur to you that he should have taken responsibility for his family rather than you?'

'He was, he said, by allowing me to help them. I know it sounds so pathetic—but I was pathetic. And every time I protested, there was a new tale of woe. You'll think me a fool, but I believed him. I had no reason not to, Luca, and he was very convincing. He could have had a career on the stage.'

He belonged in the gutter, Luca thought with a horrible premonition of what was to come. 'And then, inevitably, one day his greed caused both your downfalls, I take it?'

Becky's cheeks were chalk white. She nodded, swallowing several times before she continued. 'Crockford's,' she said, her voice barely more than a whisper. 'That's where he wanted me to play. Have you heard of it?'

'Yes.' The elite of St James's hells, where there were no limits on the stakes, where men lost and won fortunes on a nightly basis. Men like Don Sarti. The parallels were beginning to make Luca feel sick. 'Go on,' he said.

'I didn't want to. I told him I wouldn't. It was far too dangerous. They have people walking the floors, constantly on the lookout for sharps operating. And the players—they're men with influence and a long reach. I didn't want to risk it.'

'But he told you a tale which melted your heart,'

Luca said viciously. Becky flinched and he cursed his insensitivity. 'Forgive me, but I find the way this man used you difficult to stomach.' Even as he uttered the words, he wondered if he was being a hypocrite.

Becky, however, shrugged. 'I let him use me. It was my own fault. I knew what he wanted me to do was wrong. I knew it was dangerous, but I did it all the same. It took him some doing to persuade me, but I was persuaded. He told me that his father had died in prison, leaving his mother and brothers destitute with no prospect of any income now the family breadwinner was dead. Jack wanted to raise one final significant sum, enough to pay for them to travel to Ireland, where they had relatives, and establish them there. After that he would have discharged his duty and I would no longer have to play the hells, and we could concentrate on building a life together. So...'

Becky's composure snapped. A tear trickled down her cheek, but she brushed it away angrily, shook her head when Luca reached for her hand, though she accepted a fresh cup of tea. 'So we duly visited Crockford's,' she said. 'And I was winning. Jack was with me. As you know, I couldn't have crossed the portal of Crockford's without a male escort. But he was nervous. I was playing for such high stakes and it showed on his face. I was so focused on the cards, I didn't notice, but one of the Crockford's men did, and they watched Jack watching me. Their suspicions were raised. Well, it was only a matter of time before they were on to me.'

Becky drained her tea. She was staring out at the sky, her eyes unfocused, lost in what was, judging by the way she clutched at her empty teacup, a terrifying memory. 'Jack gave the game away but it was me who paid the price. I felt a hand on my shoulder. I looked up, thinking it was Jack, but he was already halfway out the door with my winnings and making a run for it. I shook myself free. Someone shouted, "Stop, thief!" from the other side of the salon—they'd noticed Jack running by then. It was enough of a distraction for me to be able to flee out of a window. It was my only bit of luck, for it faced out on to the back of the building.' Becky's smile was mocking. 'My head for heights came in very handy. I escaped across the rooftops and finally made it home, where I waited, my nerves shredded, for Jack to turn up.'

'A wait that continues to this day, I'll wager. If he is ever foolish enough to break cover, mine will be the last face he sees.'

Becky shivered. 'Then I'm very glad he's not here. Oh, don't get me wrong,' she added hurriedly. 'At the time I would have happily ended his miserable life myself. But coming here in search of a fresh start has made me realise something. It is done, and cannot be undone. It's futile for me to rail against the past or seek revenge. The future is what matters.'

Luca stared at her in amazement. 'The man betrayed you. He lied to you. He deserted you.'

'And he broke my heart too, or I thought he did. It's mended now, thanks to you.' Becky coloured. 'I mean thanks to your faith in me. I haven't told you the worst part yet. I went in search of him. Of course I did. That's when the house of cards came tumbling down, so to speak. The landlord at his lodging house informed me there was no family, never had been. Jack had left for America, leaving nothing behind but an unpaid rent bill. All that money I'd won, he'd been salting away. Right from the moment he set eyes on me at Covent Garden, he'd been planning it, I reckon. Making me fall in love with him, leading me on, before leaving me high and dry and with a price on my head to boot. The man I had been fleecing when I was caught cheating turned out to be a member of the royal family! The full fury of the establishment was turned on me, my name blackened and my crime plastered all over the scandal sheets. The Runners were set on me, and if they'd caught me…'

Luca stared, utterly horrified. 'They would hang you?' he whispered.

'In a heartbeat.'

'That is what you meant when you said you couldn't go back to England, even if you wanted to?'

'When The Procurer found me, I was in fear of my life, Luca. I don't know what I'd have done if she hadn't offered me this opportunity. You saved my skin.'

He poured himself the dregs of the cold coffee, unsurprised to see that his hand was not quite steady. He pictured the guillotine in Piazza San Marco. 'Only to put it in danger again.'

'No,' Becky said firmly. 'That's what I'm determined won't happen. That's why we can't afford to be distracted, not when we're in the *ridotti*.'

The coffee was cold and gritty, but it was sufficient to calm him. 'I would never abandon you to your fate.'

'Of course not!' she exclaimed scornfully. 'You're not Jack, you couldn't be more different. I've known that from the start.'

'Grazie mille.'

'I mean it.' Becky smiled painfully. 'I hated working with him, he was always the weak link, but I couldn't play without him. I know I can rely on you. I can trust you, because I understand, I truly do, why it matters so much to you to make amends for what happened to your father. I brought what happened to me on myself—most of it,' Becky said. 'My form of atonement is to move forward, to claim my life back on my own terms. It's— what do you call it?—serendipity that I'll be able to do that by giving you your life back too.'

'You are a very brave woman, Becky Wickes. I know no one like you.'

She blushed, shifting on the bench. 'Well, that's just the problem though, isn't it? I've never met anyone like you, and together we've both allowed that fact to…'

'Get in the way?'

'We can't risk getting any closer. Do you see?' Her cheeks were fiery red, but Becky continued determinedly. 'Passion always fades, you said, but it doesn't feel like it's fading at the moment, and I think it's time we made an effort to put the fire out, rather than to stoke the flames.'

He laughed drily. 'Sometimes you sound as if you are speaking in a play.'

'Sometimes playwrights say it better than I ever could. To put it bluntly, I need to stop thinking about anything other than what you brought me here for.'

Luca sighed heavily. 'You are right,' he admitted most reluctantly. He couldn't argue with her. Her confession had shocked him to the core, but her determination and courage were admirable. 'You have already risked your life once. I have no wish to jeopardise it a second time.'

'But when you wrote to The Procurer, you must have known that whoever she sent you would be risking their life?'

'Not in such stark terms. It is like the difference between drawing up a battle plan and fighting a battle. The danger only strikes home when hostilities commence. I don't know that in all conscience I can make you…'

'I wish you would rid yourself of the notion that you can make me do anything. You didn't make me come here. You didn't make me deceive your mother's friends into thinking I'm your cousin. You didn't make me kiss you. You can't force me to play the Queen of Coins. It's my choice, Luca. And, yes, it's a risk, but it's a manageable risk.'

'Provided we refrain from complicating matters.'

'Now you understand. It's your future at stake here as well as mine. You told me, remember, that you couldn't build your ships until this was done. Think of those ships, Luca.'

She was persuasive. And heaven forgive him, but he wanted her so much. He couldn't bear to be responsible for putting her in danger. Yet if he did not, he would be denying them both their futures—for he knew that she would accept no money from him if they abandoned their plan. His head was spinning. 'I need time to think.'

'A luxury we don't have. We return to the *ridotti* tonight, Luca. We need to agree…'

Looking into her pleading eyes, he felt his heart skip a beat. He could happily forget everything and everyone when he looked into her eyes. And that was when it finally struck home what she had meant about distraction. This wasn't mere passion. Something much more fundamental had developed between them. Something that could easily grow into a heart-breaking problem if they let it. Something that could very easily lead to their downfall in the *ridotti* too.

Luca released her, getting to his feet again. 'Your anonymous playwright is in the right of it,' he said. 'We must snuff out this fire burning between us.'

Chapter Eleven

Carnevale—January 1819

'You remember the secret signal?' Luca asked.

'Yes.' Becky checked the ties which held her mask in place. They were perfectly secure, as they always were. It was a habit, this little ritual she performed as Luca steered their gondola to the jetty. Check the ties. Check her secret pocket. Check the laces on her gown. Unnecessary, since none of them ever needed adjusting, but it had become something of a superstition. As if, somehow, if she forgot to do it, her luck would change. Luck did not enter into it, she reminded herself. She and Luca had proved such a successful duo that all of Venice was talking about the Queen of Coins and her mysterious protector.

'You have the stake?' Luca asked.

'Yes.' He too had a routine, questions in his case, to which the answers were always positive. He always had an escape plan worked out too, meticulously re-evaluated for each of the *ridotti* they visited, the number growing as Carnevale progressed. Becky had lost track of the different locations. Each night he made her recite a different set of precise directions, designed to lead her to a rendezvous spot, where she could safely wait for him to find her in an emergency.

It was reassuring, for it proved he never underestimated the dangers they faced. But every night, just at this moment as they stepped out of the gondola on to a jetty or a walkway, when he could legitimately allow his hand to clasp hers, when she could legitimately allow her fingers to twine with his, there was a frisson. Not of danger, but of awareness, of the passion still smouldering between them, which lurked, barely contained, beneath the surface. And then he let her go, and she gathered the Queen of Coins's skirts up to protect them from the perpetual damp of Venice's watery landscape, and it was over.

'Will Don Sarti be here tonight, do you think?' Becky asked.

'The play is deep here, deeper than any of the salons we have so far visited, so it's highly likely,' Luca replied. '*Bene*. You are ready?'

'Ready.'

It was the final part of their litany. Luca led the way through the gloom, to a double door under a portico far more elegant than any they had visited thus far. As usual, the windows were heavily curtained, the merest flickers of light showing. As was always the case, a burly sentry stood guard, giving them a knowing glance before ushering them in. As she always did, Becky took a moment to accustom herself to the blaze of light, the heat, the air redolent of scent and wine and nervous excitement. And as usual Luca stood at her side, a solid, comforting presence, achingly familiar, agonisingly remote. But as they made their way into the first salon, Becky sensed instantly that this was a *ridotto* in a very different league from all the others.

The room was huge, lit by several glittering chandeliers. A great many of the clientele were women, perhaps as many as half, as far as Becky could see. Many wore a simple *moretta* mask of black velvet covering most of their face, their hair concealed under a flowing veil, but there were several much more elaborate constructions, half- and full-face. Feathers, turbans, silk flowers and spangled scarves were variously utilised to make elaborate coiffures. Though dominos were the most popular garment, some of the female clientele wore gowns so low-cut that they revealed far more than they concealed. Her own costume was positively demure in contrast. The prize in some of these games, she suspected, watching a very dishevelled couple emerging from a door at the rear of the salon, was a currency very different from gold. This was a very decadent Venice on display, a city of excess and vice.

'I should have warned you,' Luca whispered. 'You need not fear that you will be propositioned.'

'I do not,' Becky replied. Few men dared to importune the Queen of Coins, her haughty demeanour being sufficient to warn off all but the most ardent, and when it was not, a few choice words from her protector sufficed. Only once had Luca been forced to manhandle a would-be seducer, and it had been carried out with such astounding efficiency that the man was on the banks of the canal before Becky had even called for help.

'We won't find our prey in this salon,' Luca said. 'Let's try upstairs.'

The chamber on the first floor was a very different place. Dimly lit, chequered with card tables and their players, the atmosphere had the distinctive hush and almost palpable tension that accompanied serious gambling, the acrid tang of fear a top note to the sweeter scent of perfume and powder. Their entrance caused a stir. Though not every occupant of every table looked up, most did. As Luca led their customary progress around the room, dealing with the various discreet overtures from those eager to pit their wits against the Queen of Coins, Becky maintained her aloof bearing, though her heart was pounding. It always did at this point in proceedings, marking her entrance on to the stage, her assessment of her audience, her prelude to the show, but tonight there was a sharper edge to her nerves. Don Sarti was here. She was sure of it.

A table was set out for her. Several fresh decks were placed upon it. A man sat down with a nod and flexed his fingers. The little finger on his left hand was crooked, the nail missing. Becky made a point of remembering such things. If their paths crossed again she would remember his style of play. He was not a poor player, certainly no novice, and was cautious at first, but as he began to lose he became more reckless.

The stakes here started high and the man opposite her wanted to raise them again despite his already heavy losses. Entry to this *ridotto*—which was, like all the other Carnevale *ridotti*, essentially a private gaming hell—was limited by the mysterious hosts to those who could demonstrate the means to play. Becky was

torn, unwilling to take any more gold from her opponent, unable to force him to leave the table until their
agreed number of hands were completed, unable, in
her role as Queen of Coins, to deliberately lose. She
hated this aspect of the game they played. She could
ensure that she did not play this man again, but there
were nights in the *ridotti* when it seemed to her that
Venice was populated entirely by such men, set not
upon winning but playing, their world narrowed to
the turn of a card, the gold they staked of no impor-
tance at all, save only to provide their quota of danger and excitement.

Luca didn't understand. He thought they had a
choice, but the worst of them had no more choice than
an opium addict, inexorably drawn to their preferred
drug. He thought Becky's conscience would be eased,
knowing their losses were added to the coffers to be
returned to Venice. It helped, but only a little.

Her opponent was betting wildly now, his concentration so entirely on his own cards that it would have
been easy to turn the deck in his favour for the last
two hands, reducing the point differential in the final
tally, thereby curtailing his losses somewhat. But there
were too many onlookers for that. When he tried to
insist on playing on, Becky gave the secret signal to
summon Luca. She had no idea how he did it, cloaked
and masked, but the authority which must have made
him a formidable captain in the navy made him a very
formidable protector. With a final mumbling protest,
the man left the table. The used deck was replaced.
Luca discreetly pocketed her winnings and summoned
her next adversary.

She did not need the fleeting touch on her shoulder to warn her. She knew as soon the black-cloaked figure with the white *bauta* mask approached that it was Don Sarti. His walk betrayed his sense of superiority, the arrogant tilt of his head, the length of his stride, the faux-humble way he clasped his hands. She had studied him closely on the few occasions they had met socially, her actor's eye noting what others might have missed. He made only the briefest of bows to the Queen of Coins before taking his seat. She wondered briefly what had betrayed his identity to Luca.

She was glad to have one game against a wild player already under her belt, to have had the opportunity while doing so to observe the room, to have settled her customary stage fright. The endless nights of playing at the other *ridotti*, Luca's endless hours of meticulous preparation, her complete trust in him as her protector, left her free to concentrate on the turn of the cards now. She did not know where he stood now, but she knew wherever it was, he would be on hand if she needed him. He seemed never to watch the play. No chance of her protector being accused of aiding or abetting. Not this time.

Becky deliberately allowed Don Sarti to win the cut for the privilege of dealing the first hand. He was not wearing his heavy gold ring with its flashy diamond, but he couldn't remove the tiny mole on his right knuckle she had noted previously. He dealt the cards for the first hand, and she turned her mind to the game.

'We did it!' Luca exclaimed triumphantly, appearing in the doorway of the secret room behind the library with a tray containing a bottle of grappa and two glasses. His eyes blazed with excitement. 'All our hard work—all *your* hard work, I should say—has paid off. Tonight, for the first time, Don Sarti crossed swords with the Queen of Coins and lost. I think that deserves a toast.' He poured two glasses of grappa and handed one to Becky, who was seated on the chaise longue, having just removed her mask. 'To the Queen of Coins, Don Sarti's nemesis and my avenging angel. I know we have only taken the first step, but there is no doubt he'll be back, and he'll keep coming back until he has returned all of Venice's money. We have him, Becky. *Salute.*'

'*Salute.*' Becky took a cautious sip, coughing as the fiery liquid burned her throat. 'Assuming it *was* Don Sarti?' she teased.

Luca laughed. 'I spotted him the moment we walked into the salon. It took all my self-restraint not to approach him before he approached me. I did not have to wait long.' He lifted his glass to Becky and tossed the remainder of the contents back. 'He tried, but he could not contain his own eagerness. Your reputation for invincibility has him in thrall already.'

Becky tipped the remainder of her grappa into her mouth. The tension of the night, the strain of the many games she had played after Don Sarti had departed, began to ease as the *digestivo* hit her stomach. She relaxed back on to the chaise longue. If she needed any reassurance as to how much this meant to Luca, she had it now in the form of his euphoric expression. A glow of satisfaction suffused her, and she smiled at him, quite forgetting that she had resolved not to smile in that particular way at him again.

Ever since her first outing as Queen of Coins and

the aftermath in this very room, Luca had taken to bidding her a curt goodnight, leaving her alone immediately upon their return. Now here he was, smiling back at her, and her heart was racing, and she was thinking about all the things she had been trying so hard not to think about. Becky sat up abruptly. 'It's late,' she said meaningfully.

But Luca for once didn't take his cue. 'What kind of player was he, Becky?'

'He's very good. Possibly the best I've played.'

Luca frowned. 'Yet he loses.'

'Everyone loses if they play often enough. Trappola is not only a game of skill. All card games involve an element of chance.'

Within the confines of the little room, they were as far apart as it was possible to be, but it was still too close. Or not nearly close enough. She mustn't think this way.

'You never lose,' Luca said.

'Because I remove the element of chance. I control the cards. Or, to put it another way, I cheat.' Let him leave now, Becky thought, though she wanted him, she so desperately wanted him to stay. Five weeks since they made their pact not to distract one another, and only that one sign, when their hands touched as he helped her from the gondola, suggested that they had not successfully doused the flames.

'If he is such a good player, why doesn't Sarti quit when he is winning?' Luca asked, still showing no signs of departing.

'He is not content with winning,' Becky replied. The reality of the situation was beginning to dawn on her. *We have him, Becky.* Her excitement began to fade. 'The more he wins, the more he wants to win. Tonight I kept the point difference between our scores low to encourage him to believe he could beat me when we meet again.'

Luca leaned back against the door to the library. It clicked shut, but he didn't seem to notice. 'I still don't understand. As a skilled player, he should win more than he loses when he plays anyone other than you.'

He truly didn't understand, Becky thought, despite her attempts to explain. His poetic justice would destroy the man and possibly also the man's family. And she was aiding and abetting him.

We have him, Becky. Justice required a price be exacted, she knew that, but still, it left a nasty taste in her mouth, that her role should be so ambiguous. 'When he loses,' she said, 'he cannot resist the urge to recoup those losses. When he wins, he foolishly believes he is fated to win more. Don Sarti, like the first man I played tonight, is irrational when in the grip of gambling fever. He must feed his craving. It is why he will come back to the Queen of Coins again and again, as a drunkard will to the bottle.'

'If Sarti lived in London, he'd have been ruined years ago,' Luca said, shaking his head. 'Only Venice's strict rules, which limit gaming to Carnevale, have spared him until now. Yet ironically, it is our city which funds his play. Tonight we made a start on taking back from him everything he has stolen.'

'You mean your father's estimate of what he stole. You can't know the exact figure, Luca. Black-market fences—men who deal in stolen goods—they don't pay the full value, far from it.'

'Sarti is hardly likely to have sold Venice's treasures through a common— Fence, did you call it? Many heads of state throughout Europe are renowned collectors. The Russian emperor, for example, is an avid acquirer of important artefacts.'

Sometimes the gulf in social class between them seemed like a chasm, Becky thought. 'Regardless of who bought them, they will not have paid the full value,' she said patiently.

'What Don Sarti was paid is immaterial. What matters is what my father believed the treasures were worth. And the truth is they were priceless.'

Becky sighed. 'So we must take everything he has. His *palazzo*? His wife's jointure? His daughter's dowry?'

'The crime is Sarti's. If others suffer, then the blame lies squarely with him.'

She could point out that Luca was in the grip of a compulsion of his own, so intent on his thirst for vengeance that he did not care if innocent people were caught in the crossfire. *We could aim lower*, she wanted to say, but what would be the point? He wouldn't listen, any more than the man who had been the Queen of Coins's first victim tonight, and she was too tired to argue. She didn't want to argue at all. Especially not with Luca.

He had taken off his mask and his cloak, loosened the buttons on his coat and waistcoat. His hair, limp from the heat of the salon, flopped over his brow. Their eyes met, and he smiled, and her tummy flipped. She hadn't forgotten that smile, but she'd tried very hard not to think about it.

'You saw the darker side of Carnevale tonight,' he said. 'I am sorry I had to expose you to it.'

'It was all a game to them, in that downstairs salon, wasn't it? I thought the females were doxies, at first, but they weren't.' Becky wrinkled her nose in distaste. 'I thought I'd seen it all, but otherwise respectable women gambling their favours just for the hell of it, hiding what they no doubt call their minor indiscretions behind a mask, that was something new to me. I'm not sure I like this Carnevale very much.'

'That's because you've not seen the lighter side.' Luca sat down on the chaise longue beside her. 'Would you like to?'

'Very much.'

'Would Cousin Rebecca like to see the sights tomorrow?'

'I'm due to visit...'

'I'll clear it with my mother. You've earned a break, Becky, and it would be a pity if your memories of Carnevale were restricted to its seamier side.'

'Thank you. I will look forward to it.'

'We'll be amongst the crowds,' Luca said with a small smile. 'Quite safe from temptation.'

For the second time that night their eyes met and held. For the second time that night, Becky's stomach lurched, and now her pulses began to race, her blood heat. Just one kiss, surely just one kiss would do no harm. She forced herself to remain perfectly still.

'I know how they feel, those men who look at the Queen of Coins,' Luca said. 'Forbidden desire. A seductress who cannot be touched. I know how they feel. I wish I did not want you so much.'

'All passion dies,' Becky said. 'You told me so.'

'I did, and it was the truth until I met you.'

He reached out to push her hair back from her brow.

His fingers trailed down the column of her neck to rest on her bare shoulder. She could tell herself that his hand compelled her to lean towards him, but it would be a lie. 'I'll be gone soon,' Becky said.

'Yes. You will.'

She caressed his cheek with the flat of her hand. It was rough, his beard soft in contrast. Her touch made him exhale sharply, and the warmth of his breath made her lean into him, and their lips met. For an agonising moment, they were quite still, each waiting on the other to break the contact, neither able to move. And then it was too much. She opened her mouth to him, he opened his mouth to her, and they kissed.

It was a searing kiss, dark with desire and over before it had begun. They jumped to their feet. Becky's heart was racing. Luca, hands shaking, poured two more glasses of grappa. 'Another toast,' he said with a mocking smile. 'This time to the beginning of the end.'

It was very cold the next day, the sky leaden, turning the Grand Canal a palette of brown tinged with copper, pink and grey. Though Isabel had appeared content to release Rebecca from her scheduled round of social calls, Becky knew better. The Contessa was going along with her son's plan, but under duress. The lure of spending the day with Luca was a much more attractive proposition than a tedious day spent making calls, however. Becky slipped into her warmest coat of dusky-pink wool. With a dove-grey velvet collar, belt and cuffs, gloves, boots and a charcoal-grey hat, she looked as if she had chosen her outfit to complement the colours of the canal.

Luca was waiting on the jetty, dressed in his customary black, but a long greatcoat with several capes replaced his preferred short cloak. There was no sign of the gondola. 'I thought we'd walk, if you're amenable,' he said.

'Very. It will be a relief to feel the ground beneath my feet for a change.'

He tucked her hand into the crook of his arm and led her away from the Grand Canal, along a footpath which followed one of the narrower bodies of water. 'Though Carnevale is not so celebrated as it was in the last century, it is still a festival of the people, as you will see today. Unlike the *ridotti*, the spectacle at Piazza San Marco is open to everyone, and a good many go in disguise.'

'In masks, you mean? In the daytime?'

'And costumes far more elaborate than any you have seen in the *ridotti*, where they would make some of the nocturnal activities somewhat problematic,' Luca said drily. 'In Piazza San Marco it takes the form of an informal parade. Of course, part of the fun is that no one knows who is parading. It has been known for a high-born *donna* and her maid to wear the same costume on different days. At Carnevale you must be on your guard. You never know who you're talking to.'

'Or liaising with? Are you speaking from experience?'

Luca laughed. 'No. It is true that some people take pleasure in such encounters, and many more visit Venice during Carnevale with such encounters in mind, but I am not and never have been one of them.'

He pulled her away from the edge as a gondola bedecked in garlands swept past, waiting for the wake splashing on to the walkway to die down. 'You take such enormous pride in being a Venetian,' Becky said, 'but there are times when I wonder if you are a Venetian at all.'

She'd meant to tease him, but he took her seriously. 'While I was away, I thought myself Venetian to the core. Now I am not so sure. I think perhaps there is more of my mother's blood in me than I realised.'

'It is your mother's blood that sent you to England and then to sea.'

'I always thought that was my Venetian blood,' Luca said, taking her other arm as they resumed their walk and the pathway tapered, placing her on the inside, away from the canal. 'Because that was what my father always insisted.'

'It seems to me that he made sure your mother had very little influence on you, even as a child.'

'A son is raised by his father,' Luca said, frowning. 'It is the custom here, especially for an eldest son. And you forget I was sent to England with my mother's blessing.'

'It's true. Isabel said that you were so restless no school could contain you.'

He smiled at that. 'And for many years, my mother's family gave me a home, so you see, she has had a great deal of influence on me.'

'Yes.' Becky concentrated on the shallow, moss-covered flight of steps which led first down and then straight up again, before the walkway came to an abrupt halt and they were forced to turn sharply through one of those dark passages populated by feral cats and no doubt a quota of rats. Fortunately, this one was short, emerging in a run-down *campo* with an empty fountain.

A flock of startled pigeons flew up into the air. Luca made for the canal at the other side of the *campo*. 'You do not sound convinced.'

'I suppose it's because I could never be happy with this way of life. I can't see that you could either.'

He stopped at the edge of the canal, where a hump-backed bridge to the other side seemed to be the only route. 'You are referring to my marriage. You know it's not exactly imminent. In fact I've been thinking that it would make sense to concentrate on putting our winnings to good use before considering anything else. A year, perhaps two or three, to accustom myself to the idea.'

'Don't you think it's significant that you feel the need to accustom yourself, Luca?'

He laughed shortly. 'I can trust you always to get straight to the point, Becky.'

'That's because I'm not Venetian.'

'No.' They climbed the steps up to the top of the bridge. There was an odd little stone bench built into the centre of it. Despite the cold, of one accord they sat down. As ever, the green shutters of the overlooking houses seemed to Becky like closed eyes. Beneath them, the canal reflected the crumbling stone, the grey lowering sky. 'You're right,' Luca said. 'I'm not as wholly Venetian as I imagined I was. I don't want a marriage such as my father's, I do not think that my mother is more suited than I to select a wife for me.' He slanted a smile at her. 'You see, Becky, I do listen.'

'What do you want, then?'

He sighed impatiently. 'I will know that nearer the

time, I hope. I must marry to continue the line. My wife must possess suitable lineage. But at this moment—since I have no idea how I, as Conte del Pietro, wish to live my life—I am hardly in a position to say how I expect my wife to live hers.'

'You don't think she'd wish to have a say in it?'

He laughed. 'She will not be Becky, determined to lead her own life on her own terms.' His smile faded abruptly. 'She will be as unlike Becky as it is possible to be.'

Something she'd always known, but for some reason the words were like a punch in the stomach. 'I should think not,' she said with an attempt at a smile. 'A woman who was dragged up rather than raised, who doesn't even know who her father is, who's made a living by cheating gullible men.'

'Don't say that.' Careless of the fact they were in public, Luca grabbed her hands. 'You are the bravest, most honest, most loyal woman I've ever met. With your talent, you could have made a fortune for yourself, whereas the truth is I suspect that there are times when your principles have left you both cold and hungry.'

Lord, she wished he didn't understand her so well. She wouldn't cry. Not here. Not in front of him. 'You make me sound downright noble,' she jested.

'You are.'

'A noble savage, perhaps,' Becky said sardonically.

'I wish you would not demean yourself. You are extraordinary, and I will be forever grateful to have known you.'

A lump formed in her throat. Her heart felt as if it was being squeezed. She had a horrible premonition of what life was going to be like without him. 'Better not to say that, not until the Queen of Coins has finished her task,' Becky said brusquely. 'And better we don't sit here any more, lest people think we're taking advantage of Carnevale, only without our masks.'

She got to her feet and Luca followed suit, but before she continued over the bridge he caught her arm again. 'I meant it, every word,' he said. 'You have to believe me.'

She didn't doubt him, not the way he was looking at her. 'I know you do,' Becky said, blinking away a tear. 'It would be better for both of us if you didn't.'

Piazza San Marco was crowded, the cafés which lined the terraces packed. Becky, clutching Luca's arm, eyed the huge sea of colour and faces in astonishment. 'It's like Covent Garden multiplied a hundred times,' she said. 'No, that's not true. It's like all of the theatres in Covent Garden had spilled all of their actors on to the piazza in their stage costumes. I had no idea it was going to be so spectacular.'

When Luca had likened it to a parade, she hadn't taken him literally, but that was exactly what it was. A couple strolled past, clad in cloaks of scarlet and black silk stripes, beneath which they were dressed like court jesters. Huge feathered hats sat upon their heads. Chalk-white masks covered their faces. They were identical save that one was clearly a man, the other equally clearly a woman. There were a great many hooped gowns in garish colours, blue teamed with gold, cherry with emerald, red with burnt orange. The wearers swayed seductively, their tall powdered wigs adorned with stuffed birds and dried flowers, their masks, the type attached to a baton, painted to match their gowns. Not all of them were female, Becky realised, as one picked up his skirts to show a decidedly masculine pair of legs. He ran at speed towards a petite figure dressed in a vaguely Turkish outfit of scarlet spotted with gold, a gold mask on her face, a gold turban trailing a long red scarf on her head.

As they made their way slowly around the perimeter of the piazza, Becky noticed a good number of people in similar costumes. 'Characters from the *commedia dell'arte*,' Luca explained. 'That is Mattacina, all in white, save for his red shoes. Then over there, you can see Pantalone, the emblem of Venice, in a red waistcoat and black cloak. In fact, you can see several more of them over there,' he added, pointing at a group of men all dressed very similarly. 'The costume preferred by those lacking in imagination, I think.'

Becky laughed. 'What about that one?' she asked, nodding at a man in an outfit patched with red, green and blue triangles which bordered on the obscene, so tightly did his pantaloons and jacket fit.

'Arlecchino,' Luca said. 'You might know him as Harlequin.'

'I doubt *he* shares his costume with anyone else,' Becky said wryly, 'unless he has an identical twin.'

A woman began to sing an aria, her voice amplified by the arcade under which she stood. As they proceeded up towards the imposing arches at the entrance of the basilica, Becky was slightly shocked to see coloured booths set up on the steps of the church. There were turbaned fortune tellers in bright silks with tarot cards and shimmering crystal balls. There was a man with skin like parchment clad in a sorcerer's gown offering horoscope readings. Quacks stood on

wooden boxes, proclaiming their wares, offering elix-
irs and pills which would cure baldness and child-
lessness, which would make an angel of a harridan, a
daredevil of a coward. A tooth puller stood outside his
tent, wielding a terrifying pair of pliers. A slight man
clad only in a pair of white drawers and a turban was
seated on the cobblestones. To Becky's astonishment,
as he began to play a discordant tune upon a pipe, a
snake emerged from the basket in front of him. Poets
declaimed, minstrels sang and played, adding to the
cacophony of sound.

By the campanile, on a high rope strung between
two poles, two men were balanced precariously, juggling wooden clubs. Beneath them, a group of child
acrobats climbed on to each other's shoulders to form
a pyramid, waiting only for a smattering of applause
before they leapt down, tumbling and leapfrogging
each other in a blur of sequins and satin. Then came
the magicians, the illusionists and the conjurors. A
pierrot rolled up the sleeve of his tunic, brandishing
a knife. The crowd gasped as he sliced into the flesh
of his own arm, and blood seemed to gush from the
wound. Cheering and applause followed as he towelled
the arm dry to reveal not a trace of a scar.

Becky, who had seen such tricks before, was more
interested in the next stall. A white *volto* mask and a
plain black domino was the magician's disguise. His
props were as simple. A ball. Three large cups. 'He'll
find someone in the crowd to shout out which one the
ball is under,' Becky whispered to Luca. 'There, see.'

A well-dressed youth stepped cockily forward and
proceeded to wrongly guess the location of the ball
every time the magician moved them around. Becky

whispered the correct location to Luca and the crowd jeered at the victim's every mistake. 'If he's wise,' Becky said, noting that the lad was becoming aggressive, 'he'll allow him one win.' Almost before she had finished her sentence, the magician did exactly that.

Luca chuckled. 'A pacifier before he passes the hat round, I think.'

'Exactly.'

They moved on, past a man juggling knives and a puppet show to another magician with a pack of cards, and Luca stopped. 'He's doing your trick,' he said, 'the one where I had to guess the card. Do you think Cousin Rebecca might take him on?'

She was tempted, remembering how impressed Luca had been that night by her silly card tricks, confident, watching him, that her own skills were superior to the sharp plying his trade. 'No,' she said firmly, turning away. 'This is his pitch, Luca, his livelihood.'

She was rewarded with a warm smile, the slightest pressure on her gloved fingertips. 'I should have known,' he said. 'My most honourable card sharp.'

She couldn't help but laugh at that, trying to ignore the glow inside her, caused not only by his admiration but by his nearness, for the continually jostling crowd had forced them more closely together. At least that was what she told herself.

It was a perfect day out of time. Against the odds, they did not encounter a single acquaintance. As a result, Becky forgot to be Cousin Rebecca and was herself for the duration, embracing the spirit of this bright, alluring side of Carnevale with the same innocent, endearing joyfulness Luca remembered from their trip to the Lido.

It was infectious. He found himself calling out a warning to Pulcinella's wife at the puppet show, surprised to discover that Becky was as familiar with the characters as he was, for it was a popular show in Covent Garden, she told him. They shared a bag of roasted chestnuts, which he had the tortuous pleasure of peeling for her, popping them into her mouth in order, he claimed, to save her from soiling her gloves. They watched a balloon ascend from the centre of the piazza and come perilously close to colliding with the campanile before it disappeared over the rooftops, apparently intending to land on Guidecca, though the stiff breeze seemed intent on taking it directly out to sea.

Florian's was crowded, but for once Luca was happy to be recognised, the Conte del Pietro and his cousin being ushered into the warm interior to a quiet table where Becky marvelled at the gilded ceiling and frescoes he was so familiar with as to fail to notice, leaving him free to marvel at her, her cheeks pink with the cold, her big violet eyes bright with delight as the waiter set a hot chocolate and sugared pastry down in front of her. She ate delicately but with relish. It touched his heart to think that this too was a result of deprivation. He couldn't bear to think of her, a young, vulnerable version of the glowing woman beside him, fending for herself, peering into the steamed-up windows of cafés such as this one.

As the sun sank, the atmosphere in the piazza subtly altered. The necromancers and the quacks packed up. The music became seductive, in tune with the changing mood of the crowd, now seeking entertainment of a very different nature. 'We should go back to the *palazzo*,' Luca said reluctantly. 'My mother will be expecting us for dinner.'

'Our little holiday from reality is over. It's been truly wonderful Luca, a day I'll never forget.'

The way she smiled up at him gave him that odd sensation again, as if his heart was contracting. It was because he'd miss her, he thought. Of course he would. After all they had been through it was natural enough. Something of his thoughts must have shown on his face. Becky looked away, started walking, forcing him to follow, away from the throng, out of the piazza, back in the direction they had come, though she faltered at the first junction, and he took the lead once more.

The air was heavy and still, the sky already darkening to night, the temperature plummeting. They walked on, their steps muffled. He thought it was rain at first, the cold sensation on his cheek, but Becky's surprised exclamation made him stop, look up at the sky.

'It's snowing,' she said, her voice hushed.

She tilted her face up to the sky, closing her eyes as the snow began to fall thick and fast, flakes landing on her cheeks and her lashes. When she opened her eyes again and turned to him, smiling, he caught her in his arms. Time stopped. It truly felt as if time stopped as he held her, as she reached her arms up to twine around his neck, tilting her face to his with an inevitability that could not be resisted.

And then they kissed, cold lips meeting, melding into the sweetest of kisses, warming his blood, stirring him into an aching desire. It was wrong, yet when it was over their lips clung, the tips of their tongues touching. And then came more kisses. Little kisses that shouldn't mean anything, butterfly kisses that were surely harmless, though the way they were pressed together now, her back against the stone wall of a shuttered building, his body covering hers, hers arching against his, though there were layers and layers of clothes between them it felt as if they were stripped bare.

Their kisses deepened, their tongues tangled and he gave himself up to the moment, forgetting everything save for the taste of her, the heat of their kisses, the agonising delight of them, so longed for, so illicitly dreamed of and so much better than any dream. Drugging kisses, impossible to resist, so sinuously, deceptively languorous that he could pretend he wanted nothing more than this, just this, warm lips, tangled tongues, cold snow framing their faces.

But he wanted a great deal more. He was so hard he was throbbing. Dragging his mouth from hers, Luca saw his own desire clearly writ on Becky's face, her big eyes glazed, her cheeks flushed. There was nothing to be done about it, nothing to be said. She slipped her hand on to the crook of his arm, and they continued the short walk back to the *palazzo* through the swirl of the softly falling snow.

Chapter Twelve

'My mother sends her apologies,' Luca informed Becky when she joined him in the drawing room before dinner. 'She has gone to comfort a sick friend and will not return until tomorrow.'

Their escape from reality was not over after all, Becky thought. The Fates were conspiring to test their resolve.

Her evening dress was one she had not worn before, of turquoise silk trimmed with silver ribbon. 'Your gown is the colours of the canal on a winter's morning,' Luca said, handing her a glass of Prosecco.

His hair was still damp from his bath. His cheeks were freshly shaved, his beard neatly trimmed. Their eyes met as their glasses touched in a silent toast, and she knew that he, like she, was thinking of those kisses in the snow, so achingly sweet, a refrain of longing and yearning. A refrain which surely deserved to be sung to the end, just once.

Smiling inwardly at this flight of fancy, attributing it to her new-found passion for the opera, which she had now been to see six times, Becky made for the windows, pulling back one of the heavy curtains which had been drawn against the cold of the winter's night. It was still snowing heavily, huge flakes tumbling like snippets of lace, coating the moored gondolas in a cloak of white, giving an eerie light to the night sky.

'It's so beautiful,' she said, entranced by the view, still caught up in the enchantment of the day, acutely aware of Luca standing just at her shoulder. 'Even more unreal than usual.'

She felt the whisper of his lips on the nape of her neck. She felt the whisper of his breath on her ear. She turned, lifting her hand to caress his cheek, the merest touch causing such an upsurge of longing as to make her catch her breath. 'Luca,' she said, and he reached for her, and then the door opened, and they jumped apart as Brunetti appeared to announce that dinner was served.

But still the heightened mood lingered as they ate, scarcely aware of the servants pouring the wine, bringing the different courses, leaving them, at Luca's behest, to serve themselves. The fates continued to smile, Becky thought to herself, as she sampled some of her favourite dishes, *calamaretti*, the little baby squid fried in batter, the razor clams which the Venetians call *capelonghe* cooked in butter and parsley, the baked fish which they called John Dory at home and which here was known as *sanpiero*, served with a fragrant pesto.

They talked of Carnevale, of the sights they had seen in the Piazza San Marco. A perfectly innocuous conversation to anyone listening, but there was another unspoken conversation continuing between them all the while. It was there in the slanted glances, in the lingering gazes, in the grazing of their fingers as they passed the dishes. The day was far from over.

After dinner, they retired to the small parlour, where the dark red walls, the tightly drawn curtains and the well-stoked fire gave the palatial room an illusion of cosiness. They had sat here many times before, practising cards, but tonight there was no question of cards.

They sat on the sofa facing the fire. Becky knew that nothing had changed, that nothing could alter the ending which loomed, but tonight she didn't care. This was a moment out of time. Tomorrow, they would return to reality, see the dangerous game they played to its conclusion and then she would leave Venice and Luca for ever. Tonight was their only chance. She knew that if she didn't grasp it, she would regret it.

Luca poured them each a cup of coffee, downing his in one gulp as usual. 'I shouldn't stay here like this, alone with you. I can't trust myself to keep our promise if I do.' He shifted on the sofa, his knees brushing hers. 'We agreed,' he said, 'that we must extinguish the attraction between us.'

But the fire was burning in his eyes even as he spoke. His hand was already covering hers, he was already leaning towards her. 'Do you think we've succeeded?' Becky asked.

His laugh was a low growl. 'We've succeeded in making it burn ever brighter.'

She leaned closer, so that they were within kissing distance. 'Do you think if we allowed ourselves this one night, it would douse the flames?'

They both knew her question was sheer sophistry. Luca was more honest than she. 'You know it would not be enough, Becky.'

Her fingers tightened on his. 'But if it is all we can have?'

'Then I would rather have this than nothing.' His free hand touched her cheek, pushing her hair back behind her ear. 'Are you sure?'

Looking into his eyes, she felt such a surge of emotion that it twisted her heart. She knew then, though she refused to acknowledge it, that something profound had just occurred. She reached for him, twining her arm around his neck. 'I'm absolutely certain,' Becky said, and then she kissed him.

He kissed her back fiercely. The restrained yearning from those earlier kisses in the snow was unleashed as their mouths clung, ravaged each other, desperate to sate the hunger which had been far too long suppressed. It was as well that Luca, tearing himself free, retained a modicum of sense. 'The door,' he said, dragging himself away from her to lock it, but when he returned to her, instead of more kisses, he pulled her to her feet. 'We have waited so long,' he said with a smile which made her burn inside. 'We can wait a little longer.'

He kissed her again, but slowly, smoothing his hands over her back, as if to calm her. He shrugged out of his coat and his waistcoat. Turning her around, he kissed the nape of her neck, the pulse at her collarbone, untying the laces of her gown, sliding it down her shoulders, over her hips. She had never been undressed before, not by anyone. She was facing the mirror above the mantel. She could see her reflection,

Luca behind her, his hair dark against her skin, his hands cupping her breasts over her corsets. She shuddered. She arched her bottom against him, feeling the ridge of his arousal, and shuddered again.

He released her only to untie her corsets. When he cupped her breasts again, there was only the thin film of her cambric chemise between them. In the mirror, she could see his thumbs circling her nipples, felt her nipples harden, saw the result in the mirror, felt and saw his sharp intake of breath, and then he turned her around and their mouths met again in a savage kiss.

She tugged his shirt free of his breeches, gazing hungrily as he pulled it over his head, her hands already roaming over the muscle-packed flesh, pressing wild kisses over his chest, relishing the way her touch made him groan. The bow which held her chemise in place was undone, the garment slid down her arms to pool on the floor beside her gown, and for a moment Luca simply gazed at her breasts, and the stark longing in his eyes swept away any embarrassment, and then he pulled her into his arms, naked flesh to naked flesh, and Becky thought she would die with the bliss of it.

They sank to the rug. He eased her on to her back and he kissed her, her mouth, her throat and then her breasts, making her writhe and beg, making her moan and arch under him, his mouth tugging at one nipple, his fingers tugging at the other until she thought she could take no more and told him so. And he laughed, telling her that she could, and kissed her again. The valley between her breasts. Her belly.

They were both breathing heavily now. She could see the beguiling rise and fall of his chest in the firelight. His cheeks were slashed with colour, his eyes dark pinpoints. He sat up to remove his boots and pantaloons. She stared unashamedly, hungrily, at the sleek lines of his body, the muscled buttocks, thighs, and as he turned, the thick curve of his erection. She wanted him so much. She ached for him to enter her, was twisted so tight with desire that she needed him inside her before she unravelled. When he knelt between her legs, covering her body with his, his erection pressing between her legs she moaned, their kiss a deep, passionate prelude of what was to come next.

Save it did not. Luca smiled at her, a wicked smile which made her heart bump, and began to press kisses down the length of her body again, and this time he did not stop at her belly. The strings of her drawers were undone. Her undergarments were tugged down her legs, and Luca's kisses began again. The backs of her knees. The inside of her thigh, and only then did she realise his intention, crying out a startled protest which instantly became a moan of delight as his mouth covered her sex, and he licked into her.

She clutched at his shoulders. She bucked under him. She clenched her teeth in an effort not to fall immediately over the edge, for his tongue worked such delicious, delightful magic, making her feel as if she were being turned inside out, licking and kissing and stroking, making her so tight she could not bear it. She clenched her fists. Tight, tight, tight, so sweetly aching she was inside, and then he sent her over the edge with one last flick of his tongue. Becky spiralled out of control into a climax so intense she was senseless, pulsing, throbbing, tugging mindlessly at him, begging him equally mindlessly, 'Now, now, now.'

'You are sure,' he panted, his voice rough, and she

could only nod, urgent for him to be inside her, needing him to be inside her.

'Sure,' she said.

He kissed her mouth. She could feel him shaking. And then shuddering. Bracing himself. And then shuddering again. And with an agonised groan, he lost control, collapsing on top of her as his climax shook him.

Luca was mortified. Sitting up, he found his handkerchief and mopped up the evidence of his shame, cursing under his breath. 'I am sorry,' he said, forcing himself to meet Becky's eyes. 'That has never happened to me before.'

To his utter astonishment, Becky laughed. 'That is one compliment I'm more than happy for you to pay.' Sitting up, she wrapped her arms around him, nestling her breasts against his back. 'That has never happened to me before,' she whispered, nuzzling his ear. 'What you did to me, I had no idea it could feel like that.'

'So I pleased you?' he asked, already feeling considerably better.

She laughed again, and her breasts shook delightfully. '*Pleased* is not a remotely strong enough word to describe how you made me feel.'

'I am sorry,' he said again. 'Witnessing you achieving satisfaction, well, it was too much for me.'

'Luca, just kissing you was almost too much for me. All this waiting,' she said, nipping his earlobe, 'it was too much for both of us.'

'But I wanted it to be perfect.'

She chuckled. 'It will be. We agreed to one night, not one act.'

And then she kissed his neck, fluttering kisses with her lips and her tongue, tasting the hollow at his shoulders, and Luca felt, to his astonished delight, that it would not be long at all before he was ready to remedy matters. She slid her arms around him, stroking his nipples, tugging at them, mimicking what he had done to her, and his shaft stirred into life. She slid out from under him, laying him on his back and rolled on top of him, her smile playfully wicked, a smile she had never bestowed on him before, and the blood surged to his groin.

Becky's eyes widened. 'An encore, so soon?' Then she kissed him, and Luca forgot all about his untimely release and felt only the most aching of wanting, wanting such as he had never felt before. He was urgent to be inside her, but once again she took her cue from him, slowing their kisses, sliding down his body to kiss his neck and his chest, to kiss his nipples, down his belly, wriggling further down until she was between his legs and her breasts were grazing his skin making him writhe beneath her, and then he felt her hand on his shaft.

She stroked him, watching him, and he groaned. She stroked him again and felt him getting harder in her hand, and so did he. She dropped her gaze from his eyes to his shaft, watching the effects of her touch with a fascination that aroused him even more. And then she dipped her head, and her tongue touched his tip, and Luca cried out. She stopped. Studied his face. A slow smile dawned on hers. She licked him again and then again. Sweet torture. Luca clenched his fists. He curled his toes as she licked again and again, and then she took him into her mouth and he knew it would not be long before she sent him over the edge, and he was determined that that was not going to happen again.

When she released him, he took her by surprise, rolling her on to her back, wrapping his legs around her. His shaft nudged at the heat between her legs. She shuddered. They kissed. He thrust his tongue into her mouth, and he entered her, just enough to make her cry out, to arch her back, and he pushed higher. She was so hot and so wet and so tight, he was almost overwhelmed. He waited, bracing himself on his arms, and they kissed again. Slow kisses, slow thrusts, each one making her tighten around him, making him throb, and then harder thrusts, and she wrapped her legs around him, her heels digging into his buttocks and he could thrust higher, and their kisses became frantic as she opened up to him and tightened around him, until he felt her shudder and heard her cry out, and her climax shook her and he felt his own gathering, tightening, pulling himself free with a cry as it shook him, from the depths of his being, and he held her tightly against him, skin against skin. He had the absurd notion of wanting to climb inside her, felt as if they could never, ever be close enough.

Becky watched the dawn arrive, huddled in her dressing gown. The snow had melted. The Grand Canal was grey, the sky iron, but she was still glowing from their lovemaking. And it had been true lovemaking, on her part at least. She was in love with Luca. She loved him with her heart and her soul. Hugging her precious secret tightly to herself, she couldn't help smiling. She loved him so much, she thought she might burst with it.

Leaning her forehead on the cool glass, she closed her eyes, remembering last night. It was like nothing she had ever experienced before, beyond anything she could have imagined. Such passion. Such intensity. Such complete closeness. There were times when she felt as if they truly were one. No need for words. Only afterwards—lying in his arms, sated—she had struggled not to say those particular words. She loved him so very much.

I have never lost myself so completely before, Luca had said, looking embarrassed, with no idea just how much his words meant to her. He didn't love her, but she was like no other woman, unique to him. It was more than she had allowed herself to wish for. Besides, she would not truly wish for him to love her, for they must part and she couldn't bear to hurt him.

This sobering thought forced her eyes open, sent a chill running down her spine which the draught seeping through the tall windows never did. Shivering, Becky stoked the embers of the fire and curled up on the chair by the hearth, for once heedless of what Chiara would think when she arrived with her morning tea. Luca didn't love her, but after last night, knowing her as he did, there was a danger that he would realise that she had fallen in love with him. He must not know how deep her feelings ran. He would feel sorry for her. He would worry about hurting her. Those were complications they could not afford.

She groaned. Had it been wrong to surrender to her feelings last night? But yesterday had been so perfect and so magical, and it truly had been their one and only chance. She'd been fooling herself for so long that she didn't care for him, telling herself that it couldn't be love because it wasn't what she'd felt for Jack. Though she hadn't known it at the time, she'd been playing a part with Jack, imagining herself in love, acting her heart out in an effort to make reality fit her idea of what love should be, seeing Jack himself through her misty-eyed vision. He'd lied to her, yes, he had, and he'd used her too, but as to breaking her heart—no, she'd done that herself, by trying to mould him into her idea of a perfect man.

While Luca was anything but perfect. There were aspects of Luca's character she didn't agree with—this thirst of his for vengeance, for example, and his misguided belief that doing his duty would make him happy. No, Luca was far from perfect, but she loved him, every bit of him, exactly as he was. How long had she loved him? For ever. At least from the moment she met him, it seemed now. It didn't matter. She loved him, and when he kissed her in the snow yesterday, her heart had, ironically, simply melted along with her resistance. She loved him. She had made love to him.

And now it was over. *Time to stop dreaming*, Becky told herself sternly. In a sense, nothing at all had changed. She loved Luca, but it was a love with no future. There was no need to recite the many facts which made her an impossible bride for him, because even if she truly was his virginal, well-born cousin Rebecca, it would make no difference. This stifling life was not for her.

It was time to face reality. No more distractions. And no more questions either. She might not like his plan, but it was what she'd signed up to see through. Don Sarti's family was, as Luca repeatedly said, his own concern and none of hers. Vengeance in Venice, she thought with a twisted smile. It sounded like a play. If that was all she could do for Luca, then she'd better make sure she did it properly because it was her future she was gambling with too.

It had been a very successful night at the *ridotto*, Luca thought to himself as he rowed the gondola back to the *palazzo*. The second time Don Sarti had sought out the Queen of Coins, the second time she had beaten him. Sarti's losses were bigger tonight, for the stakes Luca had agreed had been higher. So why was he not more elated? His satisfaction was muted, his thoughts far from the card tables of the *ridotto* and centred on Becky.

He had not allowed himself to dwell on the previous night. Not with this night looming. But now it was over, he could hardly believe it had happened. Their lovemaking had been even more passionate than he had imagined. His loss of control was no longer embarrassing but part of what made the entire night unique. It frightened him now, looking at Becky, head back on the seat, clutching her mask, exhausted, the feelings she roused in him. He wanted her even more, his body craved her, but there had been moments, in the aftermath of their lovemaking, when he'd wanted to cradle her close, to keep her safe, to keep her with him and never to let her go. Those moments scared the hell out of him. He had known from the instant he met her that Becky was unique. He had nothing to compare his feelings for her with. But he knew, in his gut, that he had to put a stop to them before they got any stronger. On both their parts. Because he knew, knowing Becky, that she would not have made love to him unless she cared a great deal for him. And if she cared deeply, it would pain her to leave him. He didn't want to hurt her. She was his path to the future but she couldn't be part of it.

He knew this, but it made him sick to his stomach all the same, making him lose his hold on the oar. The gondola bumped against the side of a bridge, startling them both, and Luca caught the oar just before it fell into the canal.

Becky sat up, blinking staring around her. 'I fell asleep.'

Hardly surprising, he thought but did not say, for they had agreed, in the hour before dawn when they finally parted, that they would not mention what had happened. 'We'll be back at the *palazzo* soon.'

Becky nodded.

'You played Don Sarti perfectly tonight,' Luca said.

'Yes.'

'Four more weeks and Carnevale will be over. More than enough time for us to take back what he stole,' Luca said, because he needed to say it aloud.

'I would prefer it if that were sooner rather than later.'

'Are you anxious to be on your way, Becky?' he asked, thinking only that it meant she wanted to leave sooner.

'Oh, Luca.' She shook her head, her mouth trembling. 'You know what I think. I agree Don Sarti must pay, but do we have to bleed him dry?'

'Don Sarti!' he exclaimed, realising that they were at cross purposes, annoyed at himself for his contrariness. It would probably be better for both of them if

Becky left as soon as possible. 'I thought you understood why I must aim so high,' he said.

'I do understand.'

They had arrived back at the *palazzo*. He tied up
the gondola, but when Becky made no move to get
out, he sat down opposite her. 'What is it?'

'You thought I meant that I wanted to leave, didn't
you?'

He sighed, smiling ruefully. *Trust Becky to say
what anyone else would have left unsaid.* 'Yes. I have
waited so long to see justice done for my father, if you
had asked me when you first arrived, I would have said
the sooner the better. But now—now I will speak the
plain truth to you, and prove once again that I am not
the true Venetian I thought I was. It is inevitable that
you leave, but...'

'We have so little time to accustom ourselves to it,'
Becky finished for him, 'that we would feel cheated
if we deliberately cut it short.'

'Yes.' He covered her hands. 'Though if you feel
differently...'

'No.' Her fingers tightened on his. 'If this is all we
can have—and I know it is—then I want it all.'

Which ought to set alarm bells ringing in his head,
but which instead made him giddy with some other
feeling he did not care to scrutinise. 'When you do
leave, what will you do? Clearly you cannot return
to England.'

'Oh, maybe some day I will, when the dust has long
settled on my indiscretion.' She extricated her fingers
from his. 'The truth is, Luca, I'm someone who wants
to be settled. It's what most women like me yearn for.
To have a roof over my head, to be safe and warm and

not hungry. When Mum died, it was the workhouse or the streets. For a while, it was the streets. Eventually I scraped enough from my acting to rent a room in the rookeries but many other less fortunate urchins slept rough under the stars. They deserve better, and now I might be in a position to help.'

'The world you describe, it's beyond my comprehension,' Luca said, both appalled and touched.

'Exactly, while I understand it all too well. Which is why I'm thinking of doing something about it. I don't know what, precisely, but I'd like to give people a place to go when they need a roof over their heads. Do you see?'

Luca was beginning to, and he was beginning to think himself very ignorant. 'I think that you would make a far better fist of spending Venice's money than I ever will.'

'You're doing yourself a disservice. Hospitals, schools, fountains supplying fresh water, the things you're contemplating, they aren't high-minded, Luca. They're very much needed and they'll cost a lot more money than I have. I'm thinking smaller. Refuges, I suppose you could call them. Safe havens where women and children can go without fear they'll be separated, without being judged for not being able to make ends meet. Rooms that are home until they're on their feet again or fit to fend for themselves.'

'Where will you found such places?'

'Oh, I don't know. Wherever I lay my hat, as the saying goes. I don't suppose London is any different from other cities. You could probably do with a few here in Venice.'

'And you, Becky? What will you do once you have established these places?'

'Sit by my fire and eat sweetmeats,' she said flippantly, getting to her feet. 'I won't be doing any of it if I don't earn it.'

She jumped on to the jetty, and he followed her. She made her way swiftly up the stairs to the secret room. He hesitated. He wanted to kiss her. But it would be wrong. Utterly wrong. And Becky—honourable, admirable, fearless Becky—deserved to be treated with the utmost respect.

Bidding her goodnight, knowing he would be unable to sleep, Luca returned briefly to his own bedchamber to change, then quit the *palazzo* once more, this time by the front door, taking the night porter by surprise. He headed along the wide banks of the Grand Canal all the way to the lagoon, past the Doge's Palace and on to the Arsenal, the district known as the machine, once the greatest shipbuilding concern in the world. It had been dubbed the eighth wonder of the world in its heyday, the engine that made Venice a world power. Now, in the grey light of the early winter's morning, it looked exactly what it was: outmoded, run-down, a ghostly reminder of past glory, the few ships still constructed here like dinosaurs of ancient times. The proud *arsenalotti* who built the ships lived in poverty now, in an enclave set apart from the city, struggling to survive without work or any prospect of it.

The ships Luca would build, modelled on the sleek, modern Clyde clippers, would require very different skills. He'd have to remodel the whole dockyard, buy and assemble new, modern equipment. The *arsenalotti* notoriously resisted change. His father had been disparaging of them, urging Luca to import Scottish labour, certain that the Venetians would refuse non-traditional work. What basis had his father had for such sweeping assumptions? Luca had not thought to question him. Wandering morosely around the crumbling extent of the Arsenal, he saw that he'd been more concerned with building his ships than with who would build them. Ships would make Venice great again, his father had said. Luca had sailed in the finest vessels of their day, fought some of the greatest battles. Ships were his life, but oughtn't he be more concerned, as Becky would be, with the power in his gift to grant new life to the people who would build them?

Unaware of the cold and the rain which was starting to drizzle down, he propped himself against one of the docks' defensive towers and gazed out sightlessly to sea. Thoughts of the future, of the daunting task which lay ahead of him, of putting Venice's money to good use, were depressing rather than uplifting. He'd assumed he knew what was best for Venice because that was what he'd been raised to believe. It had been his father's tenet, his raison d'être, working for Venice, thinking only of Venice, risking his life to keep Venice's treasures safe, at the cost of all else. Was it arrogance? Or a compulsion, like Don Sarti's fascination with gambling? The comparison made Luca deeply uncomfortable, but it could not be ignored. His father had wanted to restore a Republic that no longer existed. He'd claimed he was working towards a new future for the city, but it was in reality a shadow of the past. He had spent his life looking backwards. His last act, or at least his last words to his only son, had been an exhortation that he do the same. His father wouldn't approve of Luca's charitable intentions. His father had wanted Venice's treasures restored, her heritage, her history reinstated, regardless of the fact that her people needed food and work and schools and clean water.

Becky saw that clearly enough. How was it that it had taken Luca so long to see with equal clarity? Surely he couldn't question his father's motives, his father's principles, his father's ideals? Guido del Pietro had loved Venice so much that he had put his own life in danger by threatening to expose Don Sarti. And also the life of his wife. And to an extent Luca's life too, for if his father had been tried as a traitor along with Sarti, he would have forfeited everything. Just as Don Sarti was risking forfeiting everything, his wife, his home, his children's future, by gambling.

But, no, the two were not the same. Luca jumped down from the high wall on to the muddy shoreline, where the retreating tide exposed the detritus of Venice's shipbuilding past in the ribs of a rotten galleon. He was not thinking clearly, the result of two nights without sleep. He had been planning Don Sarti's downfall for months. He had to honour his father's wishes before he faced any sort of future. Those were the facts, he reminded himself, picking an ancient rusty nail out of the sand, turning it over and over in his hand. His plans was too far advanced to contemplate rethinking them now.

It was Becky's fault. He cast the nail into the shallows. Becky, who said she understood his desire for justice but whose wrong-minded doubts were encouraging doubts of his own to surface. He had to put a stop to them, else where would he be? Justice would not be served.

And Becky would still be gone.

He didn't want her to go. Luca stumbled, only just preventing himself from falling into the mud. He didn't want her to go, she didn't want to go, yet go she must.

What was it she had said? *If this is all we can have, then I want it all.* He swore viciously. He didn't want to hurt her, but it was already too late, he saw that now. Too late for Becky, because what was that other than a tacit admission of love? And too late for him. Because he loved her with every fibre of his being.

Luca staggered back up the muddy shore, hauling himself on to the sea wall. He loved her. Love was the cause of all the feelings he'd never felt before, for the way his stomach churned and his heart protested at the thought of her leaving. He loved her, and it was utterly impossible for him to love her, because even if he'd been asked to specify the most unsuitable woman in the world for the Conte del Pietro to fall in love with, he doubted he'd have invented one less suitable than Becky Wickes.

Or more perfect. For a few blissful moments, Luca allowed himself to imagine a future with Becky by his side. Becky, the antithesis to all that was Venetian, forthright and outspoken, an old-fashioned woman who believed in love and fidelity and marriage and family, who was, contrarily, a card sharp and, if seen through the eyes of Venetian society, a low-born wanton. And yet he loved her.

There was no question of her becoming his wife.

She was not even suited to become his established lover, for her lowly birth made her utterly ineligible. Besides, the idea was repugnant to Luca now. He understood, finally, Becky's own repugnance at the arranged marriage he must make, the loveless future which lay ahead of him. Whatever happened, he knew that he could no longer go through with that.

Which left him where, precisely? A man with a duty to discharge to his father, justice to dispense, whose life was on hold until he had done both, which he was well on the way to achieving. A man with a vision for the future which would also serve his city and the needs of many of her people. Which was all very well and very noble, but he couldn't be the one person he wanted to be above all else. A man who was proud to call Becky his wife.

Chapter Thirteen

Two weeks later

Becky was alone in the small parlour. Cousin Rebecca was required to pay less and less house calls as Carnival progressed. There were almost no evening parties now—at least none of the respectable kind. All of Venice was immersed in the festivities. The canals resounded day and night with music as revellers called to each other from their garlanded gondolas. There were bull runs in the narrow streets, too terrifying and too cruel to be classed as entertainment, in Becky's view, after she had witnessed the start of one from her rooftop viewpoint. The fireworks, on the other hand, which she also watched from the terrace, she would never tire of. She watched all of it unfold alone.

Luca was distant and morose, in her company only as her protector at the *ridotti*, or as her cousin, in the servants' presence in the *palazzo*. It was how she ought to want it. There was a good chance he had guessed the depth of her feelings for him—if not that she had actually fallen in love with him, at least that she cared far too much. He wanted to spare her any further hurt, she guessed, or perhaps he was simply paving the way for the day when they would never see each other again. She missed him dreadfully. Her heartache was like a nagging toothache, a constant unignorable presence. Luca dominated her thoughts, taking up every free moment, until she wanted to scream or to weep or to seek him out and throw herself into his arms in a desperate search of oblivion.

She did none of these things. Instead, she practised her cards. She tried to plan her unimaginable future. She watched Carnival play out on the streets and canals below her from her rooftop kingdom. She had never felt so alone.

In the last two weeks, the Queen of Coins had played Don Sarti seven times, his losses increasing incrementally with each game, his desperate determination to win increasing at the same rate. She dared not even think about the sum they had amassed, the gold which must by now surely have filled the coffer which Luca kept hidden somewhere in the *palazzo*. He never told her the exact total, only that they had not yet reached his target. She loved him, but this aspect of him, his determination to see his plan through to the last *scudo*, she could no longer sympathise with. Though he insisted it was justice, to Becky it was beginning to seem like a vendetta, an aspect of his Venetian heritage that did him no credit.

She was reminding herself yet again that Luca's motives were of the purest, that the money would be well spent, that Don Sarti's family was Don Sarti's responsibility, when the door to the parlour opened.

'Oh, Rebecca, I didn't realise you were in here.'

Isabel stopped short on the threshold. 'Do not let us disturb you,' she said as Becky got hastily to her feet. 'Come, Anna…'

But Donna Sarti had already entered the room. 'To what do we owe the pleasure of your company?' Becky asked nervously, concerned that Isabel's horrified expression was going to betray her.

Donna Sarti was always pale, but today her complexion had an ashen hue. There were dark circles under her eyes. 'I have come to discuss a matter of some delicacy with your aunt. I would not wish to burden you with the unsavoury details.'

Without another word, Donna Sarti left the room, Isabel in her wake, only to reappear alone half an hour later. 'She is gone,' Isabel said, sinking down on to the sofa in front of the fire. 'Poor woman. She is at her wits' end over her husband's gambling.'

'She would be better served raising the matter with her husband, rather than sharing her concerns with you,' Becky said with a sick feeling in the pit of her stomach. She didn't want to have this conversation with Isabel. It was bad enough that she had it with herself almost every night.

'It would be futile. He won't listen. He believes that the next night he will win, the next night he will make good his losses, the next night will see him triumph. Which he might do, who knows, if the cards were not stacked against him.'

Becky flinched. Isabel's eyes were hard, her mouth set into a tight line. She was very much the aristocratic Contessa, not at all Becky's friend and confidant. 'You know why the cards are stacked,' she said evenly. 'You know too, that this is Luca's doing, not mine.'

'Luca is not the one taking Don Sarti's money from him.'

This was Luca's game. If Becky did not play it, she would be left with nothing except a broken heart. 'Don Sarti took the money from Venice.' It was Luca's argument, not hers, but she had no option save to repeat it.

'Venice!' Isabel jumped to her feet. 'I am sick to death of hearing about Venice. I have sacrificed everything for Venice. Years spent doing my duty at my husband's side, time I could have spent with my son, or my own family. I surrendered the opportunity to have more children for Venice. I listen to Anna Sarti's descriptions of her husband's blind obsession, Rebecca, and do you know what it reminds me of?' She smiled bitterly. 'I can see from your face that you do.'

'Your husband, Isabel, he— I imagine he always did what he thought was for the best. He was not like Don Sarti...'

'Not true.' Isabel sank back on to the sofa, wringing her hands. 'That is not true. Anna's husband will ruin her life and blight their daughter's future with his gambling. In the same way, my husband's obsession with Venice dictated our lives, and by writing that damned letter, threatens to destroy our son.'

'Isabel!'

'No, listen to me, Rebecca.' Isabel clutched at her wrists, her carefully manicured nails digging into the soft flesh of Becky's skin. 'You can stop him. He'll listen to you. You can put an end to this.'

'I've tried, but my words have fallen on deaf ears. He desperately wants to put things right, Isabel. Let's not forget that Don Sarti had your husband killed for the sake of those treasures.'

'If Guido had left well alone, he would still be alive.'

'And Don Sarti would have gambled away Venice's heritage,' Becky said. 'At least, thanks to Luca, the money will benefit the city. Some good will come of it. Do you have any idea what you're asking me to do? If I don't fulfil my part of the bargain, I get nothing.'

'I have funds…'

'I don't want your money. I thought you knew me better than that.' Tears welled in her eyes. Becky brushed them furiously away. 'If you wish to discuss the subject further, I suggest you speak to your son. Now, please, leave me alone.'

She waited, dimly aware of the irony of ordering the Contessa from her own room, but though Isabel got to her feet, she did not leave. When she spoke, her tone was not cold, it was worse. It was full of pity. 'You don't approve of his plan, any more than I do, do you?'

'It doesn't matter what I think. Luca has my loyalty, he knows that.'

'Does he know that he has also captured your heart?'

It was quite beyond Becky to deny it. 'It's true, but it's also irrelevant.'

'You will not believe me, Rebecca,' Isabel said with a twisted smile, 'but I am truly sorry for that. Contrary to your very low opinion of me—one which I fear is at least partly justified—I have a very high opinion of you. If you were truly my niece, I could think of no more suitable wife for my son, and would have made every effort to make the match our society has assumed I'm trying to make from the moment I introduced you. But as you say, unfortunately the circumstances render your feelings irrelevant. I have said more than enough, forgive me.'

The door closed softly behind her. It was so unfair of Isabel to challenge her, even if Isabel did say what she was already thinking. Don Sarti would ruin his family, because she, as the Queen of Coins, would ensure he continued to lose. That Isabel had, at the same time as condemning Becky's actions, demonstrated her true affection made everything much more painful. If only she had been Isabel's niece! Ridiculous, preposterous thing to wish for. Luca would never have cared for such a one as Cousin Rebecca. Not as he cared for Becky. And he did care. She knew he did.

The air in the parlour was suddenly stifling. She felt as if the *palazzo* itself was closing in on her. Becky threw open the door of the parlour and ran full tilt down the stairs, making for the front door. The footman called to her. She had no hat or coat. Standing motionless on the jetty, she hesitated for a moment as the sleet fell, then turned away from the Grand Canal and began to run, with no thought as to where she was going.

She was very quickly lost and disoriented. Narrow pathways came to sudden dead ends, forcing her through dark passageways, down shallow steps, across one bridge, back over another. The momentary relief of a courtyard that seemed familiar turned into panic as the narrow passageway she was sure took her back to the *palazzo* instead took her back to the same dead end she had reached fifteen minutes before. She met not a soul as she ran, though as ever she felt a thousand eyes watching her from behind the shutters of the shadowy buildings looming over her. Her footsteps echoed too loudly, pigeons scattered at her approach. The sound of the canal water lapping at the crumbling brickwork took on an eerie, beckoning quality. As she stood, trying to remember which of the exits from a deserted *campo* she had already taken, the thick silence was pierced by a wail that made her jump. A child, she thought, but it was only one of the feral cats. The sound of footsteps gave her hope, but when she followed them, called out, there was no one there.

Thoroughly frightened, chilled to the bone from the mist which was swirling around her, Becky sat down on the rim of a dried-up fountain. Silent tears streamed down her face. Anxiety gnawed at the pit of her stomach. Isabel's words rang in her ears. Donna Sarti's face swam before her eyes. She had no reason to feel guilty, she told herself. She was not forcing Don Sarti to play. She had justice on her side—or at least Luca's form of justice. This was not her plan. She was merely the executioner.

A sob escaped, quickly stifled, but it echoed around the *campo* all the same. She thought she'd come so far from London, left that poor shattered Becky who had been Jack's puppet far behind her. She'd known instinctively that what Jack wanted her to do was wrong, yet she'd done it, thinking she loved him, thinking that what she was doing was for a good cause. Was it happening all over again?

'No!' Her voice, echoing again, made her jump. Luca's cause was real, it was just, it was no lie. And her love for Luca—that was real too. So very, very real. So why, then, did she have this awful feeling that there was something wrong? She covered her face,

hot, bitter tears seeping through her fingers, and surrendered to despair.

He might have been a ghost, the tall, cloaked figure who appeared at the far entrance to the *campo*, but no ghost walked so purposefully, and no ghost made her heart leap the way it did, and as she threw herself into his arms, no ghost felt so solid and so reassuring. 'I got lost,' Becky mumbled, wriggling closer, as Luca pulled his cloak around her.

'You're safe now,' he said.

There was a crack in his voice that made her look up, and his expression squeezed her heart, for she saw her own feelings reflected there. 'Oh, Luca, I—'

'Don't say it.' His arms tightened around her. 'Please, don't say it.'

Perhaps it was to stop her declaration of love, or to stifle his own. It didn't matter. Their lips met. They kissed and their kiss said more than words ever could.

There was only a week of Carnival left. The Queen of Coins and her protector chose not to take the gondola that night, but walked instead, taking a circuitous route from the back entrance of Palazzo Pietro which led to the side entrance of another *palazzo* only a short distance away, facing the Grand Canal. They were infamous now, ushered past the downstairs salon where the play was neither deep nor serious, up the wide marble staircase to the first floor. The salon they entered must look out on to the canal, but the crimson damask curtains were firmly drawn across all the windows. Their arrival caused a stir as it always did. They stood just inside the doorway as was their custom, allowing them both the opportunity to assess the room in their different ways.

Though Becky had grown accustomed to the opulence of the various Venetian *palazzos*, this room was so sumptuous as to be worthy of one of the former doges. High above her, bordered by a cornice of white and gold more elaborate and deeper than any she had seen, the ceiling was painted with a bloodthirsty hunting scene. On each wall was another such scene, presumably depicting a story from antiquity, the characters probably members of whichever aristocratic family owned the palace. There were six chandeliers, making the room garishly bright, and two fires blazing in the hearths at opposite ends of the salon made it uncomfortably hot, the heat blending the scent of perfume and sweat and red wine, and the peculiar, dusty smell of masks worn too often, into an unpleasant miasma that had a metallic quality.

She knew Don Sarti was already there. The hairs on the back of her neck alerted her to his piercing gaze before he made his way across the salon towards them, the small cluster of other gamblers vying for a game with the Queen of Coins parting to make way for him. There was no pretence now, that she would pit her wits against any other. All of Venice knew that this was a duel. All of Venice watched each fresh game with bated breath.

She sensed the change in Don Sarti immediately as he took his place opposite her at a table in the centre of the room. Luca took up his usual position, close enough to be at hand should he be needed, distant enough to avoid any accusation of collusion. The tension which usually crept up on Don Sarti as he lost was there from the beginning tonight as he cut the cards. She let him win, allowed him to deal the first hand. The sense of anticipation, the confidence with which he began every game between them was also absent. He sat too straight in his chair, his voice was strained, he dealt the cards with a snap.

'We do battle again, Queen of Coins. I hope that tonight the outcome will be very different.'

Beneath his mask, his eyes glittered feverishly. Tonight, he was afraid to lose. Becky suspected he would not be staking Venice's gold but his own. Total ruin was, quite literally, on the cards.

Don Sarti played with a recklessness born from desperation. When it came to Becky's turn to deal, she gave him a hand where Swords was the obvious suit to lead with, for he held the Foot Soldier, a ten and a seven. Yet he instead chose Cups, in which he held only the Ace. By the time all the cards of this hand had been played, she could tell without having to add up the complicated scoring system, that he had already lost deep.

The sixth hand was the last, and Becky was once again the dealer. Their audience was two deep now. Luca had been forced to move away from the door to a further corner of the room in order to maintain his view of the table. When she first played, what seemed like a lifetime ago now, Becky thought as she shuffled the deck, he had been nervous of any witnesses, afraid that her tricks would be detected. But though some clearly suspected her reputation as being unbeatable relied on some trickery and watched her closely, she was too skilled to betray herself, and Luca realised that the audience lent her credibility.

She wanted it over. Having shuffled the cards into the order she required, the Queen of Coins executed another fancy false shuffle and dealt. Four cards to Don Sarti, a mixture of suits, all low save one Cavalier. Four to herself, all Batons. Five more to Don Sarti. Another five to herself, including two Kings and two Foot Soldiers. As she expected, Don Sarti discarded all nine of his cards, drawing the next nine blind from the pack, calculating the odds were good that he would select more of one suit or higher value cards, oblivious that the odds were fixed. His hand was shaking. His fingers left damp traces on the cards. A bead of sweat trickled down from his mask on to his neck. She waited, for he had the right to discard one more time, but he did not.

The game was over very quickly after that. With a sick feeling in the pit of her stomach, Becky totted up the scores, adding in the extra points for three of a kind, for court cards taken, for the tricks won with a deuce, all the extra points she had engineered for herself, which she had ensured Don Sarti could not win. The total brought a gasp from the crowd. Hoarsely, his voice muffled by his mask, Don Sarti demanded the paper from her and began to recount. Unable to reduce the tally, he threw the pencil across the table, pushing back his chair so violently that it toppled over.

'I will give you your winnings before tomorrow night's play.'

At his words, Luca stepped forward. 'You have no right to play if you cannot pay.'

His voice was softly menacing. Don Sarti took an involuntary step back. 'You have my word as a gentleman,' he said and then, taking both Luca and Becky

by surprise, made a lunge across the table, leaning
so close that the grotesque nose of his mask almost
touched Becky's. 'Tomorrow,' he hissed, 'I will return,
and vengeance will be mine.'

'Did you hear him?' Luca asked with derision as
Becky removed her mask in the secret room hours
later. 'Little does he know that the vengeance being
administered is mine, not his.'

'The entire salon heard him. Haven't we punished
him enough?'

'Not nearly enough.'

'Will it ever be enough, Luca? He's sick. He can't
help himself. He'll keep coming back to the Queen of
Coins until he has absolutely nothing left.'

'This sickness you claim he suffers from is what
compelled him to steal from Venice, to have my father murdered. It is only right and proper that the same
sickness brings about his downfall.'

'But it will eventually, regardless of what we do,
can't you see that?' Becky exclaimed wretchedly. 'Perhaps not at this Carnival but the next or the one after
that, depending how deep his pockets are. He'll en-
gineer his own downfall, he doesn't need you or me
to do it for him.'

'I am honour-bound to do see this through to the
bitter end,' Luca said. 'It was my father's last wish. I
thought you understood that.'

'I understand it's what you believe,' she whispered.
'Hasn't it occurred to you that your father was every
bit as reckless as Don Sarti? That he was in the grip of
his own compulsion to restore Venice to some mythical vision of the past? And you too. Don't you think

that this compulsion to do your father's bidding is misguided?'

Her words, spoken only in desperation, made him flinch. Luca was leaning against the door, his mask dangling by its strings from his hand, his cloak over his arm. 'I am neither blind nor obsessed,' he said.

'No.' Becky swallowed. 'That's not what I'm saying.'

'All I'm doing is seeking to right a wrong.'

'I know.' She couldn't take her eyes from him. She loathed the fact that her words must hurt him. His cause was just, she still believed that, but his method— Oh, why the devil had she started this conversation? 'I'm sorry.'

'What for?'

For no longer being able to be completely on his side. But she couldn't say that. For falling in love with him. But she could never regret that. She shook her head helplessly. Did he love her? A week ago, when he had rescued her, kissing her so desperately at the fountain, the question had crept into her mind, but she had instantly shied away from answering it. Best to leave the impossible unsaid. But he must have read it in her eyes, for his own darkened, he dropped his cloak and mask, moving towards her as if in the grip of an irresistible force.

'The only compulsion I have is for you,' Luca said.

Becky's heart was pounding. She felt both sick and giddy. She loved him so much. This was so wrong, yet it was so right. The only thing she was certain of at this moment was that she loved him and she was incapable of denying it. One more time, she thought desperately, lifting her face to his, just one more time.

There was no finesse to their lovemaking. Their kisses were frenzied, the kisses of two people at the ends of their tethers, made frantic by the knowledge that soon they were to be parted for ever. Passion ripped through them as they tore at each other's clothes, as they ravaged each other with kisses, as they clawed at each other's skin, wanting to mark and to claim, seeking to merge, to lose themselves in each other. Becky kicked her way clear of her costume as Luca pulled his shirt over his head, kicked off his boots.

She scattered wild kisses over his torso, breathing deep of the heat of his skin, her hands restless over his back, his buttocks, the tautening response of his muscles rousing her as much as his mouth on her breasts, licking, then tugging on her nipples, setting up the sweetest, most aching, dragging tension inside her. She flattened her palm over the ridge of his arousal, felt him pulse at her touch through his breeches, and then she could wait no longer, pulling at the buttons, an agony of suspense as he freed himself, the sweet delight of him, silken and hard as she curled her fingers around him, the rasp of his breath, and then the drugging rapture of his kisses as he sank down on to the chair, pulling her on top of him, sliding inside her.

She shuddered. She wrapped her arms around his neck, claiming a deep, thrusting kiss, and then it began, the frenetic ascent to completion. His arms were on her waist, lifting her as she tightly clung then thrust, drawing a feral groan from him, taking him so deeply inside her that she cried out, tightened around him, felt the first prelude to her climax, clung more tightly. Another thrust, and she was already lost, pulsing around him, but as he lifted her, she thrust again, panting, kissing, clutching, saying his name over and over as wave upon wave caught her, and still he thrust until a hoarse cry was ripped from him and the pair of them tumbled to the floor together as his own climax shook him, and still they kissed, clutched, kissed, clung and kissed.

For a few perfect moments they were one. Becky lay on top of Luca, their skin slick with sweat, her face hidden in his hair, thinking of nothing, save how much she loved him. And then she opened her eyes, and saw such devastation in his and she knew it was over. All of it.

'I don't know what I'm going to do without you,' Luca said.

Becky sat up. The room was lit by a single lamp, but it felt like a blinding light. Save that she wasn't blinded. She saw painfully clearly what she must do. 'I'm sorry,' she said, this time utterly sure of what it was she apologised for. 'I'm so sorry, Luca. I love you with all my heart, but I can't be party to this, not any more. The Queen of Coins has played Don Sarti for the last time.'

Chapter Fourteen

'What do you mean?' Hazy from their lovemaking, Luca watched in a daze as Becky jumped to her feet and began to gather various bits of her costume from the floor, where they had been discarded.

'Exactly what I said.' She turned to him, clutching a handful of silk and ribbons, her hair dishevelled, her eyes blurry with unshed tears. 'I'm not winning another *scudo* from Don Sarti.' She began to fold up the bundle of clothes in an alarmingly final manner, as if she were already consigning the Queen of Coins to the history books.

Luca cast about for his own clothes, hastily pulling on his breeches and shirt while Becky, taking off the tunic of her costume, tied the sash of her dressing gown securely and made to leave the room. He caught her by the wrist. 'You don't mean that. We are so close to achieving our goal…'

'No! Luca, I'm sorry, but I simply can't do it.'

Her reservations had grown steadily, she'd told him so often enough, but he'd always been able to persuade her she was wrong. Or at least to persuade her to continue, which was the same thing. Wasn't it? 'What has made you change your mind?' he asked, trying to ignore the sinking feeling in the pit of his stomach.

'It was obvious tonight that he desperately needed to win, Luca. You must have sensed that.'

'He always needs to win. It's what drives what you call his compulsion.'

'But tonight it mattered in a different way.' She spoke gently, and gently led him over to the chaise longue where she sat down. He didn't like the way she looked at him, as if she pitied him. 'Tonight I'm convinced that Don Sarti was playing with money he didn't have. Not Venice's money, Luca.' Becky held her hand up when he made to speak, shaking her head. 'You have this fixed notion that when we reach a certain sum, you'll no longer feel guilty for not being able to prevent what happened, that it will compensate you for the loss of your father, for the loss of your freedom—because that is part of it too, isn't it? Your father's death has forced you to give up the life you love.'

'It's not about that.' But even as he denied it, Luca knew in his heart she was right.

'This quest of yours has become all-consuming, and I think you resent that more than you're prepared to admit.'

She had no right to question his motives, he thought frantically. He just needed her to do what she had been hired to do. Anger, a blessed relief from doubt, began to take hold. 'You can't leave until you have completed the terms of our contract.'

Becky flinched. She paled. But she did not falter. 'I'm aware that I'll forfeit everything.'

'I didn't mean…' He stopped. What had he meant? Not to send Becky away with nothing. No, no, no, a thousand times no! She could not go back to that life. She could not go back to England, where the shadow of the gallows loomed over her.

Luca jumped to his feet. 'You don't mean this. You're overwrought. I've asked too much of you, pushed you too hard. I see that now. There's still a week of Carnival left. We can leave Don Sarti in suspense tomorrow night, you can take a well-earned break, rest…'

'Luca, you're not going to change my mind.' Becky hadn't moved from the chaise longue. She looked at him, those big violet eyes of hers unwavering, her expression quite tragic, and he knew she meant it. He thought he was going to be sick.

'You don't need to ruin Don Sarti,' she continued, still in that soft, inexorable voice. 'He'll destroy himself, sooner or later.'

'But what about justice?'

'Your quest for justice has turned into a vendetta I want no part of. It's wrong, Luca. It's as simple as that. I feel it here,' Becky said, placing her hand over her heart. 'Once before, I allowed my feelings to override my conscience. I can't do that again.'

'You are comparing me to that lying toad?'

'No! I would never compare you to Jack, never. What I feel for you is utterly different to anything I've felt before, but if I carry on doing what you ask of me, I'll never be able to look myself in the eye again. Can't you see?' Becky got to her feet. 'Please think about what I've said. More than anything, what I want is for you to be happy.'

'Happy?' He stared at her as if she were speaking a foreign language.

'Forget Don Sarti. Build your fountains and your hospitals and your schools in your father's name, and build your ships in your own. Stop allowing your father to dictate your life from beyond the grave, Luca.' Becky took his hand. 'Stop looking over your shoulder. What is done is done. I love you so much. I beg you, find a way to be happy. Trust me, my darling, this is not the way.' She lifted his hand to her mouth and pressed a kiss to his palm. A tear splashed on to his fingers. She let him go. He watched, stunned, frozen to the spot as she left.

He lost all track of time. For moments or minutes or hours, Luca stared in utter disbelief at the closed door of the secret room, telling himself foolishly that as long as he stood still there was a chance Becky would return. The sound of someone moving about in the library gave him a brief, flaring hope, but then he heard the rattle of the brass curtain hooks on the pole, the clatter of a bucket on the grate, and realised that it was one of the chambermaids doing her early-morning chores. Quickly and quietly he finished dressing, now desperate to escape. It was nearly dawn as he untied the gondola, snow falling from the lightening sky. He began to row, making instinctively for the lagoon, the freedom and privacy of the Lido.

A vigorous gallop did not clear the fuzziness in Luca's head. Over and over, as his horse pounded the length of the Lido and back again, all he could think of was that Becky was leaving. Which made him miserable to the core of his being but was hardly helpful. Becky was always going to leave, he'd known that from the start.

Handing his steaming horse back to his groom, Luca made his way disconsolately down to the beach, throwing himself down on a sand dune. A foolish mistake, for the place was redolent with memories of Becky. Becky laughing as she curled her toes into the wet sand. Becky's innocent joy as she tried to hurdle the waves. Her surprise when the force of one of them nearly toppled her over. The way she had wrapped her arms around his neck when he caught her, teasing him. Then kissing him. The wild rush of pleasure as he touched her, lying right here in the sand. How long ago? A decade. A minute.

He dropped his head into his hands, groaning aloud. Why the devil did he have to love her so much? Why the devil did she have to be so stubborn? And so damned sure she was right. Because she wasn't right. Not about any of it. Save that she loved him. His chest tightened. She loved him. So why wouldn't she do what he wanted?

That she had dared to compare him to Jack Fisher! Luca swore viciously, curling his hands deep into the damp sand. But she hadn't, not really, he was forced to acknowledge, recalling her exact words. It wasn't her feelings she was comparing, it was her conscience.

If I carry on doing what you ask of me, I'll never be able to look myself in the eye again. Can't you see?

He did see. He didn't want to, but he did, and he was filled with awe at her bravery. She was willing to sacrifice everything, all her dreams to help others like herself, and, worse, her own security, in order to stand by her principles. He couldn't let her do that. For the first time since their return from last night's *ridotto*, Luca was certain about something. He could not let her do that. No matter what.

But what did that mean? The truth was…

His heart began to race. The truth was, he didn't want her to go anywhere. The truth was, he wanted her to stay with him, by his side, for evermore. For a glorious moment it seemed that the grey snow-laden clouds parted and the sun came out as he imagined that happy fate. He and Becky, together. He and Becky married. He and Becky with a brood of little children cast in their image. He smiled, half mocking himself for this sentimental vision, but at the same time tears stung the backs of his eyes. Becky loved him. Becky wanted to make him happy. And what would make him happy, he saw now, wasn't vengeance or justice or whatever name he wanted to give it. It wasn't even building ships. It was Becky.

He jumped to his feet, running down to the shore, stopping just short of the waves, staring out at the Adriatic, past the white-crested waves, as if there was an answer somewhere on the horizon, if only he looked hard enough. Even if he could reconcile himself to giving up on his plan, to failing to complete the task his father had bequeathed him—yes, she was right about that too—there were so many obstacles keeping them apart. Conte del Pietro could not marry Becky Wickes, a wanted criminal and one born without a father's name to call her own. What was more, Becky Wickes wasn't in the least bit interested in becoming the Contessa del Pietro and living the stifling life of a Venetian society hostess. Luca grinned at the very notion of it. No, Becky would not endure that life any more than he would.

He wasn't his father. He was not going to live in his father's shadow. Becky—forthright, clever Becky, who knew him better than he knew himself—had opened his eyes. It was time for him to stop looking over his shoulder and start looking forward. To claim his life back. He had no idea how. He had no idea what it might mean, but by the stars, he was going to do it. It had been so long since he had faced the challenge of overwhelming odds that he'd forgotten that stirring in his blood, that grit inside him that relished a fight. There must be a way to make it right. There had to be a way, and he had to find it quickly, because he couldn't let her go. He simply couldn't countenance losing her.

It was the early hours of the afternoon before a heavy-eyed Becky finally forced herself to leave the sanctuary of her bedchamber. Outside, snow clouds filled the sky, the Grand Canal below her window as grey as her mood. She had a headache, she'd told Chiara, and wished only to be left alone. But the maid, most likely concerned by Becky's red-rimmed eyes and chalk-white colour, besieged her with tisanes and teas and cold cloths and hot broth and fruit until Becky had no option but to claim she felt much better.

She felt, in fact, utterly devastated, and though her conviction that she was right was unshaken, she couldn't think about the consequences without trembling. She had been in worse straits, she reminded herself, significantly so. In the years immediately after her mother died, for example, when she hadn't even a room of her own, when she'd left the theatre at night with no idea where she was going to sleep. And more recently, hiding out in the rookeries following Jack's betrayal. Yes, she'd been considerably worse off, she told herself stoically. Even if her dreams were well and truly shattered. Even if the vision of a future free from trickery and cold and hunger had taken root. Even if she must leave the man she'd given her heart to, knowing that she could not give him the one thing he thought he craved. And so Becky steeled herself, as she made her way out of her bedchamber and down the stairs, to ask Isabella to help her to leave Venice for a destination unknown, as soon as practicable.

She entered the drawing room to discover the Contessa deep in conversation with a stranger, and would immediately have left with an apology for interrupting, had Isabel not beckoned her over, smiling. 'My dear Rebecca, come and be introduced to my brother, Admiral Riddell. Mathew, this is Rebecca, who is, as you know very well, *not* your long-lost niece.'

Mortified, Becky made a very shaky curtsy, her cheeks flaming with embarrassment, but to her consternation and surprise, Admiral Riddell seemed not to care a jot that she was an impostor. 'My sister has informed me of the reason you are here. I must confess to finding the tale reminiscent of something from a lurid novel. Odd sort of plan that my nephew has concocted, I think he must be turned in the head, to imagine— But there, none of my business.'

The Admiral was a tall thin man who bore a strong resemblance to his sister, though the same features which made Isabel beautiful, made him appear more formidable than handsome, his nose tending to hawkishness and his chin to squareness.

'Please join us, Rebecca. I have ordered tea,' Isabel said. 'Mathew has come all the way to Venice to escort me to England for a visit. Luca wrote to him. I had no idea. It is a lovely surprise. I was just saying to Mathew that his timing could not be better, for he plans to take in the remainder of Carnival, to set sail at Lent, which means we will be back in England for Easter.'

'I see,' Becky said vaguely.

'No, my dear, you don't. It means we will be able to take you with us. You won't have to travel back to England alone. How you made the journey yourself in the first place... But now I don't have to worry about your safety.'

'Oh.' Brother and sister were gazing at Becky expectantly. Becky bit down on the hysterical bubble of laughter which rose as she contemplated informing them that the Royal Navy would be transporting a capital criminal back to face trial. She couldn't possibly go with them. 'Thank you,' she said.

The door to the drawing room opened. Thinking that it would be the tea Isabel had ordered, Becky got to her feet to help with the tray, only to drop back down on to her chair as Luca entered the room. He was soaking wet. He had not shaved. He was still wearing last night's clothes. Where had he been? Her hand lifted, beckoning him. Their gazes locked. He took two steps towards her then stopped, shook his head, little sparkling crystals of snow scattering on to the floor. 'Uncle,' he said, extending his hand, meeting the Admiral in a warm embrace. 'I've just been informed of your arrival. I did not expect you so soon.'

'Isn't it marvellous, Luca, a wonderful surprise,'

Isabel said, beaming. 'And such fortuitous timing, I was just saying to Becky, it means we can take her back to England with us. What do you think of that?'

'Not a lot.'

Becky jumped. Isabel's mouth fell open. The Admiral, however, simply narrowed his eyes. 'I understood from your mother that this odd undertaking of yours would be completed by the end of Carnival.'

'This undertaking, as you call it, has turned out to be a damn sight odder than my mother could possibly imagine,' Luca said with the strangest of smiles. 'And if I have my way, it will be over today.'

'Today!' Isabel clapped her hands together. 'Luca, do not tell me that Rebecca has persuaded you to—' The Contessa broke off, covering her mouth.

'I didn't speak to him on your behalf, Isabel,' Becky said dully, wondering how much worse this conversation could get, 'but on my own. It made no difference.'

'But it did.'

Luca was smiling at her now. There was a light in his eyes that she didn't recognise and didn't dare name. It made her silly heart leap. It made her think that perhaps love did conquer all, just as it did in the theatre. And then she remembered that this wasn't a play, and before she could stop them, tears began to cascade down her cheeks. She covered her face, but not before she saw Isabel's horrified expression, the Admiral's perplexed one. She stumbled to her feet, muttering her excuses, making for the door. A strong arm guided her from the room. She wanted to burrow her head into Luca's shoulder and sob, but what would be the point. She shook herself free.

'I listened, Becky,' he said urgently, holding her

by the wrists. 'I don't know how yet, but I'm going to find a way to resolve this mess. I love you so much.'

She couldn't wish the words unsaid, but she wished he had not uttered them, all the same. 'I know you do, but it doesn't make any difference.'

'It will,' Luca said fiercely. 'I'll ensure it makes a difference. We'll talk later, *cara mia*, and I'll explain, but I have something I must do first.'

She watched him go, fighting the ridiculous thought that she'd never see him again as he hurtled down the stairs, still unshaven, still wearing last night's clothes, throwing open the door before the footman had a chance to reach it and disappearing, hatless, back out into the snow.

Unable to face more of Chiara's ministrations, Becky joined Isabel and her brother for dinner. They were then heading off to La Fenice to see a rare revival of Vivaldi's *Griselda*. Becky excused herself on the grounds of a headache, and Isabel, who had several times during dinner asked her to explain Luca's strange behaviour, questioned her again.

'Let the lass alone,' the Admiral intervened, much to Becky's relief. 'Can't you see she's as much in the dark as you? I dare say I know that son of yours better than you do yourself. His methods are not the most conventional, I'll grant you, but by heaven, Luca gets results, and he's as straight as the day is long. So we'll leave them in peace to sort things out between them while we're at the opera. I can't tell you how much I'm looking forward to it.'

The Admiral steered his sister out of the door. Becky retired to the library, pulling one of the huge leather chairs forward to the fire, curling up there with a book of librettos, which she failed to open. Her mind darted about like a starling trapped in an attic. She struggled to make sense of Luca's remarks, for while her silly heart veered off in the direction of un-realistic hope, her head veered in the opposite direc-tion, telling her there could be none. Luca loved her. In the end, as the clock struck eight, Becky wrapped this knowledge around her like a soft woollen blanket. He loved her. Until he returned, she would allow her-self the bliss of pretending that was all that mattered.

She must have dozed off, for she did not hear him entering the library, opening her eyes to find him standing over her, gazing down at her with the most tender of smiles. Still caught up in her dream, Becky scrabbled to her feet, allowed him to wrap his arms around her and to hold her tightly against his chest.

'Becky,' he said as she gently freed herself. 'Becky, I've just confronted Don Sarti.'

She dropped back down into the chair, her legs giving way under her. 'Please tell me you didn't do anything foolish.'

Luca poured himself a glass of grappa, drinking it in one gulp before pouring another and taking the seat beside her. 'I didn't need to. You were right,' he said heavily. 'He needs no one's help to destroy himself.'

'Tell me what happened.'

He did, recounting the full, sorry tale, in stark terms that left her in no doubt that, finally, Luca un-derstood the true nature of Don Sarti's compulsion. 'I thought he'd deny it all,' he said. 'The theft. My fa-ther's murder. But he didn't. He cried like a baby when

I told him that the Queen of Coins was my avenging angel…'

'You told him! Why, Luca? That was never part of your plan.'

'No, no, it wasn't, but it should have been.' He set down his glass, a heavy frown marring his brow. 'Having spoken to him, I can see what you have seen all along. He is already a broken man.' He shuddered. 'He was even pathetically grateful that we had saved him from himself, taught him a lesson he would never forget. Not that I believe we have.'

'No. He won't be able to resist returning to the tables,' Becky said sadly.

'No. I pity him, but I pity his family more, for he will take them down with him. I dreamed of serving poetic justice,' Luca said wryly, 'but it was already being served by the culprit himself. I can never forgive Don Sarti for having my father's life snuffed out, but I am done trying to avenge it. My father's legacy will be hospitals and schools and freshwater fountains for the poor of the city, not paintings and artefacts. Venice is nothing without our people. You've made me see that, Becky. I've been trying very hard to avoid thinking about having to step into my father's shoes. I've decided that I'm simply not going to.'

'Luca! I am so happy to hear that.'

'Are you, *cara mia*? I hope that you're going to be a great deal happier when you hear what else I have to say. You said that all you want is my happiness because you love me? I finally saw, this morning, on the beach at the Lido, that the only thing that would make me happy was you. But how to make you happy—that was a very different problem.'

He was clasping both her hands now. The tenderness in his eyes as he looked at her was almost more than she could bear. 'You can't,' Becky said, too upset to prevaricate. 'All I want is you, and it's impossible.'

'That's what I thought.' He released her to get to his feet, leaning his back against the wall beside the mantelpiece. 'I will be a very different Conte del Pietro than my father, but as conte I am required to marry well. I must produce an heir. I must make my life in Venice. You could not be less suitable in the eyes of the world, yet you are the only woman I will have as my wife, Becky.'

'Oh, Luca, that is the most— But it's impossible. I wish you had not…'

He dropped to his knees in front of her. 'For myself, I've come to realise that I don't give a damn for any of these traditions. What matters to me is not my wife's pedigree or her innocence. What matters is that her heart is the truest and the bravest I've ever known, that I will be the last man if not the first for her. That she loves me, not for my name or my money but for myself, just as I am. That she wants what I want, to be always by my side, to make a family with me, not for the sake of the del Pietro name, but for the sake of our love. That's what I want, Becky, and that's why I want you and only you. But the world would not see the things that matter. They would judge you on the things that don't. Which is why, though I am determined to marry Becky Wickes, as far as the world is concerned, I'm going to marry my cousin Rebecca.'

'You don't have a cousin Rebecca.'

'I know that,' Luca said with a mischievous smile, 'but no one else does.'

'Save the most important people, your immediate family.'

'My uncle was very taken with you. He would have no objection.'

'How can you possibly know that?'

'I've been to the theatre to speak to them.'

'And your mother? She's sacrificed her entire life to the Venetian way. What does she think?'

'She does not want my wife to be unhappy as she has been, but more importantly, what she wants is for you to be happy. She's become enormously fond of you, I think you know that.'

'She guessed my feelings for you,' Becky confessed.

'She told me. She was delighted to hear that my feelings for you were exactly the same, though extremely concerned about what society would say, as you can imagine. My proposal for countering the gossip tickled her.' Luca smiled. 'Not only would she much rather have you as her daughter-in-law than her niece, she can now happily claim that she has, as is the convention, chosen a bride for me.'

'But I'm not who people think I am.'

'This is Venice in Carnevale. No one is who you think they are.' Luca took her hands again. 'When Cousin Rebecca arrived in Venice, the world assumed my mother had brought her here to be my bride. The world assumed, despite Cousin Rebecca's pious claims to have no ambitions beyond marrying a rural English clergyman, that my charms would prove to be irresistible.'

'As indeed they have,' Becky said shyly.

'So Rebecca fell secretly in love with her dashing cousin Luca. But it was only as she planned to leave, to journey back to England with her aunt, that Luca realised that she would be taking his heart with her. And so he told her.'

Becky felt giddy. Her heart was fluttering and jumping and racing with joy, and she was trying desperately to rein it in. The grey fog which had enveloped her since the early hours was lifting, replaced with a bright, golden light that seemed to be taking its place. Her heart was bursting with love, and a huge bubble of joy was threatening to burst inside her. 'What did Cousin Luca say to her?'

'He said I love you with all my heart. I cannot let you go. If you will promise to be my wife, I will spend every day of my life trying to make you happy. I will be true to you always and for ever. My darling Rebecca, please say you will marry me.'

'Oh, Luca. Oh, my darling, if only…'

'No, no, those aren't your lines. You must ask me how I can possibly make you happy as Contessa del Pietro, when it would stifle you, to live as my mother does.'

'And what is your answer to that?'

'That you are no more obliged to live in my mother's shadow than I am to live in my father's.' Luca grinned. 'My father, along with Don Sarti, was the most influential man in Venice. I'm his son. If I choose, I can wield just as much influence. Where the del Pietro family lead, society will follow. We will set a trend, my darling, for fidelity and for togetherness in our good works. You understand, in a way that I never could, what it is to suffer, and what is needed to alleviate it.' He laughed, embarrassed. 'That sounds very worthy, very stuffy. I don't mean to imply that we'll be either, but…'

'You want me to help you?' Becky squealed.

'I want you to be at my side, to realise both our dreams, not only mine.' His smile faded. His frown returned. His clasp on her hands tightened. 'Would that make you happy, Becky? Do you think that we could forge a life together here?'

'I can't even begin to imagine how happy I would be to— But, Luca, how are we to be married? Not here, in a church— I don't know what official documents are required, but I doubt I have them.'

'We will be married at sea by my uncle, who, fortunately for us, has the power to do so invested in him as a ship's captain. We will honeymoon in England, and when we return, the story of our shipboard romance will be old news.'

'England! I can't go to England.'

'Becky Wickes most assuredly cannot go, but the Contessa del Pietro can have nothing to fear. I want you to meet my mother's family, Becky. I want you to feel part of my family, before we make a start on establishing our own.'

Heat flamed in her cheeks. 'I can't believe what you're saying.'

'I mean every word,' Luca said fervently. 'I know it must sound as if I've turned everything I believe in on its head, but I feel quite the opposite, as if I'm seeing straight for the first time since I returned to Venice, and it's because of you. This morning—was it really only this morning?—when you said you were leaving, I knew that I couldn't bear to let you go. On the beach later, I still had no idea what I needed to do, only that I must do something. I love you. It changes everything—or at least it means that I'm willing to change almost everything to have you by my side. I love you. The future is ours to shape together. Becky, if you are willing to take the risk.'

'Luca, I've been trying to reconcile myself to a future without you, without the means to put a roof over my head, in a foreign country...'

'Then marry me. At least that way you'll always have a roof over your head.'

'I'd prefer to live *on* the roof here.'

'That can be arranged. Anything you wish, if only...'

'I wish only for you, Luca. And—and not to be the Contessa del Pietro like your mother. I can't quite believe this is happening.'

Luca pulled her to her feet. 'The Procurer has a reputation for making the impossible possible. I remembered that today, and I thought, if she can do it, why, then, can't we? Do you love me, Becky?'

She twined her arms around his neck. 'With all my heart, Luca.'

'Will you marry me, Becky?'

Finally, she allowed her joy to burst through, allowed her love to show in her smile. 'Yes, my darling Luca, I will marry you.'

He pulled her roughly into his arms, holding her so tight she could barely breathe. 'I promise you that you will never, ever regret it,' he said, and then he kissed her. Tenderly at first, almost tentatively his lips touched hers, his hands crept up to cradle her face, but as Becky pressed herself against him, as their tongues touched and their kiss deepened, passion flared.

Enveloped in the sweet delight of a love they had

both come so close to losing, they surrendered to each other on the hearth in the library of the *palazzo*, affirming their love for each other over and over as they kissed, as their limbs tangled, as their bodies merged, climbing together to their climax, clinging together as one, as they would be for the rest of their days.

* * * * *

*If you enjoyed this story
be sure to check out the other books in the
Matches Made in Scandal miniseries*

From Governess to Countess
From Courtesan to Convenient Wife

*And be sure to check out the books in
Marguerite Kaye's
Hot Arabian Nights miniseries,
starting with*

The Widow and the Sheikh
Sheikh's Mail-Order Bride

Historical Note

I've never been to Venice, but thanks to Peter Ackroyd's *Venice: Pure City* and John Julius Norwich's *Paradise of Cities*, I feel as if I have. Any inaccuracies or mistakes about the Venice of Luca and Becky's time are all my own doing.

Norwich mentions Contessa Isabella Teotocchi Albrizzi, and I came across her again in Benita Eisler's epic biography of Byron, *Byron: Child of Passion, Fool of Fame*. Known as the Madame de Staël of Venice, hers was only one of two surviving salons from the heyday of the Republic. The renowned sculptor Antonio Canova was a regular there, and the bust of Helen of Troy, which he is delighted to show to Becky, was a gift from him to his hostess.

The other salon was run by Contessa Maria Querini Benzon. Byron, on his last visit to the Venice Carnival, decided that hers was more interesting than her rival's, perhaps because the Contessa was happy to include his low-born mistress into her drawing room. Contessa Benzon was notorious for having danced in a skimpy tunic around the Tree of Liberty, and she did indeed inspire a ballad, 'La Biondina in Gondoleta', which, according to Norwich, is still sung by today's gondoliers. In Becky and Luca's time she was more fond of food than dancing, particularly polenta, which she carried around with her, stuffed into her ample cleavage in winter—hence the name the gondoliers gave her: El Fumeto, The Steaming Lady.

Gambling was illegal in Venice in 1819, though a blind eye was turned during Carnival, when many of the large *palazzos* opened up private gaming hells called *ridotti*. Both women and men could play, provided they were masked, and the stakes were not always financial but a very different currency indeed.

Much of the Carnival atmosphere, both seamy and fiesta, I've taken directly from Byron's descriptions quoted in Benita Eisler's book.

Byron—obnoxious man, but excellent source— called marriage Venetian-style a social convenience rather than a sacrament. Though he was more than happy to avail himself of the custom for married women to take a lover, he was hypocritically scathing of the practice. By the time in which my book is set Venice was very much in decline, and the rich were forced to be careful with their wealth, thus the custom to try to limit the number of sons who could inherit, and the expectation that only the eldest would marry.

Regular readers of my books will notice that shipbuilding is a recurring feature, and in particular Clyde-built ships. The reasons are simple: my paternal grandfather built ships on the Clyde, my maternal grandfather captained them, and my writing view is of the Clyde estuary. If you'd like to read about an actual Clyde shipbuilding hero, then I can offer a choice of two: Iain Hunter in *Unwed and Unrepentant* and Innes Drummond in *Strangers at the Altar*.

Finally I owe a debt to Jeffrey Steingarten, for his exhaustive index of Italian and Venetian terms for all things from the sea in *The Man Who Ate Everything*. I had enormous fun creating dinner menus—and worked up a huge appetite in the process!

COMING NEXT MONTH FROM

HARLEQUIN

HISTORICAL

Available October 16, 2018

All available in print and ebook via Reader Service and online

CONVENIENT CHRISTMAS BRIDES (Regency)
by Carla Kelly, Louise Allen and Laurie Benson
Delve into three convenient Regency arrangements with a captain, a viscount and a lord, all in one festive volume.

A TEXAS CHRISTMAS REUNION (Western)
by Carol Arens
Bad boy Trea Culverson returns, bringing excitement back into widow Juliette Lindor's life. With the town against him, can Juliette show them *and* Trea that love is as powerful as any Christmas gift?

A HEALER FOR THE HIGHLANDER (Medieval)
A Highland Feuding • by Terri Brisbin
Famed healer Anna Mackenzie is moved by Davidh of Clan Cameron's request to help his ailing son. But Anna has a secret that could jeopardize the growing heated passion between them...

A LORD FOR THE WALLFLOWER WIDOW (Regency)
The Widows of Westram • by Ann Lethbridge
When widow Lady Carrie musters the courage to request that charming gadabout Lord Avery Gilmore show her the wifely pleasures she's never had, he takes the challenge *very* seriously!

BEAUTY AND THE BROODING LORD (Regency)
Saved from Disgrace • by Sarah Mallory
Lord Quinn has sworn off romance, but when he happens upon an innocent lady being assaulted, he marries her to protect her reputation. Quinn must help Serena fight her demons, and defeat his own...

THE VISCOUNT'S RUNAWAY WIFE (Regency)
by Laura Martin
After many years, Lord Oliver Sedgewick finally finds his runaway wife, Lucy. The spark between them burns more intensely than ever, but does their marriage have a chance of a happy future?

YOU CAN FIND MORE INFORMATION ON UPCOMING HARLEQUIN® TITLES, FREE EXCERPTS AND MORE AT WWW.HARLEQUIN.COM.

HOME on the RANCH

YES! Please send me the **Home on the Ranch Collection** in Larger Print. This collection begins with 3 FREE books and 2 FREE gifts in the first shipment. Along with my 3 free books, I'll also get the next 4 books from the Home on the Ranch Collection, in LARGER PRINT, which I may either return and owe nothing, or keep for the low price of $5.24 U.S./ $5.89 CDN each plus $2.99 for shipping and handling per shipment*. If I decide to continue, about once a month for 8 months I will get 6 or 7 more books, but will only need to pay for 4. That means 2 or 3 books in every shipment will be FREE! If I decide to keep the entire collection, I'll have paid for only 32 books because 19 books are FREE! I understand that accepting the 3 free books and gifts places me under no obligation to buy anything. I can always return a shipment and cancel at any time. My free books and gifts are mine to keep no matter what I decide.

268 HCN 3760 468 HCN 3760

Name	(PLEASE PRINT)	
Address		Apt. #
City	State/Prov.	Zip/Postal Code

Signature (if under 18, a parent or guardian must sign)

Mail to the **Reader Service**:

IN U.S.A.: P.O. Box 1341, Buffalo, New York 14240-8531
IN CANADA: P.O. Box 603, Fort Erie, Ontario L2A 5X3

* Terms and prices subject to change without notice. Prices do not include applicable taxes. Sales tax applicable in NY. Canadian residents will be charged applicable taxes. This offer is limited to one order per household. All orders subject to approval. Credit or debit balances in a customer's account(s) may be offset by any other outstanding balance owed by or to the customer. Please allow 3 to 4 weeks for delivery. Offer available while quantities last. Offer not available to Quebec residents.

Your Privacy—The Reader Service is committed to protecting your privacy. Our Privacy Policy is available online at www.ReaderService.com or upon request from the Reader Service.

We make a portion of our mailing list available to reputable third parties that offer products we believe may interest you. If you prefer that we not exchange your name with third parties, or if you wish to clarify or modify your communication preferences, please visit us at www.ReaderService.com/consumerschoice or write to us at Reader Service Preference Service, P.O. Box 9062, Buffalo, NY. 14240-9062. Include your complete name and address.